- J

The Magic Jacket, Broomsticks, Alice's Godmother, Lucy
. . . what memories these titles weave for long-time lovers
of stories by Walter de la Mare, and what promise they
hold for newcomers to his art! Here, in a companion vol-
ume to the beautiful *A Penny A Day*, are more stories by
the master of the uncanny and magical. These are also
stories he told to his own family that have been beloved
for three generations.

In a rare communication of spirit with the author, Paul
Kennedy in his fine illustrations has captured the very
essence of that unique combination of roguery, eerieness,
and innocence that makes these stories classics.

❀ ❀

Other Storybooks by
Walter de la Mare

Books of Poetry by Walter de la Mare

And coming in the Fall . . .

The Magic Jacket

❀ ❀

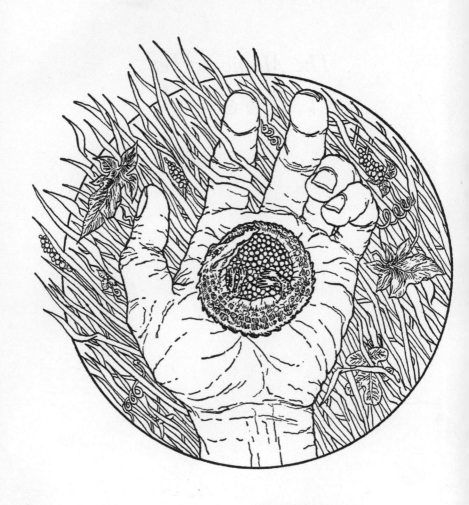

❀❀❀❀ ❀ THE ❀ ❀❀❀❀

MAGIC
JACKET

by

Walter de la Mare

Illustrated by

Paul Kennedy

❀ ❀

Alfred A. Knopf, *New York*

L.C. Catalog card number 62–9467

THIS IS A BORZOI BOOK,
PUBLISHED BY ALFRED A. KNOPF, INC.

Contents

3 2 5 ‿

By ᴿ o ᴨ

11 - 64

The Magic Jacket

❀ ❀

The Magic Jacket

When, that May Day morning, Admiral Rumbold stepped out of his four-wheeled cab at the corner of Pall Mall, he was carrying a small brown-paper parcel. Why he had not told his cabman, who—hunched up on his box—looked older even than his horse, to take him on to exactly where he wanted to go, he hardly knew. He paid the old man his fare; and he added an extra sixpence.

"Thank'ee," he said with a curt nod, then turned to continue on his way. Admiral Rumbold was not exactly a stout man, but in his navy-blue clothes, his neat boots, and brown billycock hat, he looked rather tightly packed. His broad face shone almost as red as a tomato above his white linen collar and blue-and-white spotted silk sailor's knot. He clasped his neat little brown-paper parcel closely under his elbow and at a good round pace proceeded along Pall Mall.

He glanced neither to right nor left of him, but kept his sea-bleached blue eyes fixed steadily ahead. Nor did he show the least sign of recognition when he caught sight of an old friend brandishing a silver-headed cane in his direction from under the hood of a hansom-cab. On this particular morning—and the houses and shops looked sparklingly gay in the spring sunshine—Admiral Rumbold wished to be alone. He marched straight on, his eyes fixed, his mouth tight-shut, almost as if he were walking in his sleep.

He turned sharply up St. James's Street, past the saddler's with the jockey caps and jackets behind the glass, past the little bow-windowed snuff-and-tobacco shop, and so into King Street. From King Street he turned off into Duke Street, and then on into Great St. Ann's. After the bustle and traffic now behind him, the quiet sunshine and shadow of Little St. Ann's beyond it was like port after stormy seas.

Now a few paces past the hatter's shop that stood at the corner of Little St. Ann's lay a wide smooth stretch of flat paving-stones under a high old brick wall. It was here that a screever or pavement artist had made his pitch; and here in the sunshine Admiral Rumbold came to a halt and looked about him.

The street was still and, at this early hour of the morning, almost deserted. For a while, firm as a rock, he continued so to stand. But having failed to catch a glimpse of what he was after, he began to survey a little vacantly the pictures chalked on the stones at his feet.

The first of them was of a ship with bare masts and lanky spars, tossing on an indigo sea, its waves yeastily crested with spray. Next to this there was a windmill in a gaudy country green, the miller himself standing up like Shem, Ham, and Japhet at the little rounded door above the wide wooden ladder. Next, there was a gaping brace of rainbow-coloured, rather flabby-looking mackerel. Next, a loaf of bread, a cut cheese, and a neat little long-tailed mouse at her supper. And last—and best of all to some tastes—there stood a lonely country mansion among its wintry trees, a wild full moon gleaming down on its walls. Scrawled beneath this picture, in a flowery lettering, was the one word, "HORNTED."

Admiral Rumbold had taken a good long look at these pictures only the evening before. They showed a little livelier in the morning sunshine. Still, he had come back not to have another look at them, but to have a word with the young artist. Few street chalkers, the Admiral had noticed in his walks abroad, are much less than forty. The one he now had in mind could not be more than fourteen. The Admiral had taken a liking to him at first sight, had often watched him at his work, and had dropped many a tuppence into the old cloth cap that usually lay (as if with its mouth wide open) beside the pictures. Now he wished to speak to him.

To an old gentleman with a temper as peppery as the Admiral's it was therefore an unpleasant jar to find that when he wanted the boy he was nowhere to be seen. Besides, he was anxious to get rid of the brown-paper parcel under his arm. He had a dislike to carrying anything at all —even an umbrella so massive that it looked more like a war-club. On the other hand he was a man who, having once made up his mind, kept it made up.

He crossed the street, and spent the next few minutes pacing solemnly up and down, glancing ever and again as he did so down the area railings or up at the upper windows of the houses on that side of it, in order to pretend to himself that he was not being kept waiting. And every time he turned smartly on his heel, he glared first up the street, then down the street, and then into the deep-blue empty sky.

At last he had his reward. Shuffling along close to the

railings from out of a neighbouring alley, in shoes that even
at this distance looked a good deal more roomy than comfortable, appeared the boy the Admiral was in wait for. A
coat that was at least two sizes too large for its present
wearer hung down from his bony shoulders. But he had
turned the cuffs up over the sleeves, so that his claw-like
hands came out free from beneath them.

His odd, almost ugly face was pale and not too clean.
His brown hair was lank and tousled. But as the Admiral
had noticed before, the skull beneath the hair was nut-
shaped and compact, clear over the forehead and wide towards the back. It looked as if it closely fitted something
valuable inside it. Besides which, the boy had a pair of eyes
in the pinched face looking out from under that skull which
once seen were not easily forgotten.

Admiral Rumbold, at sight of him, had slipped in under the carved shell-shaped porch of one of the neighbouring houses. From here he could see without being seen.

First, the boy glanced into his cap, then took it up,
turned it upside down, shook it, and replaced it on the
pavement. He then drew a large dingy rag that might once
have been the flap of a man's shirt or a woman's petticoat
out of his pocket. With both hands he waved this to and
fro above his pictures to waft away the dust and straw and
soot-smuts. He then pushed the rag into his pocket again,
and had a steady look at the pictures, as if he had never
seen them before and could not make up his mind whether
or not to give himself a penny. He then sighed—a sigh
that in the morning quietness was clearly audible. At this
Admiral Rumbold stepped out of his hiding-place, crossed
the road, and accosted him.

"Good morning, my boy," was his greeting. "How's
business?"

The boy looked up into the round red face of the old gentleman, with its small beak-like nose and sky-blue eyes, and a timid smile passed over his own as he shook his head.

"So, so!" said Admiral Rumbold bluffly. "Nothing much, eh? There's a bit of east in the wind this morning, and perhaps that keeps folk moving. Or perhaps . . . Well, there we are! Had any breakfast? No? Good! I want a word with 'ee. Is there a place handy where we can sit and talk?"

The boy coloured, glanced swiftly from right to left, and told the Admiral of a coffee-shop near at hand where he sometimes went himself. Then he looked up at the old Admiral again, became redder than ever, and broke off.

"Full steam ahead, then," said his friend. "And do you lead the way."

The boy buttoned his coat; away they went together; and in a minute or two the pair of them were sitting face to face on two benches between wooden partitions—like the high pews in old churches—and on either side of a table in an eating-house halfway up the neighbouring alley. The Admiral asked the boy what he would take. He said a mug of thick.

At this the Admiral cocked one of his bright blue eyes, and enquired if he would like anything to eat with it. The boy hesitated and suggested a door-step.

"H'm!" said the Admiral, "and anything for a sweet tooth to follow?"

The boy said he would like a cat's-eye. Whereupon Admiral Rumbold rapped smartly on the table. A man with greasy black hair, of a dark face, and wearing a rather dingy apron, appeared from his den behind the shop.

"Good morning," said the Admiral. "Two mugs of thick, a door-step, and a cat's-eye." And he said the words as if he had been used to them all his life and knew exactly what they meant.

The mugs of thick proved to be cocoa; the door-step, a slab of bread with a scrimp of butter; and the cat's-eye was a large yellow bun with a burnt raisin stuck in its crown. And while the two of them sipped their thick, and the boy from nibbling went on to munching at his door-step, Admiral Rumbold explained what he was after.

But first he asked him a little about himself and his work. He learned that the boy was pretty well alone in the world. His father, who had been a carriage painter, had died when he was six. His own business was fair in fine weather, but it was hard to find a pitch where there were neither too many passers-by nor too few. "And then there's the bobbies," said the boy. Summer was better than winter, but up to the last week or two there had been too much rain for any business at all.

"Ay, ay," said the Admiral, looking at him over the thick brim of his mug as he took another sip of cocoa, "a fine-weather trade, I take it." And he asked him what his name was. It was Mike.

"Well now, Mike," said Admiral Rumbold at last, "I've been keeping an eye on you for some little time. I've been *wanting* to keep an eye on someone of your age and looks for a good deal longer. I like your pictures; in fact, I *admire* them. If *I* were to sit down under that wall with every scrap of chalk you've got and do my level best with them, rain or no rain, I warrant my takings wouldn't be fourpence a month. It's the knack you want. And it's the knack, my lad, you have.

"Not, mind you," he went on, "that I know any more about pictures than what I *like*. I leave the rest to them that do. But I've lived a good many years in the world now, and

my belief is that every walk in life begins with a steepish bit of hill. When I was a boy—and we're not concerned just now with where *my* walk's led *me*—I had to face mine. And in this parcel here is—well, what helped me in the climbing of it.

"Here," repeated the Admiral and said no more for the moment. For he had brought his square solid hand down on the parcel beside his mug with such a thump that the man in the apron came hurrying up to see what more was wanted.

"I'll have," said the Admiral promptly, "another mug of thick and another couple of door-steps. And this time put in a slice or two more of beef and bacon by way of cement."

The sandwiches that followed were almost as much meat as bread, and Mike's eyes fairly watered as they were handed over to him.

"In this parcel, as I was saying," continued the Admiral, "is the *story* of what I've been telling you. A yarn, you'll understand. Tell me, can you *read?"* Mike nodded violently; his mouth was full.

"Good!" said the Admiral. "All I want you to do is to read it—it's about a *jacket*—what might be called a slice out of my early days, just as that bacon there maybe a slice out of the early days of the pig it came from. There's no hurry——" he glanced at the clock and then at his gold repeater—"it's seventeen and a half minutes past ten. Sit here quietly and read as much of it as you can. When you have finished, come along to me. At eleven sharp I'll be waiting near the pitch.

"Mind ye," he ended as he rose to his feet, "there's no shadow of *must* in that package whatsoever. Nor do I vouch for anything beyond what's written—and I've had it printed out on one of those new-fangled machines so that it can be read plain and easy. Take it quietly; ask for anything you want while I'm away; and in half an hour we meet again."

He put down half-a-crown on the table for the door-steps, etc., laid his hand an instant on Mike's shoulder, and looked him hard but friendly in the eye. Then he instantly flung open the swing-door of the coffee-shop and went out into the street.

To judge from his face, the old gentleman was very well pleased with himself at this moment. He returned to the pictures, and spent the next half-hour, as cautiously as before, in pacing to and fro along the street. Whenever he passed them he paused to look at them, dropped a copper or two into the cap, and went on. At this, some curious passer-by would also stop and glance over Mike's gallery. And, maybe, he too would fling in a penny to join the Admiral's—and, maybe, not.

Meanwhile, Mike, left to himself and now the only customer in the coffee-shop, took a good long swig of his mug of cocoa and a munch at his sandwich before setting to work on the Admiral's story. And this was what he read:

"Coming down to facts at once, I was born all but seventy years ago, in a town in Shropshire of the name of P——. My father was a grocer—retail. His shop wasn't much to look at from outside, but there was little that his customers wanted in the way of groceries that couldn't be found even then on his shelves.

"My father was a man of about forty when I came into the world. My mother was a good deal younger; and mightily pleased they were to have me. No doubt about that. They christened me Andrew and called me Sandy,

there being Scotch blood on my father's side. And if hard
work and steady is a short cut to success, that was my father's way.

"At first, my father and mother were content to live
over the shop—three rooms in all, not including one not
much bigger than a bandbox, which was called the nursery.
When I was six, things were going so well with the business that they decided to let the rooms above the shop,
and to move into a small but comfortable, high, and (what
they call) semi-detached house, half a mile or so out of the
town. We had a good strip of garden there—a few apple
and plum trees, some currant and gooseberry bushes, and
old country flowers.

"My mother loved that garden, and spent all the time
she could spare from the house in it, with me beside her, or
digging away at a patch of soil, three yards by one, with
scallop shells round the border, which she let me have to
do what I pleased with. That was *my* garden. *Sandy-land*,
she called it. Candytuft, Virginia stock, and Sweet Wil-
liams were my own particular crops.

"My mother, I remember, bless her soul, was a great
talker. I don't mean by this that she talked too much, or
talked to everybody, or never listened. I mean she was a
great talker to me, though not so much to my father. What
she and I chattered about when we went out shopping in
the morning together, or when I used to help her make
the beds, would fill a book. Everything under the sun, not
to mention the other side of it.

"I don't know what there was about my mother—
brown eyes, brown hair, and so on. But hanging up over
the pianoforte in what was called our drawing-room was a
portrait of her as a girl of eighteen or thereabouts which, if
I had been any kind of young man with an eye in his head,

I should have fallen in love with at first sight. But it wasn't her looks; it was her ways. How to put it I don't know, but she always seemed to be talking as if to somebody over her shoulder as well as to me myself.

"Never—and mine's a pretty long life now—never have I come across anyone with such a loving delight in birds, flowers, trees, clouds, stars, moss, butterflies, and all that. She knew them by heart. You might have thought she'd had a hand in their making. Words aren't my tools, and I must just get things down as straight as I *can*. But that was the way of it. To see her look at a toadstool, with some bright colour to its gills, or peep into a wren's or chaffinch's nest, or stand watching a bevy of long-tailed tits gossiping together for a minute or two in one of our tufted old apple-trees on their way to somebody else's, was like— well, I don't know what it wasn't like, except that it was like nothing on earth but my mother. She wasn't any *age* at all. We might have been a couple of brothers or sisters —old cronies, as you might say. We could hardly tell each other apart—except when my father was by.

"Now, I'm not going to say anything against *him*. He died when I was not much more than a quarter of the way up the ladder I was afterwards to set myself to climb. He did his best by me; and if it hadn't been for my own stubborn interference, he might have done better for me than I've done for myself. Can't say; don't *know*. What I wanted was to go my own way, as at last I went. And your own way is nobody else's way. It's a man's self—his *innards,* to speak abruptly—that counts. Not the stripes on his arm, or the cut of his jib, or the cash in his bank, or even what he's *done*.

"But enough of that. The truth is perhaps that being so much alone with my mother, and as contented in her company, at least in those first few years, as a butterfly with a flower, I became a bit of an apron-string child. She did not much care for going out, and she had a mighty small opinion of any young Two-Legs in the street except the one she herself had brought into the world, so I was only allowed to play with any small Tom, Dick, or Harry belonging to our neighbours provided I never went beyond view of her bedroom window. And that's not much of a playground for a healthy young sprat that ought to be learning what the sea looks like.

"Alone with her, and at peace, I wanted nothing else and could chatter away like a grasshopper. Away from her, I was usually little better than a tongue-tied numskull, flushing up to the eyebrows at a word from a stranger, and looked too shy and timid to say Boh to a goose—even to the goose in my own looking-glass! Well, numskull is as numskull does; and as the old wooden-legged sailor said,

> *When all you've got is a couple of stump,*
> *There's nowt to do but go* clump—clump—clump!

"My father could not see it that way. He began to think I was stupid on purpose. There was not a sharper tradesman in the county, nor a more honest tradesman either, in spite of the 'sharp.' All his wits were at his finger-tips. He had a memory like a dictionary. He knew where everything was or ought to be. He could tell a bargain at first wag of its tail and a good customer before he opened his mouth. He lived long enough to make three fine shops of his poky first one—plate-glass windows, plenty of gold paint, three smart vans and about a dozen glossy-haired assistants in clean white aprons. And he stowed a handsomer show of tea-chests, sugar loaves, jam-jars and piccalilli pots behind those windows than any other grocer in the town. I owe him unspeakably more than the little fortune he left me.

"But being what he was, he was impatient with anything else, and particularly with me, his own son. *Now,* I understand it. *Then,* the moment I saw his black hat above the hedge, or heard his key in the lock, I would scuttle away like a frightened rabbit. If we were left alone together, I would sit as glum as a cold plum-duff pudding— without any plums in it! If he asked me a question, every word would fly out of my head, like rooks at a rattle. The mere look of me at such times—fumbling and stammering —made him angry. The more angry he grew the more tongue-tied and lumpish grew I, and that would set my poor mother weeping. And I have never yet met a father who enjoyed being told that he could not understand his own son. Not that he loved me a penny the less; far from it. But love, my boy, is like coal. You can burn it, and warm and comfort yourself with its light and heat. Or you can keep it in a cellar. My father kept his in a cellar—and it was I who helped him stack it up!

"With my mother, as I have said already, everything was different. We would gossip away together for hours. And when she wasn't with me I would talk to myself. I had plenty of books in my bedroom under the roof—books that had belonged to my mother's younger brother who died at sea. And I read like a limpet. When in those days I opened a book that seemed meant for me—travels, voyages, that kind of thing—it was like exploring another world. Fancy tales I never took to—except journeys to the moon, or the middle of the earth, and suchlike—nor could even my mother win me to rhymes.

"Maybe it was all this book-stuff and solitude and having nobody to play with that began this odd habit in me of talking to myself when I was alone. And it was this talking to myself that led on to the great discovery. One evening, I remember, I was reading about the supper to which Sir Francis Drake invited the officer on his ship who had been stirring up mutiny against him, and whom he hanged next morning. And as I was listening to myself talking like the officer and putting up as stiff a lip as I could at the prospect of so harsh a breakfast, I suddenly discovered that there was not *one* of me, so to say, but two. I discovered what's called a second self—though of course he must have been there all the time. To make things plain and ship-shape, let us call the first of these two selves, Sandy One; and the second of these two selves, Sandy Two.

"There was first the Sandy One that was my father's son, and stayed at home with his mother in the high, oblong box of a house, standing up high on the hill with its neighbours, all in a row. This was the nervous, timid, stuttering Sandy, the Sandy who did not know where he kept his own tongue, the skulker, the dunderhead whom my father could not make head or tail of. There was next the Sandy who when alone did more or less what he liked and went where he pleased—desert islands, Red Indians, lions and tigers, castaways, cannibals, *bonum omens*—all that kind of thing. Ay, and the whole world over. *He* pined for freedom. He wanted to do and dare things. He wanted to eat his cake and chance the stale crusts afterwards. This happy-go-lucky, scatter-brained, dare-devil creature boxed up inside me was Sandy Two. We'll call him, as I say, Sandy Two: and, Here's good luck to him!—for he needed it!

"Now, do you see, my mother knew something of both Sandies, though more of One than Two. My father never so much as dreamt of Two and saw not much more of One than his worst. And Sandy Two, at his darndest and daringest, was at present inside my head and kept for myself and my books alone.

"Now Schooling. . . ."

Mike took a long slow look at this word before going any further. He was already a little tired of reading. He wanted to get to the jacket. Still, he had promised the old gentleman, who seemed to be an old gentleman who expected his promises to be kept, that he would do his best, and he had had an *uncommonly* good breakfast. So he swallowed another gulp of his tepid cocoa, took another huge bite of his door-step, and plodded on.

"Now Schooling. Well, I went to school like most boys of my age. It was what is called a Private School, and the headmaster's name was Smiles; and his name was not only where his smiles began but also ended. From the instant my father led me into his stuffy back-room, this Mr. Smiles took me for a dunce. One glance at my sheepish mottled face—Sandy One's—was enough for that. And as dunce he treated me almost until we parted. Dunce was his chief dish with me, from beginning to end—and plenty of cane sauce.

"I hated school. I hated learning. And as I was told to go straight home the moment my lessons were over, I was never much of a favourite with the other boys. They took me for a molly-coddle, and called me Tallow-candy. Which was true of course of Sandy One. And for some little time they never caught sight of Sandy Two. That came later. Still, whenever Sandy One warmed up so much in a scrap

as to bring Sandy Two into it, it wasn't the other fellow that
left off last!

"Well now, to make a long story short, my father's
heart, as I have been saying, was in groceries. And you can
take my word for it that there is one thing at least worse
than a quick profit on pickles, and that is a dead loss on
'em. His business was growing; he pulled his weight wherever he went; he was soon to be Mayor; and having only
one son, he hoped and meant that that son should go into
groceries too, and perhaps some day *double* his fortune,
keep a carriage, and become *Lord* Mayor. He wanted his
son to 'get on,' and what father doesn't?

"So in the old days, just to polish my wits, he would
ask me such questions as what raisins are, or where currants come from, or why peel is called candied; and then
—with a flicker of his eyelids—who discovered the Macaroni Tree, or how much fresh there is to a pound of salt
butter, or where the natives dig up nutmegs, or what is the
temperature of Cayenne pepper, or what is the cost of a
hogshead of treacle at 2¾ d. an ounce. The point is, I never
even *wanted* to know such things. And worse, I couldn't
even laugh at them!

"If my father had asked me what kind of birds you'd
be likely to see flitting about in the craters of the moon; or
what the war-whoop and scalping habits of the Objibwas
or the Cherokees were; or how many brothers riding on
white asses Abimelech had; I believe Sandy Two would
have consented to answer. But Sandy Two (apart from
toffee) had no interest whatever in Demerara or Barbados
sugar; and Sandy One was no better than a blockhead at
any questions whatsoever, except when his mother asked
them, or when he was alone.

"One Sunday morning, after I had first said I couldn't

answer, and then refused to try to answer, some such questions as these, I looked up and told my father that I hated grocery shops. I said of all shops I hated grocery shops the most. I said I detested school, and that the only thing in the world I wanted was to run away to sea. Then I burst out crying. At this moment my mother came in, so I never got the thrashing I richly deserved.

"But my father must have thought things over; for after that, Dr. Smiles paid very particular attention to the *grocery* side of history, geography, arithmetic and dictation. Even of French: 'Has your neighbour's gardener the oranges from Jaffa, the tapioca from Brazil, and the chicory for the coffee of his aunt?'—that kind of thing.

"Then one night I overheard my mother and father talking. Sandy Two had come stealing downstairs about half-past nine to see what he could find in the larder. The door of the drawing-room was ajar, and I heard my father say: 'He is not only half-witted, but as limp and flabby as a rag doll—and what's more, here's that bladder-of-lard, schoolmaster Smiles, saying exactly the same thing. And yet *you*. . . .' At these words Sandy One at once fled back to bed—taking Sandy Two with him. And I awoke next morning remembering what my father had said as distinctly as if it had been tattooed into my skin. For days together after that Sandy Two never so much as showed the tip of his nose in the house.

"Then, one afternoon, on my way home from school, I ventured down a shabby side-street, because at the far end of it I had caught the noise of a Punch-and-Judy Show. I could hear the children roaring with laughter, and the squeaking and the thumping and cockadoodle-ing of Mr. Punch. Sandy Two told Sandy One he would like to go and see it. So he went.

"Coming back, we passed a dingy little shop I had never noticed there before, and we stopped to look in at the window. *Marine Store* was printed up in white letters over the green front. There was some queer junk behind that window: old shoes and shawls and old hats, a ship in a bottle, a green glass rolling-pin, a telescope that must have belonged to Noah, a ship's compass, a brass cannon, a bed-warmer, a picture made of hummingbirds' feathers—such old curios as they call 'em as that. They looked as if they had been there for centuries—verdigris, mould, fluff, dust. Most of these articles had their prices marked on scraps of paper: '*Grate Bargin*, 3s. 6d.' and so on.

"And hanging up on a nail in a corner of the window and almost out of sight, was a kind of garment I couldn't quite put name to. But a piece of paper was pinned to it, and on that was scrawled the words: *Majick Jacket*. Just that and nothing more. But it was enough. I had already gloated on the telescope and the ship and the brass cannon. But those two words, *Majick Jacket*, fairly took my breath away. They stirred me up as if with a ladle—me myself, Sandy Two, and even Sandy One. At last I could bear the strain no longer.

"I pushed open the crack-paint little door—I can hear even now the jingle of its rusty bell—and in I went. The place smelt like an old cellar. It was as soundless as a vault. For what seemed hours nothing happened, except that I heard a far-away canary singing; then Sandy One began to be alarmed, and I tiptoed off towards the door.

"Just as I was about to whip it open and bolt out into the street again, an old man, with thick magnifying spectacles on his nose and a beard like a goat, came shuffling out of the back parts of the shop and asked me what I wanted.

"I said would he please tell me the price of the brass cannon—though I knew it already. Then I asked to see the ship in the bottle. And then, at last, with hardly any breath left in my body, I managed to point to the jacket.

" 'That,' he said, looking first at it and then at me, 'that's ten shillin'.'

"I got as red as a turkey-cock, coughed, turned about, and opened the door.

" 'I say! I say, Mister!' he called after me. 'What are you running away for? Come back and *see* it. Come back and look at it—*feel* it. No harm in that!' He was already climbing up on to a stool. Then he thrust his head in among the rags and drabs in the window, brought down the jacket, and laid it on the counter. And close-to, like this, it was nothing much, I must say, to look at.

"It was made of some kind of foreign dark Chinese-looking stuff, with a faint wavy pattern on it, and it had flat stone buttons with green crocodiles curled round on them. The braid was frayed at the neck and cuffs. I looked hard at it on the counter, but didn't touch it. Then I blurted out: 'Who made it?'

" 'Made it?' snapped the old man, 'that's a *magic* jacket. That's come from Pekin and Madagascar and Seringapatam and I don't know what, and if once you get inside of it you'll never want to get out again.'

"I swallowed. 'Have *you* ever put it on?' I enquired.

" 'Me?' he almost bellowed at me. 'Me! with all these old slops hanging round! Where should I be if I put 'em all on? Where's the *sale*?'

"Now I wanted that jacket with the crocodiles on the buttons more than anything else past, present or future in the whole wide world. But I had only two-and-ninepence

in my pocket—and that was riches for *me*. To be on the
safe side, I told the old man this. He stared at me through
his rusting spectacles.

" 'See here!' he said, as if in a violent temper, and
whisking out a piece of newspaper from under the counter:
'See here now, snap it!' And he wrapped up the jacket in a
flash. 'Give me all you've got, and come back with the rest.
There's a summat in your eye, young man, that never went
with a cheat.'

"Then I knew that the old man was charging me at
least double what he had meant to ask for the jacket. But I
gave him my two-and-ninepence all the same, and went out
of the shop. Before his door bell had stopped clanging I
had pushed the parcel up under my waistcoat and walked
off, keeping my stomach in, because I didn't want anybody
to ask questions.

"Once safely home, I crept upstairs and slipped the
parcel in at the back of a drawer, and for that night there it
stayed. I didn't dare to meddle with it, partly for fear of
what might happen, but mostly of what might *not!*

"All the next morning I was in torture. I was afraid
my mother might find the jacket—and give it away to some
tramp for a fern or a pot of geraniums. Every time I
thought of it I could scarcely breathe, and that didn't help
much in my school-work. I was kept in. And when I came
home I told my mother I had a headache—which was true
—but persuaded her at last to go out and leave me to myself. Then I stole up to my bedroom, shut the door, opened
the drawer, and with my heart in my mouth, felt for the
parcel. All safe! All *safe!* I took it out, undid the string,
opened the paper, and there was the jacket—wavy pattern,
crocodile buttons, frayed braid, and all.

"With a last wild look towards the window I took off

my own coat and put it on. I put it on. And nothing happened. Nothing whatever. At first blush, I mean. Except that I suddenly noticed that the room was full of sunshine and that a thrush was singing in a pear tree at the bottom of the garden. I noticed it because he sang so clear and shrill, and as though straight at *me*. If you could put sound for sight, it was as if I were listening to him through a telescope. I could see him, too, the speckles on his breast, and his bill opening and shutting—singing like an angel.

"And as I listened I noticed in the sunlight through the window the colours of my faded rose-patterned carpet and an old boot. It sounds silly, but I had never before seen an old boot look like that. I don't want to mince words, and maybe I didn't realise it then, but the fact of the matter is that that old boot on the carpet looked astonishingly *beautiful*—the light on the old leather, the tongue coming out, and the gleam of the metal eyelets. A landshark's word that—*beautiful*—but there you are.

"Well, I was soon a little impatient with all this—a new life seemed to have edged into things, or at least into me. Very peculiar. So, to get back to common sense again, I began Sandy One's *Physical Exercises*. Exercises! Why, it was as though all of a sudden I had become nothing but a twist of wire and catgut. I skipped through those jimminasticals as if I were half out of my senses. Then I tried tricks never so much as dreamt of before—hopping along my bedrail; standing on my head, first on the bedpost, then on my water-jug; balancing myself—two hands, then one hand—on the back of a chair. Whatever, within the bounds of reason, or thereabouts, I gave myself to do, I *did*—and with ease. Like the thrush singing. Nothing very much perhaps, but new to *me!* Mind you, I had never been quite the mollie my father thought me. And Sandy Two hadn't been idle, body or wits. But a little confidence, though not too much, is what you want. After a while I began to be a little bit alarmed at the effects of the jacket. I began, so to speak, to suspect my own company!

"So, hot and breathless, I sat down at the table where I always did (or didn't do) my homework, and began my 'composition.' The subject was the Battle of Trafalgar. Before I had finished I had written about fourteen pages on the Battle of Trafalgar! I had described how the *Victory* went to sea, and what Lord Nelson felt like—that last day coming, and why he kept his medals on, and all about Captain Hardy. And I put the weather in, and didn't forget old Froggy Villeneuve either—a gallant sailor and a bad end. When I looked up from page fourteen I could hardly see. It was as if I had come out of the heavenly Jerusalem! And then, almost at that moment, I heard my mother come in down below, and the front door shut.

"I felt like a keg of quicksilver, and yet dead beat. I undressed in less time than a lizard takes to slough its tail, and tumbled into bed, slipping my Chinese jacket in under the bedclothes.

"And no doubt I looked headachy enough when my mother came up to say good-night. She felt my forehead; it was burning hot. And she murmured faintly in a very small voice something about castor oil. Even Sandy One could put his foot down when it came to castor oil! But this time I didn't make the least fuss about it. I said, 'Right you are. Warm the glass, mother, and put plenty of lemon juice in.' I swigged it down, and even smacked my lips over it. Then I began to talk—so fast, and with such nonsense mixed up with the sense, that my mother was on the point of calling in the doctor. At that I sobered down again.

"The next day all was well, but I didn't go to school.

The next day after that saw me back in my place again, though not in the magic jacket! But I had cut off one of the pale-green crocodile buttons to carry about in my waistcoat pocket for a kind of charm or amulet. I got a caning for the French I hadn't done, and another caning for the arithmetic which I had. Mr. Schoolmaster Smiles himself read my *Essay on the Battle of Trafalger* then and there. He hauled me out again before the class, and asked me what help I had had. I said none. He glared at me: 'Are you positively sure, sir? Not even in the spelling?'

"I said, 'No, sir; none, sir.' What was queer, he believed me.

"Still, he had talked to me once or twice about the sea and the Navy. And I too had asked him questions, because while I was wrapped up in the thought of them, I wasn't so frightened of him. Besides, on looking back, I don't believe he really cottoned to groceries much more than I did. Anyhow, he gave me full marks and a bit over for my Trafalgar, but warned me another time I mustn't 'spread' myself out like that.

"I went home feeling like a turkey-cock, marched straight upstairs, sat down at my open window, and—put on the jacket again. But I had hardly got my arms into the sleeves when I heard my mother calling me. I hustled on my own jacket over the top of the other—which was not difficult, because my Chinese one was a very tight fit, especially at the armpits—and met her on the landing. She was as white as a sheet and could scarcely speak. She said my father wanted to see me at once, and that he had a friend with him, a Mr. Turner.

" 'And, oh, my dear,' she implored me, 'do try and answer your father's questions. Just *listen,* Sandy. Then perhaps you'll hear. And speak up to Mr. Turner, too, if he speaks to you. Think it's *me*. Don't be frightened; don't be *sulky*. Nobody can eat you. Fancy it's only just you and me talking. For my sake, Sandy.'

"I said, 'Right, Mother!' and slid from top to bottom down the banisters of the three flights of stairs almost before she had stirred foot to follow me. At the dining-room door I pulled myself together and went in.

"My father was sitting on the other side of the fireless hearth, talking to a stranger. I liked the look of this stranger. He was short and broad; his face was burnt with the sun; he had a fringe of reddish hair round his head, and wore thick-soled shoes. 'Here he is,' said my father to the stranger, then turned to me. 'This gentleman is Mr. Turner, Andrew. If you want to know anything about the sea, he'll tell you.' I put out my hand.

" 'I hear you've no stomach for dry goods,' said Mr. Turner, staring at me, but in a friendly fashion. 'Have a hankering after salt water, eh?'

" 'Yes,' I said, 'the Navy.' Out of the corner of my eye I saw my father start at this. He had never before heard me answer so direct a question without stammering or flushing or just goggling like a red herring with its mouth open.

" 'And what do you know about the sea?' said Mr. Turner, looking at me steadily. 'It's pretty deep!'

"I looked back at him no less steadily. I liked him more and more, and thought I would try him with a few tit-bits out of my fourteen pages on the Battle of Trafalgar. There was a queer silence when I had finished. And I realised that my mother had at that moment stolen away after listening at the door. As for my father, he sat in his chair dumb with amazement. He shut his eyes for an instant and then began to explain that I was not perhaps so backward in some things as in others. But, apart from mere book-learning, did Mr. Turner think that I had the framework, the grit, the *health* for a life in the open? 'You see, his mother. . . .'

" 'He looks a bit pasty,' said Mr. Turner, still quietly grinning at me. 'But you can't always tell by the skin. What about those biceps, young man?'

"I put out my arm, and he gripped it hard above the elbow, not noticing, perhaps, that I had two jackets on. And he said, 'Pretty good. Do they drill you much at school? Or is it nothing but book-learning?' I nodded, and said, 'Yes; and things at home, too.'

" 'What do you do at home?' says he.

"Now all this time I had been feeling like a bottle of ginger-beer before the cork pops out. So when he gave the word, so to speak, I upped with my heels and pretty nearly *trotted* across the room on the palms of my hands.

" 'Bravo,' said Mr. Turner. 'Try that on the table.'

"It was a circular, solid, old-fashioned mahogany table, made when Queen Victoria was a girl, and I circumnavigated it on my fingers and thumbs as nimbly as a cat. But now my blood was up. To give me room, a couple of tumblers, a bottle of water, and a decanter of whisky had been pushed into the middle of the table. Balancing myself on one hand, I poured out with the other a noggin of the water—for I couldn't quite venture on the whisky—into one of the tumblers, and singing out, 'Nelson, for ever!' drank it off. Then, spluttering and half-choking, I got down from the table, and at last looked at my father.

"He was so pale as to be all but green. He looked as if he was sea-sick. He said, 'Has your mother ever seen you do such things as that?' I shook my head. But Mr. Turner was laughing. What's more, he hadn't finished with me yet.

" 'Have you got such a thing as a stout piece of rope,

William—say a dozen fathom?' he asked my father. There were few things my father was *not* possessor of. We went out into the garden, and as neat as ninepence Mr. Turner flung a bight of the rope over one of the upper branches of a fine shady sycamore that grew so close to the house that its leaves in summer actually brushed against its windows.

" 'Try that, young man,' said my father's friend, Mr. Turner, when he had made it fast.

"Well, whether it was due to the devil in Sandy Two or only to the workings of the magic jacket, I don't know, but I shinned up that unknotted rope like a monkey up a palm tree. And when I reached the top, I edged along on my stomach till I was almost at the end of the bough. Then at arms' length I began to dandle on it—up and down, up and down, like a monkey on elastic. When it had given me enough swing and impetus—what's called *momentum* —I let go—and landed as pat as a pea-shooter through the open window onto the landing, the sill of which was some twelve feet from the ground.

"When I came down into the garden again, my father and Mr. Turner were having a close, earnest talk together, under the sycamore. My father looked at me as if I had just come back from the Andaman Islands.

"I said, 'Was that all right, Daddy?'

"But he made no answer; only patted me on the shoulder, turning his head away. And from that moment, and for ever after, we were the best of friends, my father and I; though he never had the ghost of a notion of what had caused Sandy Two—whom, mind you, he had never noticed before—to sprout like that!

"But then, that's how things go. And—to cut a long story short—by hook and by crook, by twisting and turn-ing—chiefly my father's—which would take too long to put down in black and white, I won free of groceries at last for good and all. And the next spring I went to sea for a trial voyage. And after *that,* though it was pretty hard going—well, I got into the Navy.

"And now, here I am, for good and all on land again. Not much short of being an old man, but still, thank God, hale and hearty, and able and willing, I hope, to do a fellow creature a good turn at need. And this, my lad, is where *you* come in.

"The fact of the matter is, I had watched you scrabbling away with your chalks at your pitch in Little St. Ann's a good many days before you knew it. And I came to two conclusions. First, that your pictures are proof that you can do good work. And second, that you could do much better. What I feel is you keep *yourself* back, do you see? It's the old story of Sandy One and Sandy Two. You haven't the confidence, the go, the guts (in a word), to forge clean ahead, *your* way.

"That's what I say. I see you setting to work in the morning like a young cockatrice, but presently you begin to waver, you become slack and dispirited. The least little mishap—a broken chalk, some oaf *walking* over the pictures, even a cloud floating up over the sun—shakes your nerve. At such times you don't seem to be sure even of what you want to do, let alone how to do it. You niggle at a picture first one way, then another, and at the end give it up in despair, the zest gone, and the fancy gone, and the spirit—what I call the innards—gone too. And when any stranger speaks to you, or drops a copper in your cap, you flush up, droop, go limp and dumb, and look as if butter wouldn't melt in your mouth.

"Now first, my boy, don't mind what I am saying. It is for your *sake.* I wouldn't be taking the trouble except only

and solely in the hope and wish of doing you a small service. And remember this, I've been through it all before you
—and may, when the end comes, again. I've known what
it is to feel my bones melt in my body, to tremble like a
jelly, my face like a plaster mask and my skull as empty
as a hulk on a sandbank. In two words, I know of old what
it's like to be *Sandy One*. So, you see, it's because I'm mor-
ally certain there's a Sandy *Two* in *you*—and maybe one
beyond anything I can conjecture—that I'm writing this
now.

"I like the cut of your jib, and the way you stick to
things in spite of all dispiritment and the dumps. I had my
eye on him when you marked the mug (for good, I hope)
of that suety butcher's boy the other day who spat on your
Old Boney. I want to give you a hand *in your own line,* and
see no better way of doing it than by just lending you my
old Pekin jacket for a bit. Now what do you think about
that?

"Maybe it won't work. Maybe its magic's gone. Maybe
I imagine as much as I remember about it. But I can say
this—the last time I squeezed into it before the toughest
engagement I ever came out of alive, I reckon it blew up
the enemy's ship at least two hours before she'd have gone
to the bottom in the usual way. Mind you, I haven't *often*
used it. When I was your age, an hour or two of it tired me
out for half the next week. A day or two of it might take a
complete month to recover from. Besides, if you look at
the matter by and large, and fair and square, you can see it
wouldn't do. In the long run we have to trust to what we
have in us that's constant and natural, so to speak, and
work like a slave at that. It's only in tight corners we need
a little extra fire and frenzy. *Then* maybe Dame Fortune will
see fit to lend a helping hand.

"So all I say is, give the jacket a trial. There is almost room for two of you in it—so if you don't want it to be noticeable, put it on under your own coat, and see how things go. And last, remember this, my boy: whatever happens, I shall still be keeping an eye on you. As my dear mother used to say, 'There may be more than one way home, Sandy—but it's trudging does it.' And here's good luck; God bless you; and *Finis*."

It was the last page of Admiral Rumbold's "yarn." Mike turned it over, looked at the back, coughed, and drank down what was left of his cold cocoa. He wiped his mouth with the back of his hand and looked up as he did so at the round yellow face of the clock that hung on the wall at the further end of the shop. At that very moment, it seemed, it had begun to tick. The long hand stood at two minutes before the hour. The old gentleman must be expecting him now—this very minute! Had he meant him to open the parcel and put on the jacket inside it there and then? His face flushed, then paled—he couldn't make up his mind. His head was in a whirl; his heart thumping under his ribs; he broke out hot and damp all over.

While he was still debating what he should do, he noticed that the man who had brought him the food— with his long tallow-coloured face and pale grey eyes—was steadily though vacantly watching him. Mike got up in haste, pushed the remnants of his last door-step of beef and bacon into his pocket, hastily snatched up the Admiral's manuscript and brown-paper parcel, and left the eating-house.

Before actually turning the corner which would bring him in sight of his pitch, he peeped round to see if the old gentleman was anywhere to be seen. He certainly was. At this actual moment he was walking away from Mike—square compact shoulders, brown billycock hat, and firm rolling tread. When once more he returned to the pictures he paused, looked them over one by one, dropped something into the cap, and continued on his way. In less than a minute or so he was back again, had taken another look, and once more paid his fee.

It appeared as if Admiral Rumbold had been so engaged ever since he had left Mike in the coffee-shop; and there could be no doubt he had by this means attracted passers-by to follow his example and look at the pictures. Many, it is true, just glanced and passed on; but a few paid their coppers. The old gentleman was now approaching the street corner where Mike was in hiding, so Mike stepped out a little shamefacedly and met him there and then.

"Aha!" cried Admiral Rumbold. "So there you are! Good! And sharp to time. Did you finish it? Good! Have you got it on?"

Mike went red, then white. He said: "I have read it, every page, sir, but the jacket's still in the paper, because——"

"Be dashed to 'Because'!" cried the Admiral. "Come a pace or two down that alley yonder. We'll soon put that right."

So they went off together into the shelter of an alley near by, above which the green leaves of a plane tree showed over the glass-bottled wall; and Mike, having taken off his own old loose long coat, slipped into the Chinese jacket as easily as an eel, and then back into his own again on top of it. Admiral Rumbold, having crushed up the brown paper into a ball, tied the string round it, and lightly flung it over the wall. "Good luck to it!" said he.

"Now," he added, and looked at Mike—then paused.

The boy stood motionless, as though he were frozen, yet he was trembling. His lips were moving. He seemed to be trying to say something for which he could not find the words. When at last he lifted his face and looked up, the old Admiral was astonished at the black-blue of his eyes in his pale face. It was the dark dazzling blue of deep seas. The Admiral could not for the life of him remember where he had seen eyes resembling them. They were unlike the eyes of boy or man or child or woman, and yet *somewhere* he had seen their like. Mike was smiling.

"The green crocodiles, sir," he said, fingering one of the buttons. "Most of them are not much bigger than ha'-pennies, but you can feel all the horny parts, and even the eyes stickin' out of their heads."

"Ay, ay," said the Admiral. "That's Chinese work. That's how *they* work—at least in times gone by. But how do you feel, how do you *feel*, my lad?"

Mike gazed up an instant at his old friend; then his glance roved on and upward towards the pale-green pentagonal plane leaves above his head and the patch of blue and sunny sky beyond. A smart north-west breeze was blowing, and a mountainous cloud was moving up into the heights of noonday.

"I'd like," he answered huskily, "to get back to the pitchers, sir."

"Ay, ay!" cried the Admiral. And again, "Ay, ay! Back we go." So the two of them set off together.

And though to all outward appearance the old gentleman, whose face was all but as red as a pimento, was as cool as a cucumber when he came stumping along beside his young acquaintance, his excitement was intense. It was Mike who had now taken the lead. The Admiral was merely following in his wake. The boy seemed utterly

changed, made over again. There was a look to him even as
he walked that was as lively as a peal of bells. It was as if
his bright and burning sun had suddenly shone out between clouds as cold as granite, lighting up the heavens.
What was to happen next?

First, Mike took up his cap, and with not even a
glance at what was inside it, emptied its contents into his
coat pocket. He then paced slowly on from one picture to
the next, until he had scrutinised the complete seven. From
the pocket with the remains of the "door-step" in it he
then drew out his capacious strip of rag and hurried off to a
dribbling water standard with a leopard's head on the
spout about twenty-five yards away. There he wetted his rag
through and through. He came back to his pictures, and
in a few moments had completely rubbed every one of them
out. No more than the faintest blur of pink and yellow
was left to show that the paving-stones had ever lost their
usual grey, and in three minutes that was dowsed out too.

When he had finished this destruction, and the warm
morning air had dried the stones again, he knelt down and
set to work. He seemed to have forgotten the old Admiral,
the Chinese jacket, everything that had happened that
morning. He seemed to be wholly unaware of the passers-
by, the dappling sunbeams, the clatter and stir of the street,
and even who and where and what he was. Skinny and engrossed, he squatted on his hams there, huddled up under
the wall, and *worked*.

Admiral Rumbold, as he watched him, became almost alarmed at the rapidity with which things were taking
shape on the blank paving-stones. As if by magic and
before his very eyes there had loomed into view a full-
rigged ship, swimming buoyant as a swan on the blue of its

waters, its masts tapering up into the heavens, its sails bellying like drifts of snow; while from its portholes pushed the metal mouths of such dogs as he himself had often heard bark, and seldom to no purpose.

It was not so much the resemblance of this picture to a real ship on a real sea under a real sky that drew out of his mouth a grunted, "Begad, begad!" but something in the look of the thing, some spirit living and lovely and ever-lasting behind it all, to which he could not have given name, but which reminded him of the eyes that had looked up at him a few minutes before under the plane leaves in the alley after their first intense glance at the crocodile buttons. Yes, and reminded him too of an evening long ago when he had made the circuit of his mother's maghogany dining-table on little more of his anatomy than his thumbs.

By this time a few other wayfarers had begun to collect and to watch the young street artist at his work. It did not seem to matter that he had forgotten to put back his cap in its customary place, that in fact it was on his head, for, oddly enough, when these idlers turned away, though every single one of them seemed to marvel at the quickness and skill of the boy, yet they all seemed *anxious* to be gone, and nobody gave him a ha'penny.

Admiral Rumbold could stand the strain no longer. He firmly placed a half-crown beside the little heap of coloured chalks, coughed loudly, paused an instant, and then, seeing that Mike had not noticed him, stole off and left him to his work.

The worst of the Admiral's anxieties were over. There could be no doubt in the world that the magic jacket had lost not one whit of its powers since first he had slipped into it himself all but sixty years ago. The only thing that troubled him was that not a single farthing had been bestowed on the young artist in the last quarter of an hour. Nevertheless, he thought he knew why.

"They're scared!" he muttered to himself. "They don't know what to make of it. They see it's a marvel and a miracle—and beyond 'em. They don't like the smell of it. They think it's dangerous. They just watch and wonder and sneak away. Well, my dear Rumbold, why *not*? Have patience. Never mind that. Wait and see!"

He loaded himself up with coppers the next morning, and returned very early to the narrow terrace behind Great St. Ann's. The night before had been rainless; only the lightest of dews had fallen. It had been windless, too, and there was a moon; so that the row of pictures which Mike had left unfinished on the pavement must have faintly bloomed under her beams that whole night long, and now were as fresh as they were at the first making of them. Admiral Rumbold had sallied out at this unusual hour to steal a glance at them alone; but Mike had been up before him.

There he was—on his knees once more—deaf and blind it seemed to everything in the world outside him, and intent only on his pictures. His old friend didn't interrupt him, but left him to himself, and went off to get some breakfast at his club. When he returned the boy had vanished for the time being. Five pictures out of the customary seven were now complete.

The Admiral stared and stared at them, part in astonishment, part in inexpressible delight, and part in the utmost dismay. Two of them—the ship, "The Old Victery" and the new "Hornted"—were more vivid and astonishing things than (with French chalks and paving-stones) he had thought even possible. The rest, he felt uneasily, were beyond his comprehension. He could hardly make head or tail of them.

One was called "Peepul at Sunset." It reminded him of Shadrach, Meshech, and Abed-nego walking in the midst of the burning fiery furnace. Another was called "The Blind Man"; it showed a chair, a table with a bowl of flowers, and a dish of fruit on it. There was an open window, too. It seemed to shimmer and glow and blaze like precious stones. But to the Admiral's eye the chair was all clumped and crooked, and the flowers looked queer—half human. He had never in all his born days seen a picture of a chair like that. Besides, there was not even a sign of a human being, let alone a blind man, to be seen! He stirred, coughed softly. He sighed; and glanced into the ragged cap. It was now a quarter to ten; the cap contained a French penny, a British ha'penny, and a three-penny bit with a hole in it. The Admiral lugged out of his pocket a handful of coppers, and added them to what was there. Off and on throughout the day he kept an eye on the young street artist. Of two things he was at last certain: first, that Mike was still wearing the jacket; and next, that he had made (apart from his own donations) practically no profit. For you cannot pick up coloured chalks in the gutter, or patch the knees of your old breeches with the empty air! The boy could hardly have taken an independent sixpence.

Admiral Rumbold began to be a little anxious as he thought this dark fact over, but decided not to interfere. Next day he knocked fairly early at the door of a lodging-house nearly opposite Mike's pitch.

"Good morning," he said, as soon as it was opened. "I'd like, if you please, to have the window again. Is it free?"

"Certainly, sir," said the woman who had answered

his knock. "I'm glad you enjoy the view, sir. It's a pity there's so much wall."

"It's not the bricks, ma'am, but the people," replied the Admiral, as he followed her up a flight of stairs into a room which immediately overlooked the street.

There—behind the Brussels curtains at the window, and seated on a rather lumpy armchair—the Admiral spent most of his morning, watching all that went on in the street below, but especially the boy. And once more he came to two conclusions: first, that Mike was *not* now wearing the jacket, and next that he was making less money even than the day before. *Life* seemed to be gone out of him. He sat hunched up beside his chalks and his empty cap—his bony face as grey as ashes. He hardly dared even raise his eyes when anybody paused to examine his pictures. Now and again, however, he would glance anxiously up and down the street as if in search of somebody.

"He's looking for me," muttered the Admiral to himself. "He wants to return the jacket. God bless *me!* Still, steady does it; steady does it."

He returned to his window in the early afternoon. The boy looked even more miserable and dejected than ever, but none the less he had begun to tinker a bit at his picture, "The Old Victery." On this occasion the Admiral had brought field-glasses with him. With these he could now watch his young friend at work so closely as almost to fancy he could hear him breathe. Indeed, he could see even a round-headed ant making its way along the crack between two paving-stones; and the tiny bits of chalk resembled coloured rocks.

Mike laboured on, now rubbing out, now chalking in, and the Admiral could follow every tint and line and stroke. At last—though by no means as if he were satisfied

—the boy stood up and examined what he had done. At sight of it he seemed to droop and shrink. And no wonder. The Admiral almost wept aloud. The thing was ruined. There was the ship, there the sea, and there the sky; but where the lovely light and airiness, the romance, the wonder? Where the *picture?*

Admiral Rumbold was at his wits' end. The day was drawing on. He began to think that his intended kindness had ruined the boy for good and all. He sat back in his chair absolutely at a loss what to do next. One thing was certain. He must go soon and have a word with the boy— hearten and liven him up. He must give him a good square meal, put some "beef" into him, and—perhaps—take the jacket back. It had been little but a deceit and a failure. He must take the jacket back, then think things over.

He leant forward to rise from his chair, and as he did so cast a last desperate glance at the opposite side of the street. Then he paused. Fine weather was still in the heavens. The first colours of evening were beginning to stretch across London's skies—shafts of primrose, melted gold, and faint crimson lighting up the walls of the houses, flooding the streets with light. And Mike was no longer alone. He was still squatting tailor-fashion under his wall and as motionless as if he had been carved out of ebony, but a pace or so away stood an odd-looking old gentleman in a sort of long curry-coloured ulster. This old gentleman had a beard and wore a high conical black felt hat with a wide rim to it. An umbrella, less neat but more formidable in appearance even than the Admiral's, was tucked under his arm.

He was not merely looking at, he was intent on, "lost" in the pictures. He stooped over them each in turn, spending at least two or three minutes over every one, except "The Old Victery," at which he just glanced and went on.

When he found himself at the end of the row, he turned back and examined them all over again. Admiral Rumbold watched these proceedings with bated breath. The old man in the ulster had now turned to Mike, who at once scrambled to his feet, leaving his chalks, his cap, and a small newspaper parcel on the pavement. The two of them in the clear-coloured evening light were soon talking together almost as if they were father and son. They were talking about the pictures, too; for every now and again Mike's new acquaintance, bent almost double, would point with the stump of his umbrella at one of them, tracing out a line, or hovering over a patch of colour. At the same time, his beard turned over his shoulder towards Mike, he would seem to be praising, or criticising, or explaining, or asking questions. Once, indeed, he stooped, caught up a piece of chalk, and himself drew a few lines on the pavement as if to show the boy exactly what he meant. "So!" the Admiral heard him end, brushing his fingers.

There could be no doubt this eccentric old gentleman in the wide black hat was interested not only in the pictures but also in Mike. He looked as if in his excitement he might go on talking till midnight. But no; at this very moment he seemed to be making some kind of proposal to the boy. He had put his hand on his shoulder as if in encouragement. Mike hesitated; then cast a long look into the sky, as if to consult the weather. After that his mind seemed to be made up. He hastily took up his cap, his chalks, and his parcel, and the two of them set off down Little St. Ann's together.

At this Admiral Rumbold paused no longer. He seized his hard billycock hat, his field-glasses, and his malacca cane, and clattered down the stairs out into the street. Keeping well behind them, he followed Mike and the old

gentleman out of Little St. Ann's into Ashley Court, and so across into Jermyn Street. At this corner, so intent was he in his pursuit, that he barely escaped being run over by a two-horse grocery van.

Mike and the old gentleman were now so clearly in sight that the Admiral had time to pause and address a policeman.

"Good evening, constable," he said. "I want you to tell me if by any chance you happen to know the *name* of that old gentleman in the hat yonder, walking with that lad there?"

The policeman fixed his eyes on the pair.

"Well, sir, to tell you the truth, sir," he said at last, "I've *seen* him somewhere though I couldn't say rightly just where. I've even been told who he *is*. But bless me, if I can lay tongue to the name of him. I wish I could, sir. He looks as if it might be worth while." Admiral Rumbold thanked the policeman and hastened on.

At the moment when he once more came within sight of the two of them a long-haired youngish young man in a dark, loose cape or cloak had but just met and passed them by. This young man was also wearing a black wide-brimmed hat. As soon as politeness permitted, he not only stopped dead, but stood intently watching the pair until Admiral Rumbold himself had come up with him. The Admiral glanced him over.

"You will excuse me, sir," he said, "but if I am not mistaken, you are as much interested in that old gentleman yonder as I am myself. A most impressive figure! Could you oblige me with his *name?*"

"His *name*, sir!" exclaimed the young man. "Gracious heavens! why, that's old B———. That's 'old B. in a Bonnet!' —the crankiest, craziest old creature in the British Isles.

But make no mistake, sir. What that old boy doesn't know about pictures and painting isn't worth a tallow candle. He's a Master. Wait till he's dead, that's all. Then the whole world will be wagging with him."

"You don't say *so!*" shouted the Admiral. "A *Master! Painting!*—eh? I am very greatly obliged to 'ee—very greatly obliged. And you think if he's taken a fancy to that lad there—*sees* promise in him, I mean—well—that the lad's in luck's way?"

" 'Think?' " replied the young man. "Bless your heart, sir, I *know*."

The Admiral detained him no longer. He saluted him and passed on. He could say no more. He was satisfied. All was well. The magic jacket, then, had *not* played him false; Mike's "steepish bit of hill" was well begun. He found himself at the further end of Jermyn Street, and in the traffic of the Haymarket. The old man in the ulster had disappeared. But no, there he was—old B.—some little distance down on the opposite side of the street, and at the window of a print-seller's shop. He was talking to the boy at his side —pointing, gesticulating, his bushy beard wagging. And Mike was listening, gazing in, entranced. Admiral Rumbold turned on his heel. He had never professed to know much about pictures. Then why should he now suddenly feel downcast and depressed? He was tired, too, and extremely thirsty. It was almost as if he missed his jacket.

The Scarecrow

The house in which old Mr. Bolsover lived was of a faded yellow primrose colour; it was a long house, but of only two storeys. Yet even its lower windows looked out far away over the meadows lying at this moment spread out beneath them, bright green in the morning sunshine. A narrow veranda shaded the windows, its sloping canopy of copper now a pale grey-green; and around its slim wooden pillars clemantis and jessamine clambered. At either end of it was a low weather-worn stone pedestal. On these stood two leaden fauns—the one ever soundlessly piping to the other across the wallflower and the pinks. And it was the pinks that were now in flower, white as snow, and filling the air with their musky fragrance.

A little clock had just chimed ten, and old Mr. Bolsover, in his cool white jacket, was coming out of the French windows of the breakfast-room with his small niece, Letitia. Letitia had a quick nimble way of walking and talking and turning her head that was like a bird's. And old Mr. Bolsover, with his eyes and his nose, was rather like a bird himself, but of the long-legged, tall, solemn kind—the flamingos and the storks. They came to a standstill together looking out over the meadows.

"Oh, Uncle Tim, what a *perfectly* lovely morning!" said Letitia.

"A *perfectly* lovely morning," said Uncle Tim. "Just as if it had been ordered all complete and to match for a certain small friend of mine!

> *Lettie's like a lovely day:*
> *She comes; and then—she goes away."*

"Ah, Uncle Tim," said Letitia, "that's called *flattery."*

"Bless me, my dear," replied her uncle, squinnying at her from under the glasses of his spectacles, "it doesn't matter a pin what it's called!"

"Ah, I know all about that!" said Letitia. "And to think it is exactly a whole year since I was here before! Yet you wouldn't believe a single pink was different. Isn't that funny, Uncle Tim? *We* are. And why, yes," she went on hastily, twisting her head on her slender neck, "there's that curious old Guy Fawkes creature over there by the willows. He's not changed a single bit either."

"So it is, so it is," said Uncle Tim, peering out over the meadows. "Though as a matter of fact, my dear, it's not quite true to say he hasn't changed a *bit*. He has changed his hat. Last year it was an old hat, and now it's a very old hat, a shocking hat. No wonder he covers up one eye under its brim. But it doesn't matter how long you stare at him, he'll stare longer."

Letitia none the less continued to gaze at the scarecrow—and with a peculiar little frown between her eyes.

"You know, he *is* a little queer, Uncle Tim—if you look at him long enough. And you can easily pretend you are not *quite* looking at him. You don't seem to remember either," she went on solemnly, "that the very last morning I was here you promised me faithfully to tell me all about him. But you didn't, because Mother came in just when I was asking you, and you forgot all about it."

"Why, so I did," said Mr. Bolsover. "That's what comes of having a memory like a bag with a hole in it. That's what comes of the piecrust promises are made of— they just melt in your mouth. . . . Still, that's Old Joe right enough. *So* old, my dear, you could hardly tell us apart!"

"You're please not to say that, Uncle Tim—it isn't true. You are the youngest, oldest, kindest Uncle Tim that ever was. So there. But what *were* you going to tell me about Old Joe? Where did he come from? What is he for— except the rooks, I mean? Isn't there a tune about Old Joe? Is that him? Tell me *now?*" cried Letitia. "Let's sit down here comfily on the stones. Feel! they are as warm as toast with the sun! And now go straight on. *Please.*"

Down sat old Mr. Bolsover; down sat Letitia—side by side like Mr. Punch and his dog Toby. And this is the story he told of Old Joe. . . .

"I must begin, Letitia," he began, "at the beginning. It is much the best place from which to get to the end. Now when I was about your age—not quite 129 years ago—I used sometimes to go and stay with an old friend of my mother's—your grandmother's, that is—whose name was Sara Lumb. She was a very stout woman, with black sleek hair, round red cheeks, and dimples for knuckles. And she used, I remember, to wear an amethyst-coloured velvet cap, flat over her ears, and a lace thingummy over

her shoulders. I can see her now—her wide face all creased up in smiles, and her fat fingers with their emeralds and their amethysts, and even the large emerald brooch she wore at her neck. She wasn't an aunt of mine, she wasn't even so much as my godmother, but she was extremely kind to me. *Almost* as kind as I am to you! She was very fond of eatables and drinkables too and had a cook that could make every sort of cake that is worth talking about—seven sultanas and nine currants to the square inch. Jams, jellies, raspberry fool, fritters, pancakes, tipsy-cake—they were the best I have ever tasted. So were her stuffed eggs and oyster patties at the Christmas parties. My eye!"

"Oh, Uncle Tim," said Letitia, "you *were* a greedy thing."

"And what's worse," said her uncle, "I have never grown out of it. You shall see for yourself at lunch. And if I'm not an unprophetic Double-Dutchman I can already smell apple charlotte. But never mind about that. It's no good—until it's ready. But in any case I am sure you will agree, Letitia, that my old friend Mrs. Lumb was just the kind of old friend for a small boy with a large appetite to stay *with*. This of course was always during the holidays; and, in those days, while there was plenty of hard tack at school, 'impots,' canings, cabbage stalks, cod, suet-duff, castor oil, bread-and-scrap, and what not, there was no such horror as a holiday task. Holiday tasks always remind me, my dear, of the young lady who wanted to go out to swim:

> *Mother, may I go out to swim?*
> *Yes, my darling daughter.*
> *Fold your clothes up neat and trim,*
> *And don't go near the water.*"

"The rhyme *I* know," said Letitia, "is 'Hang your clothes on a hickory limb.' "

"That's all very well," said her uncle, "but just you show me one! Let's have it both ways then:

> *Mother, may I go out to swim?*
> *Yes, my darling daughter.*
> *Fold your clothes up neat and trim,*
> *(So at least says Uncle Tim),*
> *Or hang them up on a hickory limb,*
> *(That's what Letitia said to him),*
> *And don't go near the water.*

What—before this violent quarrel—I *meant* was, my dear, that in those days *no* good little boy had to stew indoors in his holidays and simply *detest* reading a book which he would have given half his pocket money to read for its own sake *if* he had never been made to. Q.E.D. But that's quite between ourselves. We must never, never criticize our elders. And anyhow, at my old friend's Mrs. Lumb's there was no need to. It was bliss.

"First, hers was a queer old rambling house, much older than this one, and at least three and a half times as big again. Next, there was beautiful country round it too; fields stretching down their sunny slopes, and little woods and copses on the crests and in the folds and valleys; and a stream—with reeds and rushes and all sorts of water birds —that came brawling over the stones at the foot of her long sloping garden. But I hate descriptions, don't you, Letitia? And *there,* an orchard so full of cherry trees that in springtime it looked as if it were thick with snow. Well, well, if ever I go to heaven, my child, I hope to see that house and garden again."

"But isn't it still *there?*" said Letitia. "I mean, you know, where it used to be?"

"Alas, my dear, no," said old Mr. Bolsover. "It is gone for ever. There came a cook—*not* Mrs. Lumb's. She was frying dabs—Brighton dabs—for breakfast one morning; the cat squealed and scratched her leg; she upset the pan; there was one huge blaze; she ran screeching into the garden instead of—well, doing what she ought to have done; and the old house was burned down clean to the ground. Clean. Think of that, Letitia. Always keep your eye on cats and fat. But this, I am thankful to say, was *after* my dear old friend Mrs. Lumb had left the house and had gone out to live with her younger brother in Ceylon, where the bad cook's strong tea had come from.

"Now in those far-away days *birds* were all my fancy. The wonder is I never sprouted feathers. I loved them too much to carry a catapult, but not enough to refrain from setting traps for them, to catch them for pets. Brick traps and sieve traps. But how would you like to be a linnet or a lark or a thrush or a bullfinch caged up in one tiny room with bars for windows just to amuse a wretch of a boy like me when I was nine or ten or eleven or thereabouts?"

"I shouldn't," said Letitia. "But I'd *much* rather be in your cage than in any other horrid little boy's."

"Thank you, my dear," said Mr. Bolsover. "That's a bargain. Still, the wilder the bird the worse the cage. But then as I was a boy, I did as boys do—bless their little hearts! And I used to weep tears like a crocodile when the sparrows or finches I caught moped off and died. After the funeral I'd stick a bit of wood in the ground to mark the grave—and go off to set another trap.

"My traps were everywhere, and sometimes in places where they had no business to be. But first you must understand what I was after, really *after*." Mr. Bolsover all but whispered it. "It was *rare* birds—hoopoes, golden orioles, honey buzzards—the lovely and seldom. Deep down in me I pined for a bird unspeakably marvellous in plumage and song; a bird that nobody else had ever even seen; a bird that had flown clean out of the window of some magician's mind. Which means of course that I had become a little cracked on birds. I used even to dream of that bird sometimes—but then it was usually me myself that was in the cage!

"Well, there was one particular covert that I kept in memory to set a trap in for days before I ventured to make the attempt. This was at the edge of a field where a great many birds of all kinds and sizes were accustomed to haunt, though I never found out why. I watched them again and again, hosts of them—their wings shimmering in the light. It seemed it was their happy secret meeting place— and in spite of Old Joe!"

"*That* Old Joe *there?*" cried Letitia, pointing at the mute lank ungainly figure over against the grey-green willows, with its ragged arms, and battered old hat on one side, that stood blankly gazing at them from out of the field beyond the garden.

"Yes," said her uncle, "that Old Joe *there*. You see, between you and me, Letitia, and don't let us look his way for a moment in case we should hurt his feelings, that Old Joe there (as perhaps you've guessed) is a scarecrow. He is nothing but a dumb, tumbledown hugger-mugger antiquated old hodmadod. He has never really been anything else; though after all the years he and I have been together, and not a single unkind word said on either side, he is now a sort of twin brother. Like Joseph and Benjamin, you know. Why, if we changed places, I don't suppose you would be able to tell us apart."

"How can you dare to say such things, Uncle Tim?" cried Letitia, pushing her hand in under his elbow. "You know perfectly well that that's a sort of a kind of flattery—of yourself, you bad thing."

"All I can say to that, Miss Tomtit," replied Uncle Tim, "is, ask Old Joe. Still, we are old friends now, he and I, whereas the first time I saw him he gave me a pretty bad fright. I had come creeping along on the other side of the hedge, keeping a very wary eye open for anybody that might be in the fields—because I was trespassing. When they were not being ploughed or harrowed or rolled or sown or hoed or cropped, there never was anybody; except perhaps on Sunday, when the farmer, Mr. Jones, a large stout man with a red face and a thick stick, came round to have a look at his crops.

"It was a wide, sloping, odd-shaped field of about forty acres running down to a point, rather like the map of England turned upside down, and with a little wood of larch on one side of it. This particular morning was in April. It was sunny but cold, and the field was bare except for its flints glinting in the sunbeams. It had been sown, but nothing green was showing.

"Well, I was skirting along the hedge, as I say, but on this side of it, carrying the bird snare I had with me under my jacket, and hardly able to breathe for excitement. I knew exactly—as I peered through the hedge, on which the thorn buds were just breaking green as emeralds—which was the place for me. There was a ditch beyond the hedge, and I could see only a narrow strip of the field at the moment, because of the hedge and bushes in between. But it was truly a little paradise of birds, my dear, and particularly when spring was on its way.

"Well, on I went until I came to the corner by the rickety old gate, which was tied up with a piece of chain. Between you and me it was a shameful old gate. But that is not *our* business. And all of a sudden I caught sight of what I supposed was Farmer Jones himself, glaring straight at me across the field, and not thirty yards away. I fairly jumped in my skin at sight of him, turned hot, then cold, and waited, staring back. For that one instant it seemed as if I could see the very colour of his eyeballs moving in his head.

"But all this was only in the flicker of a moment. No Farmer Jones that, and not even one of his men! It was just Old Joe; *our* Old Joe. That Old Joe there! Come alive. And after all, what *is* life, Letitia?"

"That's perfectly true, Uncle Tim," Letitia whispered, edging a little closer to him. "He might be alive at this very instant."

"And not only that, you must remember," went on Mr. Bolsover, "this was in Old Joe's better days. He was young then. He has been peacocked up in many a fine new suit of old clothes since then, and more hats than I could count on twice my fingers. But *then* he was in his heyday, in the very bloom of his youth, the glass of fashion and the knave of trumps. And now I wouldn't part with him for a bag of golden guineas. No, not for twenty bags. And though I am very fond of guineas, the reason for that is, first, that I love him for his own sweet sake alone, and next, my dear Letitia, because one doesn't very often see—*see*, I mean—real live fairies in this world."

Letitia burst out laughing. "Real, live fairies, Uncle

Tim!" she cried, stooping forward in her amusement and dragging her skirts tight down over her knees. "Why, you can't mean to say, you poor dear, that Old Joe's a *fairy?*"

"No," said Mr. Bolsover, "I didn't mean to say quite that. Then, as now, Old Joe was the scaringest of scaring scarecrows I have ever set eyes on. But, like the primrose in the poem, he was nothing more. No, it wasn't Old Joe himself who was the fairy, no more than the house behind us *is* you and me. Old Joe was merely one of this particular fairy's rendyvouses, as the old word goes. He was where she *was*.

"That morning, I remember, he was wearing a pair of slack black-and-white check trousers and a greenish black coat, very wide at the shoulders. Apart from the stick for his arm, another had been pushed into one of his coat-sleeves for a cudgel. Another with a lump at the top made his head and on that was a hat, a hard, battered, square black hat—like the hats farmers and churchwardens used to wear in those days. He was stooping forward a little, staring across at me as I crouched by the gate. As I say, I hugged the wire snare under my jacket closer, and stared back.

"Whether it was because of the hot air that was eddying up from the stony soil under the sun, or because of some cheating effect of the light on the chalky field, I can't say, Letitia. But even while I stood watching him, his head seemed to be ever so gently turning on his shoulders as if he were secretly trying to get a better view of me without my noticing it. Yet all the time I fancied this, I knew it wasn't true.

"Still, I was a good deal startled. Quite apart from crows and such riff-raff, he had certainly scared *me*—for in those days young trespassers (not to mention the old dou-

ble-toothed mantraps, which were a little before my time)
might find themselves in for a smart walloping if they
were caught. But even when I had recovered my wits I
continued to watch him, and at the same time kept glancing from side to side at the birds that were flighting about
me, or feeding, or preening and sunning themselves in
the dust. And though by this time I knew him for what he
was, I wasn't by any means at ease.

"For even if there were no real eyes in his own head,
I was perfectly certain that somebody or something was actually looking at me from under that old black hat, or from
out of his sleeve—from *some*where about him. The birds
were already used to my being there, simply because I remained so still. After perhaps five whole minutes of this, I
squatted down at the edge of the field and began to set my
trap.

"But the whole time I was stooping over it, and softly
hammering the wooden peg in with a large flint, I was
thinking of the old scarecrow—though without looking at
him—and knew I was being watched. I say without looking at him, but whenever I got a chance I would snatch a
little secret glance at him from between my legs or over
my shoulder or from under my arm, pretending that I was
doing nothing of the kind. And then at last, the trap finished, I sat down on the grass under the hedge and steadily
fixed my eyes on him again.

"The sun climbed slowly up the blue sky, his rays
twinkling from sharp-cut stone to stone and scrap of glass.
The hot air rilled on at his feet. The birds went about their
business, and nothing else happened. I watched so hard
that my eyes began to water, but whatever was hiding
there, if anything *was* hiding there, could be as patient as I
was. And at last I turned home again.

"At the far corner of the field under an old thorn tree I stooped down once more as if I were tying up my shoe lace, and had another long look, and *then* I was perfectly certain I had caught a glimpse of something moving there. It was as if a face had very stealthily peered out of the shadow of the old scarecrow, and, on sighting me under the thorn tree, had as swiftly withdrawn into hiding again.

"All the rest of that day I could think of nothing else but Old Joe, assuring myself that my eyes had deceived me, or that a bird perched on his shoulder had fluttered down, or that a very faint breeze from over the open upland had moved in his sleeve. Or that I had made it all up. Yet I knew deep down inside me that this wasn't true. It was easy to invent explanations, but none of them fitted."

"It might, of course, Uncle Tim, you know," said Letitia, "it might have been not a bird but some little animal, mightn't it? I once saw a hare skipping about in the middle of a field, and then suddenly, though there wasn't even the tip of his ear showing before, there was another hare. And then another: would you believe it? And they went racing over the field one after the other until they went right out of sight. Or might it have been a bird, do you think, which was building its nest in Old Joe? Robins, you know, build their nests anywhere, even in an old boot. And I have seen a tit's nest with I don't know how many eggs in it in an old pump. And look, Uncle Tim, there is a bird actually perched on Old Joe's shoulder now! That's what it might have been, I think—some little animal, or bird nesting."

"Well, you shall hear," said Uncle Tim. "But I am quite certain that if you had been with me that morning, hundreds of years ago, you would have agreed that there was something different about Old Joe; different, I mean, from what he looks like now. He looked *queer*. I can't quite explain; but it was the difference between an empty furnished house and the same house with its family in it. It was the difference between fishing in a millpond which has fish in it and in one which has none. It was the difference between you yourself when you are really asleep and when you are only foxing and pretending to be. And what's more, sure enough, I was right.

"Now I had my proper bedtime at Mrs. Lumb's; and before it, always, an apple and a glass of milk. My old friend was not only a great believer in apples, but she had seven beautiful Jersey cows, which are a great help, my dear, not only at bedtime, but with gooseberry tart or apple pie. But she wasn't one of those Uncle Tims who want everything done exactly at the right moment. She didn't wait till the clock struck eight (which just shows how easy it is to rhyme if you don't try to) and then come peeping in to see if I was safe in bed."

"Why, you know very well," said Letitia, "you don't do that yourself."

"Aha!" said Mr. Bolsover, "I wonder. People who sleep with one eye open grow as wise as old King Solomon. I creep and I creep and I creep, and every door has a keyhole. But never mind that. That very evening after my first sight of Old Joe, and when, if I had been a nice, honest boy, I should have been in bed, I made my way down to his field again—slipping on from bush to bush, tree to tree, as cautiously as I could, so cautiously that I trod on the scut of a bunny, Esmeralda by name, that happened to be enjoying a dandelion for her supper on the other side of a bramble bush.

"When I reached my hawthorn tree—and hundreds of years old *that* looked—I stooped down beside its roots very

low to the ground, having made up my mind to watch until
the evening grew too dark to see across the field. It was getting into May, and the air was so sweet and still and fresh
that your eyes almost shut with bliss of themselves every
time you breathed. And in those days, Letitia, we kept clocks
by the sun. We didn't cheat him in the morning and pay
him back in the evenings, as we do now. So there was faded
gold and rose in the sky, though he himself was gone down.

"But apart from the birds and the bunnies, nothing
happened except this great Transformation Scene of day
turning into night, until it began to be dark. And then it
seemed that almost every moment Old Joe, inch by inch,
was steadily moving nearer. Seemed, mind you. And then, at
the very instant when I noticed the first star—which by its
mellow brightness and by where it was, must have been the
planet Venus—I saw—well, now, what do you think I saw?"

"The fairy!" said Letitia, and sighed.

"Full marks, my dear," said Mr. Bolsover, squeezing
her hand under his elbow. "The fairy. And the odd thing
is that I can't—can't possibly—describe her. This is perhaps partly because the light wasn't very good, and partly
because my eyes were strained with watching. But mostly
for other reasons. I seemed, you see, to be seeing her as *if*
I were imagining her, even though I knew quite well she
was there.

"You must just take my word for it—I knew she was
there. She was stooping forward a little, and the top of her
head reached, I should say, about up to what one might call
Old Joe's waist. There he is—say the third button down of
that old black coat he has on. Her face seemed to be a little
long and narrow, but perhaps this was because her fair
hair was hanging down on either cheek, straight and fine
as combed silk, and in colour between gold and grey—

rather like the colour of a phosphorescent fish in the dark, but much more gold than silver. It looks to me, now I come to think of it, that since it was now gloaming I must have been seeing her in part as if by her own light.

"She stood lovely and motionless as a flower. And merely to gaze at her filled me with a happiness I shall not forget but cannot describe. It was as though I had come without knowing it into the middle of a dream in another world; and cold prickles went down my back, as if at the sound of enchanted music.

"There was not a breath of wind stirring. Everything around me seemed to have grown much more sharp and clear, even though the light was dim. The flowers were different, the trees, the birds. I seemed to know within me what the flowers were feeling—what it is like to be a plant with green pointed leaves and tiny caterpillar feet, like ivy, climbing from its white creeping roots in the dark earth by fractions of an inch, up the stem of a tree; or to have feathers all over me, and to float lighter than the air, and to be looking out from two small bright round eyes at my bird-world. I can't explain it, Letitia, but I am sure you will understand."

Letitia gave two solemn nods. "I *think* so, Uncle Tim —a little. Though I never should have guessed, you know, that any *boy* was like that."

"Boys, my dear, are mainly animals," Uncle Tim agreed heartily, "and so was I—nine and three-quarter tenths. But it was the other bit, I suppose, that was looking at Old Joe.

"And I firmly believe that the fairy knew I was there, but that in spite of knowing it, she could not delay doing what she wished to do any longer. For presently, after a minute or two, she drew very gently backwards and out of

sight, and then began to hasten away over the field towards
the corner of it furthest away from me, keeping all the time
as far as she was able so that Old Joe stood in between us,
and so prevented me from seeing her clearly, however much
I dodged my head from side to side in the attempt to do so.
Now that, Letitia, considering that she had her back turned
to me, and was flitting along as swiftly as a shadow—*that*
was a very difficult thing to do; and I don't quite see how
she managed it. I am perfectly certain *I* couldn't—without
once looking back, I mean."

"And what," said Letitia, "was she like from behind?"

Old Mr. Bolsover narrowed his eyes, and shut his lips.
"She was like," he said slowly, "a wraith of wood smoke
from a bonfire. She was like what, if you could see it, you
might suppose a puff of wind would be in the light over
snow. She was like the ghost of a little waterfall. She
moved, I mean, my dear, as if she were hovering on her
way; and yet she never left the ground. Far, far more
lightly than any gazelle she stepped; and it was so entrancing to watch her in the quiet and dusk of that great
field, it fairly took my breath away. And mind you, I was
only a clod-hopping boy of about ten."

Mr. Bolsover took a large coloured silk handkerchief
out of his pocket and, as if in triumph, blew his nose. "I
ought to add at once," he continued, pushing the handkerchief back into his pocket again except for one bright
coloured corner, "that this is not a story at all. Not a story,
Letitia."

"But *I* think, Uncle Tim, it *is* a story," said Letitia. "It
doesn't make stories any worse if they are *true*. I mean,
don't you think, that all *real* stories seem better than true?
Don't you think so yourself, Uncle Tim? Just think of the

Seven Swans, and Snow White! Oh, all those. At least I do. Please, please go on."

"What *I* mean, my dear, is that a story ought really to be like a piece of music. It should have a beginning and a middle and an end, though you could hardly say which is which when it all comes out together. It ought to be like a whiting with its tail in its mouth—but a live whiting, of course. This one, you see, this one I am telling you, begins —and then goes off into nothing."

"I don't think," said Letitia, "that matters one atom. Just please go on with the fairy, Uncle Tim."

"Well, as soon as she was gone out of sight, my one and only desire was to steal into the field and take a look at Old Joe at close quarters. But upon my word, Letitia, I hadn't the courage. He was *her* dwelling-place, her hiding-place, her habitation: at least whenever she needed one. That was certain. Now that she was absent, had forsaken it, had gone away, the very look of him had changed. He was empty, merely a husk; he was just nothing but a hodmadod —Old Joe. Though we won't think a bit the worse of him for that. Bless me, no! When *you* have gone daydreaming, your face, Letitia, I assure you, looks still and quiet and happy. But I am afraid you must be thinking I was an exceedingly stupid boy. You see, I *was*. And I confess that I simply could not make up my mind to go a step nearer.

"Old Joe was quite alone now. I wasn't afraid of *him*. But after what I had seen I felt a curious strangeness all about me. I was afraid because I felt I had been spying, and that every living thing within view under the quiet sky knew of this and wanted to be rid of my company. I didn't— which was worse—even go to look at my bird snare. And when I went to the field again it had vanished.

"Next morning after breakfast with my old friend Mrs.

Lumb, I talked my way round until at last we came to fairies. 'I sometimes wonder if they *can* be true,' I said to her airily—as if I had just thought of it. Alas, Letitia, what deceivers we may be! But yes. My old friend believed in fairies all right. I never felt any doubt about that. But she had never seen one. I asked her what she thought a fairy would be like if she ever did see one. She sat in her chair—with her cup in her hand—looking out of the window and munching her toast.

" 'Well, between you and me, my dear Tim,' she said (*crunch, crunch*), 'I never much cared about the flibberti-gibbety little creatures which are supposed to find a water-lily as comfortable a place to sleep in as you might find a four-post bed. That, I think, is all my eye and Betty Martin. And I don't believe myself that any fairy would pay much attention to *me* (*crunch, crunch*). I expect (*crunch, crunch*) they prefer people, if they care for human beings at all, with less *of* and *to* them. And probably there are not many of them left in England now. Fairies, I mean. There are too many of *us*. Mr. Lumb, as you know, was an en-tomologist. Perhaps he would have been able to tell you more about it. Besides (*crunch, crunch*), he had once seen a ghost.' "

"Do you really mean," said Letitia, "that your friend Mrs. Lumb's *husband* had once seen a ghost, and that *he* was—was dead too?"

"That's what Mrs. Lumb meant, my dear, and I asked her what the ghost her husband saw was like. 'Well,' she said, 'it was like (*crunch, crunch*) it was like, he told me, seeing something with your eyes shut. It made him feel very cold; the bedroom went black; but he wasn't frightened.' "

Letitia sidled yet a little closer to her uncle. "Between you and me, Uncle Tim," she said, "I believe that ghost would have given *me* the shudders. Don't you? But please let's go back to your fairy. Did you tell Mrs. Lumb about that?"

"I never breathed so much as a single syllable, though if you were to ask me why, I couldn't say. It's just like small boys, I suppose; and small girls too, eh? They are dumplings, but keep the apple to themselves."

"I think I'd have told just you, Uncle Tim," said Letitia. "And what happened then?"

"Two whole days went by before I ventured near the field again, though I doubt if an hour passed without my thinking of it. The birds in my memory seemed now to be stranger, wilder, and lovelier creatures than I had ever realized. I even set free the two I had in small wooden cages—a linnet and a chaffinch—and for a while thought no more of traps and snaring. I loafed about wondering if all that I had seen might not have been mere fancy.

"And then on the third evening, I was so ashamed of myself that I determined to go down to the edge of the woods again and keep watch. This time I made my way to the upper corner of the field by the larch plantation, all in its fresh young green. It was there, as I supposed, I had seen the fairy vanish. The pheasants were crowing in their coverts, and the last birds were at evensong. I crept in between some elder bushes, and having made myself comfortable, took out a little red and brass pocket telescope which my father had given me. Through this I hoped to be able to see clearly everything that might happen near Old Joe. It would bring him as close as if I could touch him with my hand. But when I came to put the telescope to my eye I found that one of the lenses was broken.

"It was a little later in the evening than on my first visit, and though the skies were still burning, the sun had set. But my legs were all pins and needles, and my eyes nearly gone black with staring on and on, before I saw anything out of the common.

"And then, Letitia, all of a sudden I knew not only that the fairy was there again but also that again she was aware she was being watched. Yes, and though I had seen not the least stir or motion in Old Joe, she had already stolen out of her hiding-place and was steadily and *openly* gazing across the first faint green flush of the sprouting wheat in my direction. I held my breath and tried in vain to keep myself from shivering.

"For a moment or two she hesitated, then turned as before, and sped away, but now towards the very thorn tree from which I had first spied out on her. I was bitterly disappointed, *angry* and—well, I suppose it would be a queer boy who had nothing of the old hunter in him. It was clear she was pitting her wits against mine. And just as, though I was devoted to the wild birds, I would sometimes shake my fist at them and almost howl with rage when I saw one steal my bait without falling into the trap I had set, so I felt now.

"But I was stiff and aching, and it was too late to attempt to try and intercept her now. *'You wait!'* thought I to myself, 'next time we'll see who's craftiest.' So I shut up my telescope, brushed the dead leaves from my clothes, stayed till life came back into my leg, and then rather sulkily went home.

"That night was still and warm though April was not over yet. And while I was undressing a full moon began to rise. In spite of the candlelight I could see it shining through my bedroom blind. I blew out my candle, drew up the blind, and looked out of the window; and the world looked as if it were enchanted—like an old serpent that has sloughed its skin. It seemed the moon shed silence as well as light. And though I was there in my old friend Mrs. Lumb's familiar house—wood and brick and stone—it was as if no human being had ever looked out of her window like this before. And—even better, Letitia. The same feeling came over me when I had first caught sight of that Old Joe there. Just as the fairy had been aware of me watching her in the fields, so I was sure now that she was concealing herself not very far from the house and—watching my window."

"It *does* seem odd, Uncle Tim," said Letitia. "Isn't that *curious!* I know exactly what you mean. It's just as if there were things in the air, *telling* people, isn't it! And did—did you go out?"

"To tell you the truth, Letitia, no. I didn't. I didn't dare to, though it was not because I was afraid. No; I stood watching at the window until presently a bird began to sing, out of the warm hollow darkness away from the moon. It may have been a nightingale, as there was a hurst or thicket of common land not far from the house which was the resort of nightingales in the summer. Still, it was very early in the year. The song I heard was fully as sweet and musical as theirs, and yet it seemed less the song of a bird than—well, than even the song of a nightingale seems. A strange happiness and mournfulness came over me, listening to it. And even when I got to bed it was a long time before the echo of it had faded out in memory, and I fell asleep.

"Can it have been, do you think, that the fairy was beseeching me not to come to her haunts any more? I can't tell. But in my stupidity I persisted in persecuting her, just as I had persisted in persecuting the birds. I was too stupid, you see, to realize that my company in her field might be as disquieting to her as it would be for us if, when we had a few nice solid friends to tea, *she* came too."

"Oh, Uncle Tim, if only she would! Then we wouldn't ask a single soul to tea for months and months and months. Would we?"

"No," said Mr. Bolsover. "But it's no good denying it, *she* wouldn't. They don't. We ourselves may wish, even pine, to see them; but I don't think, Letitia, they pine to see us. And I am quite sure she didn't want a clod-hopping, bird-trapping boy spying about in her field. Old Joe was not only roof and house, but company enough; and her own solitude.

"None the less, my dear, I met her face to face. And this is how it happened. It was the day before I had to go home again, and two or three other visits to the field had been entirely in vain. I could tell by now almost at a glance at Old Joe whether she was there or not. Just as you could tell at a glance at me if *I* were here or not. I don't mean merely my body and bones—eyes, nose, boots and so on; but the me which is really and truly—well, just me."

"Yes," said Letitia.

"Well, she never was. And this particular evening I was in as black and sullen a temper as a small boy can be. I was full of aches and pains, owing, no doubt, to my being so stupid as to lie on the ground under the bushes after rain. Night after night too, I had lain awake for hours. It seemed that the fairy had forsaken the field. It seemed that all my cunning and curiosity and hope and longing had been in vain. I scowled at Old Joe as if he were to blame. Just vanity and stupidity.

"Besides, my old friend Mrs. Lumb had discovered somehow that I was creeping late into the house while she was at dinner; and though she never scolded me, it was quite easy to know when she was displeased at anything. And she could smile at you with her nice red apple-dumpling cheeks and black eyes, and be pretty tart of tongue at the same time."

"There's a mistress at school," cried Letitia, "called Miss Jennings that's just like that; though she's not very fat. At least, not yet. And then? . . . You saw her, Uncle Tim?"

"Yes, I saw her—face to face. I was making my way back through the copse at the upper corner of the field where two hedges met at the end of a narrow green lane. And as I came stumping along I suddenly went cold all over, and I firmly believe my cap had pushed itself up a little on the top of my head, owing to the hair underneath it trying to stand on end.

"I can't even tell you what she was wearing, but as I recall her at this moment it was as if she were veiled about with a haze like that of a full moon—like bluebells at a little distance in a dingle of a wood. That may or may not be, but I quite clearly saw her face, for I was staring steadily into her eyes. They too were blue, like the blue of flames in a wood fire, especially when there is salt in it, or the wood has come from some old ship, with copper in it. Her hair was hanging on either side her head in a long strand from brow to chin, and down the narrow shoulder. All else in the world I had completely forgotten. I was alone, an ugly small awkward human animal looking, as if into a dream, into those strange unearthly eyes.

"There was not the smallest movement between us; not the least stir in her face that she knew me or recognized me or reproached me or feared me. But as I looked—how can I possibly describe it?—there did come a faint far-away change in her eyes. It was as though while you might be looking out to sea some summer's evening from a high window or from the edge of a cliff, a flight of distant seabirds should appear out of the blue and vanish into it again. We poor mortals can smile with our eyes only—and that's a much better smile than with the lips only. But not like that. This was *her* way of smiling at *me*. Just as the angels on the ladder might have had their way of smiling at Jacob—with his sleeping head on the stone. And I doubt if they smile often. It told me in my heart of hearts that she was not unfriendly to me; and yet that she was entreating me to come no more and trespass near her lair. What she was doing in this world, how much alone she was, and where and with whom she was when not in my parts, near Mrs. Lumb's, I can't say. All she was *telling* me was that she meant me no harm but begged me not to spy on her or watch her any more. After all, what right had I to do so —quite apart from manners? And then she was gone."

"Oh, *gone!*" said Letitia, and stooped her head suddenly.

"You see, it was easy to take hiding in the evening shadow of the woods, and the field hedges were dense. Yes, she was gone, my dear, and I have never seen her since, nor anything resembling her. . . . But there, as I have said already," added old Mr. Bolsover, "you can't call *that* a story." He was blinking at his small niece like an owl caught out in the morning sun. Letitia remained silent for a few moments.

"But I *do* call it a story, Uncle Tim," she said at last. "And oh, how I wish. . . . Still, it's no good saying that. But then what about Old Joe, that Old Joe *there*, Uncle Tim?"

"Ah, Old Joe! Him, the old rascal! The fact of the matter is, I never forgot that evening. Years and years after-

wards—and I must have been a young man by then—say
twenty or so—I stayed a night or two with my old friend
Mrs. Lumb again. She, alas, was older too; and so no doubt
was her cook. But that was the only difference. The first
walk I took alone was to the field under the woods, and
about the time of sunset. Would you believe it, there was
Old Joe in his usual place, though the barley crop he was
watching over that particular summer was now well above
his knees. And whether it was because I myself was
changed, or whether the fairy had long since forsaken her
hiding-place, or whether really and truly he was merely
her way of getting into and out of *our* world, who can say?

"However that may be, Old Joe looked"—Mr.
Bolsover lowered his voice—"well, precisely, Letitia, between you and me, as he looks now: a little vacant-like,
empty, accustomed to being alone. He had brand-new
clothes on then, too, standing up there in his barley, and
an immeasurably old wide-brimmed hat, just the kind of
hat that might once have belonged to old Mr. Hiawatha
Longfellow—the kind of hat, I mean, that nobody but a
poet would wear, and not unless he had a long white beard
to match. And what do you think I did?"

"You didn't go and *steal* him, Uncle Tim?" whispered
Letitia.

"No, Letitia. What I can't help thinking was much
worse, I went and bought him," said Uncle Tim; "though
'bought' is not the word I should say out loud. I went
straight off to the old farmer—old Farmer Jones—still as
stout as he used to be, but with his whiskers all gone grey,
and asked him how much he would take for his hodmadod in the barley field, just as a curiosity. I told him I
had known Old Joe as a boy, that there was an old friend-
ship between us. There sat the old farmer in his great

wheel-back chair in his kitchen—as fat as a porpoise, with his large mulberry-red face and eyes like bits of agate. He sat there merely staring at me for a time, as if he thought I was a lunatic.

" 'Well, that's a good 'un,' he said at last. And what do you think he charged?"

Letitia pondered, her eyes fixed on the grass at her feet, though they were blinking so fast she couldn't have been thinking very clearly. "I suppose," she said, "five pounds would be a good deal, wouldn't it, Uncle Tim? Even for Old Joe? Though of course," she added, as if old Mr. Bolsover had suddenly gone much further off, "even then it would be *'strordinarily* cheap."

"No. Guess again, my dear. Nothing like five pounds! Nothing like tuppence, even. 'Give me a pipe of that plug baccy of yours,' said the old farmer, 'and he's yours for ever.'

"So mine he was. And I'm glad it wasn't money."

"So am I," said Letitia. "Baccy doesn't hurt your feelings, Uncle Tim, I suppose; does it? And . . . and you never saw the—the fairy again?"

"In a way of speaking," old Mr. Bolsover replied, "I have never, Letitia, really *seen* anything else. It's a question of what one means exactly by 'seeing,' I suppose. Words are no use. It can't be done, can it?"

Letitia shook her head violently. "No, Uncle Tim, it can't be done," she said, and fell silent again.

The low wide-windowed house, with its jasmine and clematis, crouched in the light and heat of the sun, as if it had been listening all this while. Tiny butterflies, like pale scraps of the blue sky, were circling and flitting over the flowers. The bells from their belfry in the stone tower of the village church, muffled by the leafy woods between, sounded sweet and solemn in the summer air. It was so still the great world might have stopped spinning.

And there, half in shadow of his grey-green willows, black in his old clothes, shocking hat over one eyebrow and one lank arm aloft, stood the scarecrow; and never stirred. Nor did he seem to be wishing for company. Hiding-place he may have been once (as might a bee long ago have taken possession of old Mr. Bolsover's bonnet), but whatever visitor had come, had gone. Letitia turned her head at last to look up into the old man's face.

"What I believe myself, Uncle Tim," she began again, in a voice so low it was almost as if she were talking to herself, "what I believe myself, and I am sure you won't mind my saying so—I believe it was almost as if you must have fallen in love with that fairy. Was that it, Uncle Tim, do you think?"

"Ah!" replied old Mr. Bolsover, and sat there blinking in the sunlight. Then, "Goodness me!" he muttered almost to *him*self, "I can smell that apple charlotte now, even above the pinks! . . . I'll tell you what, Letitia. It's high time we stirred our stumps. We'll go over and ask Old Joe! . . ."

Maria-Fly

Little Maria that morning—and this is a good many years ago now—was dressed in a black and white frock with a flounce to it. Her hair was tied back over her small ears with a white ribbon, and she was sitting in the drawing-room on a low armchair with a blue-cushioned seat, her stockinged legs dangling down in front of her. She was all by herself. She had wandered in there—nobody by; and after walking about for a little while looking at the things in the room, and sniffing at a bowl of red damask roses, she had sat down, looking so sleek and demure you might almost have supposed that company was present and she was "behaving."

But she was not; she was only thinking. It was a quiet morning. The room, with its two square-paned bow windows, was rather long. There was sunshine in it, and it was still, and though, as it appeared, there was no other living thing between its walls except herself, it seemed to be happy too. And Maria had begun to think—or rather not exactly to think and not exactly to dream, but (if that is possible) to do both together; though she could not have told anyone what she was thinking and dreaming about.

She had had a bowl of bread and milk for breakfast, half an apple, and two slices of bread and jam. She felt comfortable. Her piano practice in the old room by the nursery was over, and now she was alone. But she was alone more than usual. It was as if she were not only sitting there in her blue-cushioned armchair with her legs dangling down, but that she could see herself sitting there. It startled her a little when that notion occurred to her. It was almost as if at that moment she must have really slipped into a dream. And she glanced up quickly with her rather round face and clear, darting eyes to make sure. And on the white paint at the side of the door, not very far away, she saw a fly.

It was just a fly. But simply because at that moment everything was so quiet in the world, and because, maybe, unlike the chairs and tables around her, it was alive, Maria fixed her eyes on the fly. It was nevertheless a perfectly ordinary fly—a housefly. It stood there alone on its six brushy legs and clawed feet, their small, nimble pads adhering to the white gloss of the paint. But, though ordinary, it was conspicuous—just in the same way as a man in black clothes with immense boots and a high cap on the enormous dazzling snow-slopes of a mountain is conspicuous—and Maria seemed to be seeing the fly much more clearly and minutely than you would have supposed possible, considering the distance between herself and it.

On the other hand, the fly was not standing there doing nothing, as Maria was sitting there doing nothing. It was not, for example, merely standing on the paint in *its* drawing-room and looking across at another fly infinitely tinier on the white paint of the minute door to that draw-ing-room. It was busy, as flies usually are in the warm, sunny months.

Maria had been up and had dressed herself hours and hours ago; but flies seem to be dressing, or at least to be toileting and titivating themselves all the time when they are not prowling about on a table in search of food, or roving about, or sucking up water, or standing like mock flies asleep, or angling to and fro in the air under a chandelier or a fly-charm in one another's company.

Not that Maria was by any means fond of flies. She shooed them away with her spoon when they came buzzing about over her blancmange or red-currant-and-raspberry tart, or alighted on her bare arms, or walked rapidly about over her bedclothes. Once she had pulled off the wings of a fly, and had never forgotten how suffocatingly fusty and hot she had felt after doing so.

And if there was one thing Maria couldn't abide, it was a fly floating in her bath. It was extraordinary that though its carcass was such a minute thing you could at such a moment see absolutely nothing else. It was extraor-dinary that the whole of the water at such a moment seemed like fly-water.

She would ask her nurse to take the ill-happed crea-ture's corpse out of the bath and put it on the window-sill in case it was not quite dead and might come to again.

And if she remembered to look next morning, maybe it was not, or maybe it *was,* there still—just its body. She had more than once, too, heard the dismal languishing drone a fly utters when it has been decoyed into a web and sees the spider come sallying out of its round, silken lair in the corner. It had filled her with horror and hatred and a miserable pity. Yet it had not made her any fonder of flies just for their own sakes alone. But then, one doesn't always feel exactly the same about anything. It depends on where you are, and what kind of mood you are in, and where the other thing is, and what kind of mood *that* is in.

So it was this morning. For some reason, this particular fly was different; and Maria sat watching it with the closest attention. It seemed to be that just as Maria herself was one particular little girl, so this was one particular fly. A fly by itself. A fly living its own one life; confident, alert, alone in its own Fly World.

To judge from its solitude, and the easy, careless, busy way in which it was spending its time, it might be supposed indeed that it had the whole universe to itself. It might be supposed it was Sirius—and not another star in the sky. And after a while, so intent did Maria become that she seemed to be doing a great deal more than merely watching the fly. She became engrossed.

She was now stooping together in her chair almost as if she were a pin-cushion and her eyes were black-headed pins in it. She seemed almost to have *become* the fly— Maria-Fly. If it is possible, that is, she had become two things at once, or one thing at twice. It was an odd experience—and it lasted at least three minutes by the little gold clock, with the gilt goggling fish on either side its dial under the glass-case on the chimney-piece. Three minutes, that is, of ordinary clock-time.

For when Maria herself came to, it seemed she had been away for at least three centuries—as if, like the stranger in the rhyme, she had been with her candle all the way to Babylon; aye, and back again: as if she had gone away Maria, come back Maria-Fly and now was just Maria again. But yet, when she came to, everything was a little different.

She could not possibly have explained why, but she felt surprisingly gay and joyful. It was as if a voice, sweet and shrill as the angel Israfel's, had been singing in her mind from a very long way off. She looked about her in sheer astonishment. If anything, the things in the room were stiller than ever, and yet she would almost have supposed that up to a moment ago they had been alive and watching her, and were now merely pretending to be not-alive again.

She looked at the roses in the bowl: they were floating there filled with their fragrance and beauty as a dew-drop is with light. The fishes on either side the little clock seemed to be made of flames rather than gilded plaster. There was a patch of sunshine, too—just an oblong patch resting on the carpet and part of a chair. It seemed to be lovelier than words could tell and to be resting there as if in adoration of its own beauty. Maria saw all this with her young eyes and could not realize what had happened to her. She was glad she was alone. She had never felt like it before. It was as if she had ceased to be herself altogether in her black and white frock and had become just a tied-up parcel marked "Pure Happiness," with the date on it.

And as she gradually became aware how very still the room was, almost stealthy—and all quiet things, of course, seem in a way a little watchful—she felt she must go out of it. She felt she must go out of it at once. So she scrambled down off her chair. On purpose, she didn't even glance again at her friend the fly. She most particularly (though she didn't know why) wished not to see it again. So she walked sidelong a little, her head turned to one side, so that no part of her eye should see the fly again even by accident.

She went out of the room, walked along down the

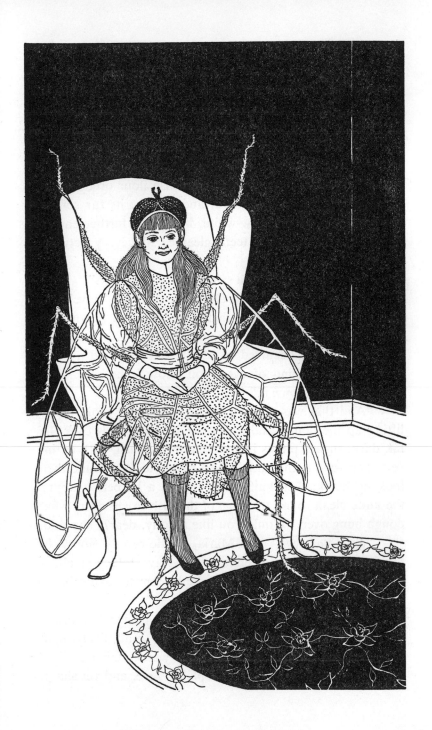

hall, and went down the rather dark side-stairs into the kitchen. There was a fire burning in the great burnished range. A green tree showed at the window, and a glass jar half-full of beer and wasps was twinkling on its sill. Mrs. Poulton, the cook, was rolling a piece of dough on her pastry or dough-board, with an apron tied with all its tape round her waist. There was an immense flour dredger like a pepper-pot beside the board, and a hare, its fur soft as wool, cinnamon and snow-white, lay at the farther end of the table. Its long white teeth gleamed like ivory between its parted lips.

"Mrs. Poulton," Maria said, "I have seen a fly."

"Now, *have* you?" said the cook. And the "have" was like a valley or a meadow that slopes up and down with wild flowers all over it. "And did the fly see you?"

That hadn't occurred to Maria. She frowned a little. "It's got lots of kind of eyes, you know," she said. "But what I mean is, I *sawn* it."

"And that was a queer thing, too," said cook, deftly lifting up the dough and arranging its limp folds over the fat, dark, sugary plums in the shallow pie-dish, with an inverted egg-cup in the middle. She gave a look at it and then took up her kitchen knife and, deft as a barber, whipped the knife clean round the edge of the dish to cut away what dough hung over. "Would you like a dolly, dear?" she said.

"No, thank you," said Maria, a little primly, not wishing to have the subject changed. "I have told you about the fly," she repeated, "and you don't seem to take a bit of notice of it."

The cook lifted her doughy knife, turned her round face and looked at the little girl. She had small, lively, light blue eyes and the hair under her cap was as fair and light in colour as new straw. It was a plump face, and yet sharp.

"And what do you mean by that, may I ask?" she said, eyeing Maria.

"I mean," said Maria stubbornly, "I *sawn* a fly. It was on the paint of the door of the droring-room, and it was all by itself."

"Whereabouts?" said Mrs. Poulton, trying to think of something else to say.

"I said," said Maria, "on the door."

"Yes; but whereabouts on the door?" persisted the cook.

"On the side where it's cut in and the other part comes."

"Oh, on the jamb," said Mrs. Poulton.

"Jam!" said Maria. "How could there be jam on the door?"

"Well, I'm not so sure about that, Miss Sticky-fingers," said the cook. "But by jamb I meant *door*-jamb, though it's spelt different—leastwise, I think so. And what was the fly doing?—nasty creatures."

Maria looked at her. "That's what everybody says," she said. "*My* fly—wasn't doing anything." This was not exactly the truth; and feeling a little uneasy about it, Maria remarked in a little voice, "But I am going now, thank you."

"That's right," said the cook. "And be sure and mind them steep stairs, my precious."

Maria glanced at the wasps hovering over the bottle, she glanced at Mrs. Poulton, at the fire in the range, at the dishcovers on the walls—and then she went out of the door.

She minded the steep kitchen stairs just as much as usual, though she was a little indignant after her talk with the cook. When she reached the top of them, she went on along the slippery hall, past the grandfather's clock with the white moon's-face in the blue over its hands, past the table with the pink-flowering pelargonium on it, and climbed on up the wide, shallow staircase, taking hold of the balusters one by one, but treading as near as possible in the middle of the soft, rose-patterned stair carpet.

And when she got to the top she came to a room where she knew she would find a guest who was staying in the house. His name was Mr. Kittleson; he was a clergyman, and this Saturday morning he was writing his sermon for Sunday, and his text was "Consider the lilies of the field. . . . They toil not neither do they spin."

After fumbling with the handle a little Maria pushed the door open and looked in. And there sat the old gentleman in a round leather chair, with his silvery-grey beard spreading down over his chest, his sermon-paper on the blotting book in front of him, and a brass inkstand beyond that. His lips were moving as he wrote. But on hearing the door open he stayed his writing, and with stooping head looked round over his gold spectacles at Maria.

"Well, well, my dear, this is a very pleasant sight, and what can I do for you?" he said, being one of those peculiar old gentlemen who don't mind being interrupted even when they are writing sermons.

"I," said Maria, edging a little into the room, "I have just seen a fly! It was standing all by itself on the—the jamb of the door in the droring-room."

"In the drawing-room? Indeed!" said the old gentleman, still peering over his gold spectacles. "And a very fortunate fly it was, to be in your company, my dear. And how very kind of you to come and tell me."

Maria was almost as little pleased by the old gentleman's politeness as she had been with her talk with the cook. "Yes," she said, "but this was not a norinary fly. It was all by itself, and I looked at it."

The old gentleman peeped down a little absently at his clear, sloping handwriting on the paper. "Is that *so?*" he said. "But then, my dear little Maria, no fly is really ordinary. They are remarkable creatures if you look at them attentively. And especially through a microscope. What does the Book say: 'fearfully and wonderfully made'? They have what is called a proboscis—trunks, you know, just like elephants. And they can walk upside down. Eh? How about that?"

At that moment, out of its shadowy lair a silvery clothes-moth came flitting across the sunlight over his table. The old gentleman threw up his hands at it, but it wavered, soared, and escaped out of his clutches.

"Cook says flies are nasty creatures," said Maria.

"Ah," said the old clergyman, "and I've no doubt cook avoids them in our food. But they have their ways, which may not please us, just as we have our ways, which may not please somebody else. But even a fly, my dear, enjoys its own small life and does what it is intended to do in it. 'Little busy, thirsty fly,' " he began, but Maria, who was looking at him as attentively as she had looked at the insect itself (before, that is, it had actually become a Maria-Fly), at once interrupted him. "It's a *beautiful* rhyme," she said, nodding her head. "I know it very well, thank you. But that was all I wanted to say. Just that I had sawn it —seen it. I don't think I could tell you anything else—so, I mean, that it would be 'xplained to you."

The old gentleman, pen in hand, continued to smile at his visitor over his beard in the same bland cautious way he always did, until she had slid round the door out of his sight, and had firmly closed it after her.

On her way back along the corridor Maria passed the door of the workroom; it was ajar, and she peeped in. Miss

Salmon, in her black stuff dress, sat there beside a table on which stood a sewing-machine. At this moment she was at work with her needle. She always smelt fresh, but a little faint; though also of camphor. She had an immensely long white face—high forehead and pointed chin—with rather protruding eyes and elbows; and she and Maria were old friends.

"And what can I do for you, madam, this morning?" she cried in a deep voice like a man's.

"Well, I just looked in, madam, to tell you I seen a fly."

"If you was to look through the eye of the smallest needle in that work-basket you would see the gates of Paradise," said Miss Salmon, stitching away again with a click that sounded almost as loud as if a carpenter were at work in the room.

"Give it me," said Maria.

"Ah ha!" cried Miss Salmon, "such things need looking for."

"Ah ha!" chirped Maria, "and that means tidying all the basket up."

"Nothing seek, nothing find," cried Miss Salmon, "as the cat said to the stickleback, which is far better than Latin, madam. And what, may I ask, was the name of Mr. Jasper Fly Esquire? If you would kindly ask the gentleman to step this way, I will make him a paper house with bars to it, and we'll feed him on strawberries and cream."

Maria's spirits seemed to sink into her shoes. "It was not that kind of fly at all," she said, "and—and I don't wish to tell you the name, thank you very much."

"*Good* morning," said Miss Salmon lifting her needle and opening wide her eyes, "and don't forget closing time's at seven."

It was strange that Maria should feel so dismal at this turn of the conversation, considering that she and Miss Salmon were such very old friends and always had their little bit of fun together. Maria looked at her sitting bolt upright there in her high-collared black stuff dress, with her high head.

"*Good* morning, madam," said Miss Salmon.

And Maria withdrew.

Opposite the workroom there was a portrait hanging on the landing in a large gilt frame. Maria looked at the lady painted in it, in her queer clothes with a dome of muslin draped on high over her head, and she said, under her breath, though not out loud, "Mm, *you* don't know I've seen a fly." And then she ran off downstairs again and met her father at that moment issuing out of his den with the topmost joint of a fishing-rod in his hand. He had on his ugly brown suit and thick-soled brown shoes.

"Daddy," she called at him, "I've just been telling him I have seen a fly."

"Oh, have you," said he, "you black-eyed young ragamuffin. And what business had you to be mousing into his room this time of morning, I should like to know? And talking of flies, Miss Black-and-White, what would you recommend for this afternoon, so as to make quite sure of a certain Mrs. Fat Trout I wot of?"

"You see, Daddy," said Maria stiffly, "you always turn things off like that. And it was something so very special I wanted to tell you."

"Now see here," said her father, flicking with the tip of his tapering rod-piece, "what we'll do is this, we will. You shall tell me all about that fly of yours when I come in to say good-night to-night. And perhaps by then you will have seen lots of other things. And you shall have a penny for every one that begins with a Q. There's plenty of flies," he added.

"I don't think I shall *care* to see lots of other things," said Maria—"but I'll see." And she walked off, more sedately even than little old Queen Victoria, into the garden.

Up till then it had been a morning like a blue-framed looking-glass, but now a fleece of cloud was spread over the immense sky. Far away in the kitchen-garden she came across the gardener, Mr. Pratt. With his striped cotton shirt-sleeves turned up over his elbows, he was spraying a rose-tree on which that day's sun even if it came out in full splendour again would shine no more. Maria watched him.

"What are you doing that for?" she said. "Let me!"

"Steady, steady, my dear," said Mr. Pratt—"you can't manage the great thing all by yourself." But he put the syringe with a little drop of the liquid left in its brass cylinder into her hands. "Now, push!" he said, "all your might."

Maria pushed hard, till her knuckles on her fat hands went white, and she was plum-red in the face. But nothing came. So Mr. Pratt put his thick brown hands over hers, clutched the tube, and they pushed together. And an exquisite little puff of water jetted like a tiny cloud out of the nozzle.

"It came out then," said Maria triumphantly. "I could do it if I tried really hard. What, please, are you doing it *for?*"

"Ah," said Mr. Pratt, "them's secrets."

"Ah," said Maria imitating him, "and I've got a secret, too."

"What's that?" said the gardener.

She held up her finger at him. "I—have—just—

seen—a—fly. It had wings like as you see oil on water, and a red face with straight silver eyes, and it wasn't buzzing or nothing, but it was scraping with its front legs over its wings, then rubbing them like corkscrews. Then it took its head off and on, and then it began again—but I don't mean all that. I mean I sawn the fly—saw it, I mean."

"Ah," said Mr. Pratt, the perspiration glistening on his brown face, and his eyes at least two shades a paler blue than Mrs. Poulton's, as though the sun and the jealous skies had bleached most of the colour out of them. "Ah," he said. "A fly now? And that's something to see, too. But what about them pretty little Meadow Browns over there, and that Painted Lady—quiet, now, see—on that there mallow-bloom! There's a beauty! And look at all them yaller ragamuffins over the winter cabbage yonder. We won't get much greens, Missie, if you can underconstumble, if *they* have their little way."

Maria could perfectly underconstumble. But she hated greens. She hated them as much as if she had eaten them on cold plates in another world. It was odd too that nobody had the smallest notion of what she wanted to say about the Fly. No one. How stupid. But she looked at the Painted Lady none the less. It was limply perched on the pale paper-like flower of the mallow, with its ball-tipped antennae, and suckling up its secret nectar for all the world like the Queen in her parlour enjoying her thick slice of bread and honey. And then the sunshine stole out again into the heavens above them, and drew itself like a pale golden veil over the shimmering garden. The Painted Lady's wings, all ribbed and dappled orange and black and white, trembled a little in its gentle heat, as if with inexpressible happiness and desire.

But though Maria admired the creature in its flaunting

beauty more than she could say, this was not her Fly—
this, at least, was no *Maria*-Fly. It was merely a butterfly—
lovely as light, lovely as a coloured floating vapour, exquisitely stirring, its bended legs clutching the gauzy platform beneath it and supporting its lightly poised, frail,
plumy body on this swaying pedestal as if the world it knew
were solid as marble and without any change; even though
it now appeared as gentle as a dream.

Maria was not even thinking as she watched the butterfly, except that she was saying over to herself, though not
using any words, that she did not want to go into the drawing-room any more just now; that she had no wish to see
her fly again; that she didn't want ever to be grown-up; that
grown-ups never could underconstumble in the very least
what you were really saying; that if only they wouldn't try
to be smiling and patient as though the least cold puff of
breath might blow you away, you might prove you were
grown-up too and much older than they—even though you
had to eat greens and do what you were told and not interrupt old gentlemen writing sermons, and must wait for
bed-time—*no,* she was not really thinking any of these
things. But her small bosom rose and fell with a prolonged
deep sigh as she once more glanced up at Mr. Pratt.

He was hard at work again with his syringe, and now,
because the sun was shining between herself and its watery
vapour, it had formed a marvellous little rainbow in the air,
almost circular, with the green in it fully as vivid as that of
the myriad aphids clustering like animated beads round
the stems of the rosebuds.

"I told you," she quavered a little sorrowfully, though
she was trying to speak as usual, "I told you about something, and you didn't take any notice."

"Well, well, well," said the gardener. But he hadn't time to finish his sentence before Maria was already stalking down the path and in a moment had disappeared round the corner of the green-house.

And there, a moment or two afterwards, she happened to come across patient Job, the gardener's boy. Job was an oaf to look at, with his scrub of hair and his snub nose and silly mouth. He was little short of what the village people called a half-wit or natural. He laughed at whatever you said to him, even when you frowned double-daggers at him. But there was no gardener's boy like him; the very roots of the flowers he handled seemed to want to net themselves about his clumsy fingers, and he was "a fair magician" with bees. Three little steel mole-traps lay on the gravel beside him where he knelt, and he was scouring flower-pots with a scrubbing-brush, and as Maria appeared he looked up with a face like a good-humoured pumpkin, and he grinned at her with all his teeth.

"Marning, missie," he said.

"Good morning, Job," said Maria. She stood looking at him, looking at his tiny pig-like eyes in the great expanse of his good-humoured face, and hesitated. Then she stooped a little and all but whispered at him.

"Have you ever seen a fly?"

"Oi, miss, seen a floi?" he replied, opening his mouth. "Oi, missie, oi've seed a floi."

"But have you," and Maria all but let all her breath go—over just those first three words, "But have you, Job, ever seen the only teeny tiny fly there ever was: *your* Fly?"

Job scratched his head and looked so serious for an instant that Maria feared he was going to burst out crying. "Oi, missie," he suddenly shouted at last with a great guffaw of laughter, "that oi 'ave, and avore I could catch un ee was gawn loike a knoifejack clean down Red Lane ee wor. Oi and ee *wor* a floi, ee wor."

Maria burst out laughing: they laughed in chorus; and then she found tears were standing in her eyes and she suddenly felt silent and mournful. "And now," she said, "you had better get on with your pots."

She turned away, her small head filled as if with a tune ages old, and as sorrowful as the sounds of the tide on the unvisited shores of the ocean. There was a little old earwiggy arbour not far away that always smelt damp even after weeks of fine hot weather—though then it smelt dry-damp.

Maria went into its shadow and stood there by herself a moment. Why she had gone in she didn't know. It was very still. But mustily, stuffily, gloomily still—quite different from the sunny coloured stillness of the drawing-room. There was a wide droning in the air outside. Millions of minute voices were sounding in concert like the twangling of the strings of an enormous viol. A bird hopped on to the roof of the arbour; she could hear its claws on the wood. Its impact dislodged a tiny clot of dust. It fell into the yet finer dust at her feet. The arbour's corners were festooned with cobwebs.

Maria gave yet another deep sigh, and then looked up around her almost as if in hopes of somebody else to whom she might tell her secret tale—about the fly—about Maria-Fly. She paused—staring. And then, as if at a signal, she hopped down suddenly out of the arbour, almost as lightly as a thin-legged bird herself, and was off flying over the emerald green grass into the burning delightful sunshine without in the least knowing why, or where to.

Alice's Godmother

Though Alice sat steadily looking out of the small square pane of glass in the railway carriage, she was not really seeing the green and hilly country through which the train now clattered on its way. While everything near—quickening hedges, grazing cattle, galloping calves, wood, farm, and stony foaming brook—swept past far too swiftly for more than a darting glance; everything in the distance— hill, tree and spire—seemed to be stealthily wheeling forward, as if to waylay the puffing engine and prevent it from reaching her journey's end.

"If only it would!" sighed Alice to herself. "How much—much happier I should be!" Her blue eyes widened at the fancy. Then once more a frown of anxiety drew her eyebrows together; but she said nothing aloud. She sat on in her corner gently clasping her mother's hand and pondering in dismay on what might happen to her in the next few hours.

Alice and her mother a little prided themselves on being just "two quiet, ordinary people," happy in each other's company, and very seldom going out or paying calls and visits. And the particular visit that Alice was about to make when they reached the little country station of Freshing, she was to make alone. It was this that alarmed her. The invitation in that queer, scrabbling handwriting had been to herself only. So though her mother was with her now, soon they would be parting. And every now and again Alice would give the hand she held in hers a gentle squeeze of self-reassurance. It was the Good-bye—though it would be only for a few hours—that she dreaded.

And yet their plans had all been talked over and settled again and again. Alice must, of course, take a fly from the station—whatever the expense. After telling the cabman when she would need him again, she would get into it and her mother would wait for her in a room at the village inn until she herself returned in the early evening from her visit. Then everything would be safely over. And to imagine the joy of seeing all these fields and woods come racing back the other way round almost made Alice ill.

It was absurd to be so nervous. Alice had told herself that a hundred times. But it was no use. The very thought of her great-great-great-great-great-great-great-great-grandmother filled her heart with a continuous foreboding. If only she were a little stronger-minded; if only this old, old lady, who was also her godmother, had asked her mother to come with her; if only her heart would stop beating so fast; if only a wheel would come off the engine!

But then, after all, Alice had never before so much as seen her godmother. Even now she could not be quite certain that she had the number of "greats" to the "grandmama" quite right. Not even strong-minded people, she supposed, are often suddenly invited to tea with relatives aged three hundred and forty-nine. And not only that

either; for this day—this very Saturday—was her godmother's birthday: her three hundred and fiftieth!

Whenever Alice remembered this, a faint smile stole
into her face. At seventeen a birthday is a real "event."
Life is galloping on. You are sprouting up like a beanstalk.
Your hair is "put up" (or at least it was when Alice was a
girl), your skirts "come down," and you're soon to "come
out." In other words you are beginning to be really and
truly "grown-up." But three hundred and fifty! Surely by
that time. . . . It must be difficult even to be certain you
have the total right. Surely there can't be *any* kind of a
change by then! Surely not!

Still, Alice thought, it is perhaps the *name* of the
number that chiefly counts. She herself had known what
an odd shock it had been to slip into her teens, and could
guess what the shivers would be like of the plunge into her
twenties. Yet even if it were only the name of the number—
why, at the end of three centuries you must be beginning
to be getting accustomed to birthdays.

It was a little odd that her godmother had never asked
to see her before. Years ago she had sent her a squat par-
cel-gilt mug—a mug that her godmother herself used to
drink her beer out of when she was a child of ten in Queen
Elizabeth's reign. A little sheepskin, illuminated Prayer
Book, too, that had once been given to her godmother by
Charles the First, and a few exquisite little old gold trinkets
had come too. But receiving presents is not the same thing
as actually meeting and talking with the mysterious giver of
them. It is one thing to imagine the unknown; another
thing altogether to meet it face to face. What would her
godmother look like? What *could* she look like? Alice
hadn't the faintest notion. Old ladies of eighty and upwards

are not unusual; but you can't just multiply eighty by four as if growing older were merely a sum in arithmetic.

Perhaps when you are very old indeed, Alice suspected, you have no wish to sit for a portrait or to be photographed. It is a petrifying experience even when you are young. When you are—well, very old indeed, you may prefer to—well, to keep yourself *to* yourself. *She* would.

"Mamma dear," she suddenly twisted round on her hard seat, her straight ribboned straw-coloured hair slipping over in one smooth ripple on her shoulder as she did so; "Mamma dear, I can't think even now what I ought to do when I go into the room. Will there be anybody there, do you think? Do I shake hands? I suppose she won't kiss me? I simply can't think what I ought to do. I shall just hate leaving you—being left, I mean."

She stroked hard with her fingers the hand that was in her own, and as she gazed at her mother's face in this increasing anxiety, she knew that the smile on it was just like a pretty blind over a window, and that her mother's self within was almost as much perturbed over this visit as she was herself.

"It's getting nearer, darling, at any rate, isn't it?" her mother whispered. "So it will sooner be over." Whereupon the fat old farmer in the further corner of the carriage emitted yet another grunt. He was fast asleep. "I *think,*" her mother continued softly, "I should first enquire of the maid if she is quite well—your godmother, I mean, my dear. Say, 'Do you think Miss Cheyney is well enough to see me?' She will know what you ought to do. I am not even certain whether the poor old lady can speak: though her handwriting is simply marvellous."

"But, Mummie darling, how are we to know that there *will* be a maid? Didn't they, in godmother's time, always have 'retainers'? Supposing there are rows of them in the hall! And when ought I to get up to say goodbye? If she is deaf and blind *and* dumb I really don't know what I *shall* do!"

A dozen questions at least like this had been asked but not answered during the last few days, and although Alice's cheek, with that light hair, was naturally pale, her mother watched it grow paler yet as the uncomfortable old-fashioned railway-carriage they sat in jogged steadily on its way.

"Whenever I am in any difficulty, sweetheart," she whispered close up to her daughter's ear, "I always say a little prayer."

"Yes, yes, dear dearest," said Alice, gazing at the fat old farmer, fast asleep. "But if only I weren't going quite alone! I don't think, you know, she can be a very good god-mother: she never said a word in her letter about my Confirmation. She's at least old enough to know better." Once more the ghost of a smile stole softly over her face. But she clasped her mother's fingers even a little tighter, and the hedges and meadows continued to sidle by.

They said good-bye to one another actually inside the cab, so as to be out of sight of the inn and the cabman.

"I expect, my sweet," breathed Alice's mother, in the midst of this long embrace, "we shall both soon be smiling away like two turtledoves at the thought of all our worry. We can't tell what kind of things she may not be thinking of, can we? And don't forget, I shall be waiting for you in the 'Red Lion'—there's the sign, my dear, as you see. And if there is time, perhaps we will have a little supper there all to ourselves—a little soup, if they have it; or at any rate, an egg. I don't suppose you will have a very *substantial* tea. Not in the circumstances. But still, your godmother wouldn't have asked you to visit her if she had not really wanted to see you. We mustn't forget that, darling."

Alice craned her head out of the window till her mother was out of sight behind the hedge. And the fly rolled gently on and on and on along the dusty lanes in the direction of The Grange. On and on and on. Surely, thought Alice at last, we must have gone miles and miles. At this she sprang up and thrust her head out of the window, and called up to the cabman, "The Grange, you know, please."

"That's it, Miss, The Grange," he shouted back, with a flourish of his whip. "Not as how I can take you into the Park, Miss. It ain't allowed."

"Mercy me," sighed Alice as she sank back on the fusty blue cushions. "Supposing there are miles of avenue, and the front door's at the back!"

It was a pleasant sunny afternoon. The trim hedge-rows were all in their earliest green; and the flowers of spring—primroses, violets, jack-in-the-hedge, stitchwort—in palest blossom starred the banks. It was only half-past three by Alice's little silver watch. She would be in good time, then. In a few minutes, indeed, the fly drew up beside immense, rusty wrought-iron gates on the four posts of which stood heavy birds in stone, with lowered heads, brooding with outstretched wings.

"And you will be sure to come back for me at six?" Alice implored the cabman, though she tried to keep her voice natural and formal. "Not a minute later than six, please. And then wait here until I come."

The cabman ducked his head and touched his hat; drew his old horse round in the shafts; and off he went. Alice was alone.

With one last longing look at the strange though

friendly country lane—and there was not a house in sight
—Alice pushed open the little gate at the side of the two
large ones. It emitted a faint, mocking squeal as it turned
slowly upon its hinges. Beyond it rose a hedge of yew at
least twenty feet high, and in a nook there stood a small
square lodge, its windows shuttered, a scurry of dead leaves
in its ancient porch. Alice came to a standstill. This was a
difficulty neither she nor her mother had foreseen. Ought
she to knock or to go straight on? The house looked as
blind as a bat. She stepped back, and glanced up at the
chimneys. Not the faintest plume of smoke was visible
against the dark foliage of the ilex behind the house. Some
unseen bird flew into the shadows with a cry of alarm.

Surely the lodge was empty. None the less it might be
good manners to make sure, so she stepped onto the porch
and knocked—but knocked in vain. After pausing a minute or two, and scanning once more the lifeless windows,
in a silence broken only by the distant laughing of a wood-
pecker, Alice determined to go on.

So thick and close were the tufted mosses in the gravel
of the narrow avenue that her footsteps made no sound. So
deep was the shade cast by the immense trees that grew on
either side she could have fancied evening was already
come, though it was yet early afternoon. Mammoth beeches
lifted their vast boughs into the air; the dark hollows in
their ancient boles capacious enough for the dwelling-house
of a complete family of humans. In the distance Alice
could see between their branches gigantic cedars, and others still further, beneath which grazed what she supposed
was a herd of deer, though it was impossible to be quite
certain from so far.

The few wild creatures which had long ago detected
her in these haunts were strangely tame. They did not trou-

ble to run away; but turned aside and watched her as she passed, the birds hopping a little further out of her reach while yet continuing on their errands. In sheer curiosity, indeed, Alice made an attempt to get as near as she possibly could to a large buck rabbit that sat nibbling under the broken rail of the fence. With such success that he actually allowed her to scratch his furry head and stroke his long lopping ears.

"Well," thought she with a sigh as she straightened herself, "there can't be very much to be afraid of in great-great-great-great-great-great-great-great-grandmother's house if the rabbits are as tame as all that. *Au revoir,*" she whispered to the creature; "I hope to see you again very very soon." And on she went.

Now and then a hunchbacked thorn-tree came into view, and now and then a holly. Alice had heard long ago that hollies are wise enough not to grow prickles where no animal can damage their leaves by browsing on them. These hollies seemed to have no prickles at all, and the hawthornes, in spite of their bright green coats, speckled with tight buds, were almost as twisted out of shape as if mischievous little boys had tied knots in them when they were saplings. But how sweet was the tranquil air! So sweet indeed that this quiet avenue with its towering branches and the child-like blue of the skies overhead pacified her mind, and she had almost forgotten her godmother when, suddenly, at a break between the trees there came into view a coach.

Not exactly a coach, perhaps, but a large painted carriage of a faded vermilion and yellow, drawn by two cream-coloured horses—a coachman on the box in a mulberry livery, and a footman beside him. What was really strange, this conveyance was being noiselessly driven round a circular track so overgrown with moss and weeds that it was hardly discernible against the green of the grass. Alice could not but watch it come nearer and nearer—as she stood drawn up close to the furrowed bark of an oak that branched overhead. This must be her godmother's carriage. She must be taking her daily drive in concealment from the wide wide world. But no: it had drawn near; and now, with a glimpse of the faded red morocco within, it had passed; it was empty. Only the backs of coachman and footman now showed above its sun-bleached panels—their powdered hair, their cockaded hats.

All Alice's misgivings winged back into her mind at sight of this unusual spectacle. She tiptoed out of her hiding-place, and hastened on. Her one wish now was to reach her journey's end. Presently after, indeed, the house itself appeared in sight. The shorn flowerless sward gently sloped towards its dark low walls and grey chimneys. To the right of it lay a pool as flat as a huge looking-glass in the frame of its trees. Behind it rose a smooth green hill.

Alice paused again behind yet another of the huge grey boles to scan it more closely before she herself could be spied out from any of its many windows. It looked as if it had stood there for ever. It looked as if its massive stones had of their own weight been sinking imperceptibly, century after century, into the ground. Not a blossoming shrub, not a flower near by—except only a powder of daisies and a few yellow dandelions.

Only green turf and trees, and the ancient avenue on which she stood, sweeping gently towards its low-porched entrance. "Well," she sighed to herself, "I'm thankful I don't live *there,* that's all—not even if I were a thousand

and one!" She drew herself up, glanced at her shoes, gave a little push to her ribboned straw hat, and, with as much dignity as she could manage, proceeded straight onwards.

A hoarse bell responded, after a whole second's pause, to the gentle tug she had given the iron pull that hung on the porch. It cried, "Ay, ay!" and fell silent. And Alice continued to look at the immense iron knocker which she hadn't the courage to use.

Without a sound the door opened at last, and there, as she had feared, stood, not a friendly parlour-maid with a neat laundered cap, but an old man in a black tail-coat who looked at her out of his pale grey eyes as if she were a stuffed bird in a glass case. Either he had been shrinking for some little time, or he must surely have put on somebody else's clothes, they hung so loosely on his shoulders.

"I am Miss Alice Cheyney—Miss Alice Cheyney," she said. "I think my great-great . . . Miss Cheyney is expecting me—that is, of course, if she is quite well." These few words had used up the whole of one breath, and her godmother's old butler continued to gaze at her, while they sank into his mind.

"Will you please to walk in," he said at last. "Miss Cheyney bade me express the wish that you will make yourself at home. She hopes to be with you immediately." Whereupon he led the way, and Alice followed him— across a wide hall, lit with low, greenish, stone-mullioned windows. On either side stood suits of burnished armour, with lifted visors. But where the glittering eyes of their long-gone owners once had gleamed, nothing now showed but a little narrow darkness. After a hasty glance or two to either side, Alice kept her eyes fixed on the humped back of the little old butler. Up three polished stairs, under a hanging tapestry, he led her on, and at length, at the end of a long gallery, ushered her into what she supposed was her godmother's sitting-room. There, with a bow, he left her. Alice breathed one long deep sigh, and then, having un-buttoned and buttoned up again one of her grey silk gloves, she sat down on the edge of a chair near the door.

It was a long, low-pitched, but not very wide room, with a coffered ceiling and panelled walls, and never before had Alice seen such furniture. In spite of the dreadful shy-ness that seemed to fill her to the very brim, at thought of her mother's little pink-and-muslin drawing-room com-pared with this, she almost burst out laughing.

Make herself at home! Why, any one of those chests would hide her away for ever, like the poor lovely lost one in "The Mistletoe Bough." As for the hanging portraits in their great faded frames, though she guessed at once they must be by "old masters," and therefore eyed them as sol-emnly as she could, she had never supposed human beings could look so odd and so unfriendly. It was not so much their clothes: their stomachers, their slashed doublets and wide velvet caps, but their faces. Ladies with high bald foreheads and tapering fingers and thumb-rings, and men sour and dour and glowering.

"Oho! Miss Nobody!" they seemed to be saying. "And pray, what are *you* doing here?"

The one single exception was the drawing of a girl of about her own age. A dainty cap with flaps all but concealed her yellow hair; a necklet dangled at her breast; the prim-rose-coloured bodice sloped sharply to the waist. So deli-cate were the lines of this drawing and so faint the tinted chalk, they hardly stained the paper. Yet the eyes that gazed out across the low room at Alice seemed to be alight with life. A smile half-mocking, half-serious lingered in their depths. "See, I am lovely," it seemed to be hinting, "and yet how soon to be gone!" And even though Alice had never before seen a face so enchanting, she could not but confess it bore a remote resemblance to herself. Why this should have a little restored her confidence she could not tell. None the less, she deliberately smiled back at the drawing as if to say, "Well, my dear, I shall have *you* on my side, whatever happens."

The lagging minutes ticked solemnly by. Not a sound to be heard in the great house; not a footfall. But at last a door at the further end of the room softly opened, and in the greenish light of the deep mullioned window appeared what Alice knew was She.

She was leaning smally on the arm of the butler who had admitted Alice to the house. Quiet as shadows they entered the room; then paused for a moment, while yet another man-servant arranged a chair for his mistress. Meanwhile the old lady was peering steadily in search of her visitor. She must once have been as tall as Alice herself, but now time had shrunken her up into the stature of a child, and though her small head was set firmly on the narrow shoulders, these stooped like the wings of the morose stone birds upon her gates.

"Ah, is that you, my dear?" cried a voice; but so minute was the sound of these words that Alice went suddenly hot all over lest she had merely imagined them.

"I say, is that you, my dear?" repeated the voice. There was no mistaking now. Alice ventured a pace forward into the light, her knees trembling beneath her, and the old lady groped out a hand—its shrunken fingers closed one upon another like the cold claws of a bird.

For an instant Alice hesitated. The dreadful moment was come. Then she advanced, made the old lady a curtsy, and lifted the icy fingers to her lips.

"All I can say *is*," she confided to her mother when they met again, "all I can say *is*, Mamma, if it had been the Pope, I suppose I should have kissed his toe. And really, I would have very much rather."

None the less, Alice's godmother had evidently taken no offence at this gesture. Indeed what Alice thought might be a smile crinkled, as it were, across the exquisite web of wrinkles on her face. On her acorn-shaped head rose a high lace and silver cap resembling the gown she wore; and silk mittens concealed her wrists. She was so small that Alice had to bend almost double over her fingers. And when she was seated in her chair it was as if a large doll sat there— but a marvellous doll that had voice, thought, senses and motion beyond any human artificer's wildest fancy. The eyes in this dry wizened-up countenance—of a much fainter blue than the palest forget-me-not—steadily continued to look at Alice, the while the butler and footman, with head inclined stood watching their mistress. Then, as if at a secret signal, they both bowed and retired.

"Be seated, my dear," the tinkling voice began when they had withdrawn. And there fell a horrifying pause. Alice gazed at the old lady, and like half-transparent glass the aged eyes remained fixed on herself, the bird-like hands crossed daintily over the square lace handkerchief held in the narrow lap. Alice grew hotter and hotter. "What a very beautiful old house this is, great-grandmamma," she suddenly blurted out. "And those wonderful trees!"

No flicker of expression showed that Miss Cheyney had heard what she had said. And yet Alice could not help thinking that she *had* heard, and that for some reason she had disapproved of her remark.

"Now, come," piped the tiny voice, "now, come; tell me what you have been doing this long time. And how is

your mother? I think I faintly remember seeing her, my dear, soon after she married your father, Mr. James Beaton."

"Mr. Beaton, I *think,* was my great-grandfather, great-grandmamma," Alice breathed softly. "My father's name, you know, was John—John Cheyney."

"Ah, well, your great-*grand*father, to be sure," said the old lady. "I never pay much attention to dates. And has anything been happening lately?"

"Happening, great-grandmamma?" echoed Alice.

"Beyond?" said the old lady. "In the world?"

Poor Alice; she knew well the experience of nibbling a pen over impossible questions in history examinations, but this was far worse than any she had ever encountered.

"There, you see!" continued her godmother. "I hear of the wonderful things they are doing, and yet when I ask a simple question like that no one has anything to say. Have you travelled on one of these steam railway trains yet? Locomotives?"

"I came that way this afternoon, great-grandmamma."

"Ah, I thought you looked a little flushed. The smoke must be most disagreeable."

Alice smiled. "No, thank you," she said kindly.

"And how is Queen Victoria?" said the old lady. "She is still alive?"

"Oh yes, great-grandmamma. And that is just, of course, what *has* been happening. It's her Diamond Jubilee this year—sixty years—you know."

"H'm," said the old lady. "Sixty. George III reigned sixty-three. But they all go in time. I remember my dear father coming up to my nursery after the funeral of poor young Edward VI. He was one of the Court pages, you know—that is, when Henry VIII was King. Such a handsome lad—there is his portrait . . . somewhere."

For a moment Alice's mind was a whirlpool of vague memories—memories of what she had read in her history-books.

But Miss Cheyney's bead-like notes had hardly paused. "You must understand that I have not asked you to come this long way by one of those horrid new-fangled steam-engines just to gossip about my childhood. Kings and Queens come and go like the rest of things. And though I have seen many changes, it seems to me the world is pretty much the same as ever. Nor can I believe that the newspaper is a beneficial novelty. When I was a girl we managed well enough without, and even in Mr. Addison's day one small sheet twice a week was enough. But there, complaint is useless. And you cannot exactly be held responsible for all that. There were changes in my girlhood, too—great changes. The world was not so crowded then. There was nobility and beauty. Yes." Her eyes wandered, to rest a moment on the portrait of the young woman in the primrose gown. "The truth is, my dear," she continued, "I have to tell you something, and I wish you to listen."

Once more she remained silent a moment, clutching the handkerchief she held between her fingers. "What I desire you to tell *me*," she said at last, leaning stealthily forward in her great chair, "what I am anxious that you should tell me is, How long do you wish to live?"

For a few moments Alice sat cold and motionless. It was as if an icy breath straight from the North Pole had swept across the room, congealing with its horror the very air. Her eyes wandered vacantly from picture to picture, from ancient object to ancient object—aged, mute and lifeless—to rest at last on a flowering weed that reared its head beyond one of the diamond-shaped panes of glass in the window.

"I have never thought of that, great-grandmamma," her dry lips whispered. "I don't think I know."

"Well, I am not expecting an old head on young shoulders," retorted the old lady. "Perhaps if King Charles had realised that—so learned, so generous, so faithful a monarch—I doubt if that vulgar creature Oliver Cromwell would ever have succeeded in having his off."

The acorn chin drew down into its laces like a snail into its shell. Until this moment Alice might have been conversing with an exquisite image, or an automaton—the glittering eyes, the crooked fingers, the voice from afar. But now it seemed a new life was stirring in it. The tiny yet piercing tones sank almost to a whisper, the head stirred furtively from side to side as if to be sure no eavesdropper were within earshot.

"Now listen close to me, my child: I have a secret. A secret which I wish to share only with you. You would suppose, wouldn't you, that this being the three-hundred-and-fiftieth anniversary of my natal day"—and at this the dreadful realization suddenly swept over Alice that she had quite forgotten to wish her godmother "Many happy returns"—"you might suppose that you are about to meet a gay and numerous company here—young and happy creatures like yourself. But no: not so. Even your dear mother is, of course, only my great-great-great-great-great-great-great-granddaughter-*in-law*. She was a Miss Wilmot, I believe."

"Yes, Woodcot, great-grandmamma," said Alice softly.

"Well, Woodcot," said the old lady; "it is no matter. It is you, my child, whom I have made, to be precise, my chosen. In mere men I take no interest. Not only that, but you must now be of the age I was when the portrait you see on yonder wall was painted. It is the work of a pupil of Hans Holbein's. Hans Holbein himself, I believe, was dead at the time. Dear me, child, I remember sitting for that portrait in this very room—as if it were yesterday. It was much admired by Sir Walter Raleigh, who, you may remember, came to so unhappy an end. That was, I recollect, in my early seventies. My father and his father were boys together in Devonshire."

Alice blinked a little—she could not turn her eyes away from her godmother's—that mammet-like face, those minute motionless hands.

"Now glance at that picture, please!" the old lady bade her, pointing a tiny crooked-up forefinger towards the further wall. "Do you see any resemblance?"

Alice looked long and steadily at the portrait. But she had neither the courage nor vanity to deny that the fair smiling features were at least a *little* like her own. "To whom, great-grandmamma?" Alice whispered.

" 'To whom?' Well, well, well!" came the reply, the words sounding like the chiming of a distant silver bell. "I see it. I see it. . . . But never mind that now. Did you perhaps look at this *house* as you made your way up the avenue?"

"Oh yes, great-grandmamma—though I couldn't, of course, look close, you know," Alice managed to say.

"Did you *enjoy* its appearance?"

"I don't think I thought of that," said Alice. "The trees and park were very lovely. I have never seen such—*mature* trees, great-grandmamma. And yet all their leaves were budding and some were fully out. Isn't it wonderful for trees so—so long in the world to—why, to come out at all?"

"I was referring to the house," said the old lady. "*Springs* nowadays are not what they used to be. They have vanished from the England I once knew. I remember once an April when angels were seen on the hilltops above London. But that is no matter for us now: not now. The house?"

Once again Alice's gaze wandered—to come to rest again on the green, nodding weed at the window.

"It is a very very quiet house," she said.

The childlike tones died between the thick stone walls; and a profound silence followed them, like that of water in a well. Meanwhile, as Alice fully realized, her godmother had been fixedly searching her face with her remote but intent eyes. It was as if Time itself were only a child and that of this aged face he had made his little secret gazebo.

"Now please listen to me very carefully," she continued at last. "Such a countenance as yours—one bearing the least resemblance to that portrait over there, must be the possessor of a fair share of wits. I am old enough, my child, not to be charged, I hope, with the folly of vanity. In my girlhood I enjoyed a due share of admiration. And I have a proposal to make to you which will need all the sagacity you are capable of. Don't be alarmed. I have every faith in you. But first, I want you to go into the next room, where you will find a meal prepared. Young people nowadays, I hear. need continuous nourishment. What wonder! Since they have forgotten all the manners of a lady as *I* know them, and are never still for a moment together. What wonder! With all these dreadful machines I hear of, the discontent, the ignorance and folly, the noise and unrest and confusion. In my young days the poor were the poor and the humble the humble, my child; and knew their place. In my young

days I would sit contented for hours at a time over a simple
piece of embroidery. And if I needed it, my mother never
deigned to spare the rod. But there, I didn't invite you to
visit an old woman merely to listen to a sermon. When you
have refreshed yourself you are to take a little walk through
the house. Go wherever you please; look well about you; no
one will disturb you. And in an hour's time come back to
me here again. Nowadays I take a little sleep in the afternoon. I shall be ready for you then. . . ."

Alice, with a relief beyond words, rose from her chair.
She curtsied again towards the small, motionless figure in
the distance, and retired through the dark oak door.

The room in which she at once found herself was
small, hexagonal, and panelled with the blackest of old oak.
A copper candelabrum hung from the dark moulded ceiling, and beyond the leaded panes she could see the gigantic
trees in the park. To her dismay the footman who had accompanied the butler into the room when her godmother
had first made her appearance was stationed behind the
chair at the table. Never had Alice supposed that it was
proper for men-servants, except perhaps gardeners, to wear
long grey beards. But there he was, with his dim sidling
eyes. And she must needs turn her back on him to seat herself at the table. She nibbled the fruit and bread, the rich
cake and the sweetmeats which he presented in their heavy
silver dishes, and she sipped her sweet drink. But it was a
hasty and nervous meal, and she tasted nothing of what she
had eaten.

As soon as it was over, the servant opened the door for
her, and she began her voyage of discovery through the
great, deserted house. It was as if her very ghost were her

only company. Never had solitude so oppressed her; never before had she been so intensely aware of being wide awake and yet dreaming. The long corridors, the low and crooked lintelled doors, the dark uneven floors, their Persian mats, their tapestries and hangings, only the lovelier in that their colours had been dimmed by so many suns, the angled flights of stairs, the solemn air that brooded between the walls, the multitude of pictures, the huge beds, the endless succession of superannuated coffers, daybeds, cabinets—all this in but a few minutes had tired and fatigued Alice far more even than the long journey from the home of her childhood that morning. Upstairs and downstairs, on she wandered for all the world like the goosey-goosey-gander of the old nursery rhyme.

And when at last with a sigh she glanced at the bright little silver watch which had been her mother's birthday gift, its slender hands told her that she had still a full quarter-of-an-hour before she need return to her great-great-great-great-great-great-great-great-grandmother's room.

That into which she had now admitted herself seemed to be a small library. Its walls were ranged from ceiling to floor with old leather and lambskin folios and quartos and squat duodecimos, while between them hung portraits and the loveliest miniatures and medallions of scores upon scores of persons who she guessed must be her ancestors and ancestresses of goodness knows how many monarchs ago.

One or two of the pictures, indeed, as the crabbed inscriptions showed, had been gifts to the family from those monarchs themselves. In their various costumes, wigs, turbans, and furbelows they looked as if they must have been the guests at an immense fancy-dress ball.

What tho Felicitie befal?
Time makyth shadowes of us all.

In this room a low recess filled the shallow bow window and on this lay a strip of tapestry. The leaded pane of the window was open. The sun was already westering, its beams slanting in on the gilt and ebony and ivory of the frames suspended from their nails. Alice knelt down at the window; and her mind slipped into a daydream; and her gaze wandered far away over the golden budding tops of the enormous oaks, the flat dark outstretched motionless palms of the cedars—perhaps descendants of those which Sir Philip Sidney had brought home to his beloved England from the East.

The thoughts that had all day been skittering in her mind like midges over a pool gradually fell still, and she sank deeper and deeper into the hush that lay over the ancient house. It was as if its walls were those of an enormous diving-bell sunken beyond measure in an unfathomable ocean of Time. So tranquil was the sweet April air beyond the window that she could actually detect the sound of the browsing of the herd of fallow deer that had now closely approached the lawns of the house itself.

And as, lost in this reverie, she sat entranced, she became conscious that a small living animal—the like of which she had never seen before—had crept up within a pace or two of her on the window-sill, and was now steadily regarding her with its clear bead-brown eyes. In size it was rather larger than a mole, its dark thick fur was soft as a beaver's, and it had a short, furry, and tufted tail. Its ears were cocked on its head, its silvery whiskers turned downwards above its jaws, and Alice could see its tiny ivory claws as it sat there erect on its haunches like a tame

cat or a dog begging for a titbit of meat. Alice, alas, had nothing to offer her visitor, not even a cherry-stone, not even a crumb.

"Well, you pretty thing," she whispered, "what is it?"

The creature's whiskers moved ever so slightly, its eyes fixed more intently than ever on the face of this strange visitor. Very very delicately Alice thrust out her finger, and to her astonishment found herself gently caressing the furry nose. "It was as if I was in Wonderland, myself," she explained long afterwards to her mother. Perfectly mute and still, the owner of it seemed to enjoy this little courtesy. And when she had withdrawn her finger, it looked at her more closely and searchingly than ever, as if bidding her take heed. It then tapped repeatedly with its ivory-clawed paw on the oak casement, glanced searchingly at her yet again, then shook its furry head vehemently three times, paused, turned swiftly about and pattered away into hiding behind a huge carved Moorish cabinet before Alice could so much as bid it adieu.

Quiet little events in this life, even though we cannot understand what exactly they mean, are apt to *seem* to mean a great deal. So with this small animal and Alice. It was as if—though she was not aware of it—she had been brooding over a problem in algebra or a proposition in Euclid, and it had ventured out of its living-place to tell her the answer. How fantastic a notion!—when Alice knew neither the problem nor what its solution was.

She glanced at her watch once more; her fair cheeks pinking all over at realizing that she was now ten minutes late for her assignation with her godmother. She must be gone. None the less, she had time to look her farewell at the huge dreaming park before she set out on her return journey.

Before at last finding her way, however, she irretrievably lost it. For the house was a silent maze of deceptive passages and corridors. Every fresh attempt only increased her confusion, and then suddenly she found herself looking into a room utterly different from any she had yet seen. Its low walls were of stone, its dusty windows shuttered; it contained nothing but a chair. And in that chair sat what appeared to be the life-size image of the smiling lovely creature she had seen in the portrait—eyes shut, cheeks a faint rose, hair still shimmering with gold, the hands laid idly in her lap, the fingers of one of them clutching what seemed to be the dried-up fragments of a bunch of roses. What there was to alarm her in this harmless image she could not tell; but she gazed awhile at it in horror, closed-to the door and ran off as if pursued by a nightmare, down one corridor and up another, to find herself at last by good fortune once more in the room where she had had her meal. It seemed, as she stood there, her hand upon her breast, as if she would never again recover her breath. She was no longer nervous; no longer merely timid: she was afraid. "If only, if only I had never come to this house!" was her one terrified thought.

She discovered with relief on re-entering Miss Cheyney's presence that her godmother was still asleep. Alice could see a while without being seen.

Now one of her mother's brothers—one of Alice's uncles, that is—was an old bachelor who delighted in birthday gifts. Alice had therefore been richer in dolls than most children: wooden, wax, china, Dutch, French, Russian, and even one from the Andaman Islands. But no single one of them had shown a face so utterly still and placid as that now leaning gently aside in its lace and silver cap and mantle. There was no expression whatever on its features. No faintest smile; no shadow of a frown. And yet the tiny wrinkles all over it, crooking down even from the brows over the eyelids, gave it the appearance of an exquisitely figured map.

And Alice was still surveying it as closely as some old treasure-hunter might the chart of his secret island, when the minute eyes reopened and her godmother was instantly awake and intent.

"Ah," whispered she, "I have myself been on a long journey, but I heard you calling. What happens, I wonder," and the tones sank lower, "what happens when one has ventured on too far to hear any such rumours? Answer me that, eh? But no matter. There is a more important question first. Tell me now, if you please, what you think of my house."

Alice moistened her lips. "That, great-grandmamma," she managed to reply at last, "that would take *ages*. It is marvellous: but oh, so very still."

"What should there be to disturb it?" asked the old lady.

Alice shook her head.

"Tell me," and her voice tinkled across the air with a peculiar little tang, "would you like this house for your own?"

"This house—for my own?" breathed the young girl.

"Ay, for your own, and for always—humanly speaking."

"I don't quite understand," said Alice.

The little head leaned sidelong like an inquisitive bird's.

"Naturally, my child. You *cannot* until I have gone a little further. The gift I am now offering you is one that few human beings in this world conceive to be possible. It is not merely this house, my child, with all that it contains —much as that may be. It is life. My father, you must understand, was a traveller, and in days when danger was a man's constant companion. In this very room on his return from a many years' journey, he told me as a girl of a dismal mountainous region of snow and ice and precipices that lies *there*—West of China, I believe. It was from thence that he brought back his secret. It was one that for grievous and tragical reasons he could not follow himself. And I, my child, was his only choice. You will realize there may come a day when the wish to live on may have somewhat dimmed in my mind. I confess to feeling a little weariness at times. But before I go, it is my privilege— my obligation—to confer the secret on another. Look at me!" The voice rose a little; it was as though a wren had uttered its shrill song in the low resounding room. "I am offering this inestimable benefit to *you*."

Alice sat straight as a dart in her chair, not venturing to turn her eyes aside even for a moment.

"The secret, great-grandmamma?"

"Aye," continued the old woman, closing her eyes, "you heard me aright. I will presently whisper it into your ear. Imagine, my child, the wonder of infinite time! Imagine a life in such surroundings as these, far from all the follies and vexations of the world—and one fear—the most terrible of all fears—gone, or at any rate so remote as to be of no consequence. Imagine that, I say."

For an instant Alice's gaze wavered. Her eyes glanced swiftly towards the window where shone the swiftly changing colours of the sunset, where sang the wild birds and Spring was fleeting on its way.

"Take your own time: and do not be afraid of me. I shall make few conditions. Only that you must vow si-

lence, to breathe not one syllable of what I shall tell you—
not even to your own mother. All else will be easy—com-
paratively easy. All else. You will come here and live with
me. Rooms are prepared for you—books, music, horses to
ride, servants to wait on you, all that you need. And in
due season this house, this accumulation of things precious
and old and beautiful, this wide park stretching for many
more miles than you can see from my topmost windows,
will be yours alone. You may pine for a while for old
friends. It is an unhappy thing to say good-bye, as I have
heard. But all fades, all goes. And in time you will not wish
for company. Servants as aged as mine are not difficult to
find; they are discreet, and have need to remain faithful.
I shall have many a quiet talk together. I have much to
tell you. I long, my dear child, to share memories with you
that I have never breathed to a living soul. There are
wings to this house into which you cannot have penetrated,
simply because they are shut off by bolts and bars. They
contain much to see: much to linger over; much to wonder
at. Yes, and my dear child, in you I should live on—our
two minds . . . two lives. Tell me now, what do you
think of my proposal? And remember this—not even
Solomon in all his glory could have conferred on you what
I now offer."

The aged head was nodding—as if with fatigue. The
cramped fingers fumbled aimlessly with the lace handkerchief, and Alice's poor wits were once more in a desperate
confusion. The room swam dizzily before her eyes. She
shut them a moment; endeavouring in vain to consider
calmly what that remote unhuman voice had been saying to
her. She might as well have struggled in sleep to shake off
the veils and nets of a dream, the snares of a nightmare.
One thing only was audible to her now, a bird singing in

the garden and the sound of her shoe tapping on the floor. She listened—and came back.

"You mean," she whispered, "on and on and on—like you, great-grandmamma?"

The old lady made no reply.

"May I, do you think, then, if you would be so kind, may I have time to think it over?"

"Think what over?" said her godmother. "Are you supposing a child of your age can think over three complete centuries before a single moment of them has come into view?"

"No," said Alice, her courage returning a little, "I meant, think over what you have said. It is so very difficult to realize what it means."

"It means," said the old lady, "an immeasurable sea, infinite space, an endless vista—of time. It means freedom from the cares and anxieties and follies that are the lot of the poor creatures in the world beyond—living out their few days in brutish stupidity. You are still young, but who knows? It means, my child, postponing a visit to a certain old friend of ours—whose name is Death."

She breathed the word as if in begrudged pleasure at its sound. Alice shuddered, and yet it gave her fresh resolution. She rose from her chair.

"I am young and stupid, I know, great-grandmamma; and I would do anything in the world not to—not to hurt your feelings. And of course, of course I know that most people have a very hard time and that most of us are not very sharpwitted. But you said *death;* and I think, if you will forgive my saying so, I would rather I should have to die when—just when, I mean, I *must* die. You see, it would be a very sorrowful thing for me if it came after my mother had —if, I mean, she cannot share the secret too? And even then.

. . . Why cannot we all share it? I do see, indeed I do, there is very little time in this world in which to grow wise. But when you think of the men who have——"

"You are here, my child," Miss Cheyney interrupted her, "to answer questions—not to ask them. I must not be fatigued. Then I should have no sleep. But surely you are old enough to know that there is not a human creature in a thousand, nay, not one in a hundred thousand, who has any hope of growing wise, not if he lived till Doomsday."

She edged forward an inch in her chair. "Suppose, my child, your refusal means that this secret will perish with—with *me?* Unless," the voice sank to a muttering, "unless *you* consent to share it? Eh, what then?"

Alice found her eyes fixed on the old lady like a bird's on a serpent, and the only answer she could make was a violent shake of the head. "Oh," she cried, suddenly bursting into tears, "I simply can't tell you how grateful I am for all your kindness, and how miserable I seem to myself to be saying this. But please, Miss Cheyney, may I go now? I feel a dreadful thing might happen if I stay here a minute longer."

The old lady seemed to be struggling in her chair, as if in the effort to rise out of it; but her strength failed her. She lifted her claw-like mittened hand into the air.

"Begone at once, then," she whispered, "at once. Even my patience is limited. And when the day comes that will remind you of my kindness, may you wish you had . . . Oh, oh! . . ." The frail voice rose shrill as a gnat's, then ceased. At sound of it the old butler came hastening in at the further door; and Alice slipped out of the other. . . .

Not until the house had vanished from sight behind the leaping branches of its forest-trees did she slacken her pace to recover her breath. She had run wildly on, not daring to pause or even glance over her shoulder, as if her guardian angel were at her heels, lending wings to her feet to save her from danger.

That evening she and her mother—seated in the cosy red-curtained coffee-room of the "Red Lion"—actually sipped together a brimming glass of the landlord's old Madeira. Alice had never before kept any secret from her mother. Yet though she was able to tell her most of what had happened that afternoon, she could not persuade herself to utter a syllable about the purpose which had prompted Miss Cheyney to send her so improbable an invitation. Not then, nor ever afterwards.

"Do you really mean, my own dearest," her mother repeated more than once, pressing her hand as they sat in the chill spring night under the old oil lamp post awaiting their train in the little country railway station; "do you mean she never gave you a single little keepsake; never offered you *anything* out of all those wonderful treasures in that dreadful old house?"

"She asked me, mother dear," said Alice, turning her face away towards the dark-mouthed tunnel through which they would soon be venturing—"she asked me if I would like ever to be as old as she was. And honestly, I said I would much prefer to stay just the silly green creature I am, so long as I can be with you."

It was an odd thing to do—if the station-master had been watching them—but, however odd, it is certainly true that at this moment mother and daughter turned and flung their arms about each other's necks and kissed each other in such a transport as if they had met again for the first time after an enormous journey.

Not that Alice had been quite accurate in saying that

her godmother had made her no gift. For a day or two afterwards there came by post a package; and enwrapped in its folds of old Chinese paper Alice found the very portrait she had seen on the wall on that already seemingly far-off day—the drawing, I mean, made by a pupil of the famous Hans Holbein, depicting her great-great-great-great-great-great-great-great-grandmother in the year of grace 1564, when she was just turned seventeen.

The Old Lion

There was once a sailor of the name of John Bumps. He had bright blue eyes and wore gold rings in his ears. Although, when this story begins, Mr. Bumps was still quite young, he had three children—Topsy, Emmanuel, and Kate—who lived with their mother in a nice little house with square windows in Portsmouth, and he had often been round the world. He had sailed into most of its ports in all kinds of weather; and there was scarcely an island of great beauty or marvel that he couldn't tick off on his tarry fingers.

Now one day, a little the right side of the rainy season, he came again to the west coast of Africa. His ship, *The Old Lion*—and he was her second-mate—had been sailing south down that great coast, past the Canaries and the Green Islands, past the Ivory and the Gold and the Slave Coasts to Banana and the noble Congo; and not long after that Mr. Bumps went ashore. He was paddled up the river Quanza, dark and green, past Dondo, to visit an old friend. And there in a village of the black men, for two green-and-red bead necklaces and a jack-knife, he bought a monkey.

Mr. Bumps had now and then bought other monkeys, and he knew this was a high price for one in that part of the country. But his friend, the Chief of the Mlango-Nlango tribe, who was exceedingly fat, and wore two blankets besides his beads and ivories, assured Mr. Bumps that this was no ordinary monkey.

The Chief's round black face, with its two rows of flashing teeth, broke into an immense smile as he told Mr. Bumps this. "Ee no skittle-skattle monk-ee, no," he said, for he had often traded with the English. "Ee . . ." but instead of finishing the sentence, he shut his eyes and put one black hand on the top of his head; though what exactly he meant Mr. Bumps could not tell. At first glimpse of the monkey, however, Mr. Bumps had known at once that whatever pleasant things the Chief might say of it they would be true. Besides, the Chief was an old friend of his, and wouldn't tell him lies.

On the other hand, since the hairy little fellow stood an inch or so under the common stature of monkeys of its kind, it was of no great size, and there was nothing else remarkable that showed—not then. As Mr. Bumps held it on his arm, in its long-skirted crimson coat, which one of the Chief's wives had made out of the royal cloth, it sat far less heavy indeed than would his younger daughter, Kate. And she herself was very small for her age.

But it had a neat, pretty head, wonderfully slender hands and long thumbs; and as it turned its solemn hazel eyes on Mr. Bumps, he suddenly felt acutely homesick. He had been more than once more than half round the world without feeling *that*. "It's *no good* longing," he would say, "when you've got to wait."

And then something which Mr. Bumps had not expected at all happened. It was this. His eyes, as has been said already, were of a particularly bright blue, and as the blue of his blue eyes met the gazing hazel of the monkey's, the creature stirred on his arm, opened its mouth, and made a remark. Mr. Bumps had never paid much attention to foreign tongues, and he did not understand what it said. Nevertheless, he knew what it *meant*. He knew for certain that the tiny liquid syllables which had issued from the small mouth were a message from friend to friend.

He bade a cheerful goodbye to the Chief, kissed his hand to the black lady who had brought the monkey into his hut, and went off again down to the river. He took aboard *The Old Lion* a good store of nuts, bananas, and other fruit; and as that evening he looked back at the coast, shining in the last of the sun—and *The Old Lion* was now some miles out to sea—he turned to his monkey and said, "How do you like the sound of the name of Jasper, sonny?"

The monkey softly turned to him as if to answer, but this time said nothing.

So Jasper he was called; although this was really due to a mistake on the part of Mr. Bumps. What had come into his mind, as he stood at the taffrail looking back at the coast of Africa, were the first two lines of a hymn that had been a favourite of his mother's—

> *From Greenland's icy mountains*
> *To India's coral strand.*

But in saying the words over to himself he had got the last but one word wrong. He had said,

> *From Greenland's icy mountains*
> *To India's* jasper *strand.*

Still, Jasper, he thought, was a better name than Coral, and Jasper it remained.

There never was a monkey so quick to learn, so grave in the learning, and so quiet and pleasant in manner as Jasper. Mr. Bumps could only guess how old he was, and he guessed, "p'raps five." And since the famous little son of John Evelyn even before this age could all but talk in Greek, Latin, and Hebrew, it may not be so marvellous as it sounds that Jasper soon began to pick up a few words of English. Long before this, however, he had learned to sit at table and say his grace (in his own tongue); to use a knife and fork, and a mug for his drink; to bow when spoken to; to swing his own hammock; and little things like that.

He would creep up, too, to watch the man at the wheel or the cook at his cooking in the galley or caboose. He would gaze for minutes at a time at the compass and lamp in the binnacle and would salute the captain whenever he saw him on the bridge. He knew the Christian names of every man jack of the crew and where each of them slept in the fo'c'sle; he could manage a little rope-splicing, and knew the difference between a granny and a reef knot, a loop and a fisherman's bend. In spite of his red cossack gown, he could scamper up the rigging to the truck or very summit of the mainmast twice as quick as any cabin-boy—and like every cabin-boy he had no tail to help.

Besides all this Mr. Bumps taught Jasper much else. Not that he sat him down and *made* him learn. It amused him, and Jasper enjoyed it. It was a long voyage too; *The Old Lion* edged into the Doldrums; and there was plenty of time.

As the days and weeks drew by, Jasper became as much at home on *The Old Lion* with his friend Mr. Bumps as if he had been born to the sea. Merely because he was

jimp and hairy, had a small flat-nosed face, and showed
his teeth when he talked, the sailors at first would tease
and laugh at him, treating him only as a pet or a plaything.
As soon as he began to talk King's English, however, they
teased him no more. He began to say things they remembered.

What Mr. Bumps meant to do with him when he was
safe home in his little house in Portsmouth he hardly knew.
He was sure his wife, whose name was Emma, would be
pleased to see his new friend, and there was no doubt at all
about Topsy, Emmanuel, and Kate. But how could he ever
part with Jasper now? Yet how expect him to lead a sea-
life? There was, however, no need to decide anything for
the present; and meanwhile he took almost as fond a care
of him—sought him out dainties, physicked him when sick
—as Mrs. Bumps was taking of their little Kate.

At last, and Mr. Bumps had long since made up his
mind that he could never of his own wish be separated
from Jasper, *The Old Lion* drew into the English Channel.
She was nearly home. And one misty afternoon in Novem-
ber she sailed slowly up the Thames and dropped anchor in the Pool of London. It was bitter cold, but still; and
a haze of the colour of copper hung over the mighty city.
And there in the midst, like an enormous leaden beehive
against the sullen sky, rose the dome of St. Paul's.

Mr. Bumps stepped ashore early next morning, with
the monkey hooded upon his arm, some presents for his
wife and children in his bag, and set out briskly for his
railway station. He had not been in old England for many
months, and the first thing in his mind was to get down to
Portsmouth as soon as he possibly could. But the haze that
had been high over the city the day before had now descended into its streets, and Mr. Bumps had to grope

on in the direction of the Monument and Pudding Lane through a fog which grew steadily denser.

He knew, at last, that he had lost his bearings. And when presently he came to a little public house, *The Three Swans,* its windows dimly glowing in the fog, he decided to go in and ask his way. But, somehow or other, he didn't like the notion that Jasper should go in too. He glanced into the little face under its hood and saw how cold and doleful it looked. But he was afraid the thick tobacco smoke and the smell of the beer and spirits in *The Three Swans* might make him ill.

So, "Sit you here a moment, Jasper," he said, as he put him down beside his bag beside the lamp-post, "and don't 'ee stir till I come back."

But, alas, Mr. Bumps stayed many minutes longer than he had intended to in *The Three Swans,* and when he came back, though his bag was still there where he had left it, Jasper was gone.

Indeed, Jasper had been patiently waiting in the fog in the dim light of the lamp-post for no more than five of those minutes, when there came by a stranger, with a black hat on his head, a black beard, and a coat reaching almost to his heels. If the monkey had not stirred at that moment, all might have been well. But, at sound of these footsteps in the strange cold London street, the solitary creature had lifted his face and put out a hand; for he had made many friends on board ship. And the stranger stooped, and looked at him.

Now, by a chance—whether evil or not it is hard to say—this man with the dark beard was a dealer in all kinds of animals. He had a shop in a narrow alley not far from the river. That shop went back, and every now and then up two or three steps, at least thirty paces. And from end to end of it there were cages of all kinds of birds and small beasts; besides tanks of fish and of rare snakes and lizards, and even gauze-covered cages of butterflies on rows of shelves. His larger animals he kept, though out of the rain, in a stone-flagged yard.

He stooped down, his rusty black coat brushing the paving-stones, and in the foggy gloom looked long into Jasper's face. Then he took the little, narrow hand in his, and gently shook it.

"How d'ye do?" he said, in a wheedling voice, and speaking through his nose. "Very pleased to meet you, I'm sure."

And Jasper, with his usual gentle manners, and thinking no harm of him, looked up into his face and chattered a few sounds, which were uncommonly like sea-English.

The stranger shot one swift, thief-like glance over his shoulder, then, opening a button of his great-coat, gingerly lifted Jasper from where he sat, slipped him in under it, and strode rapidly away.

Before evening, Jasper found himself, with a few monkey nuts and a can of water, squatting alone in a cage, surrounded by other cages in which, beside barking dogs and scrambling puppies, were scores of white rabbits and rats and cats—Manx, tabby, and Siamese—squirrels, ferrets, stoats, tortoises, owls, lovebirds, canaries, parrots, parakeets and macaws; and in the midst of a din and screaming of voices more deafening by far than he had ever heard in his own west-African forests, or in the middle of a storm at sea. He sat shivering and trembling in his gown, and at last pushed his head in under its furry hood, muttering to himself in small, mournful, monkey accents, "Mr. Bumps. Mr. Bumps. Oh, Mr. Bumps!"

But Mr. Bumps, having in great grief given up his

friend for lost, was long since in the train and on his way
in spite of the fog to his little square-windowed house in
Portsmouth, and back to his Emma, his Topsy, Emmanuel,
and Kate.

Jasper did not stay long in Mr. Moss's animal shop—
only for nine days and nine nights. But at the end of them
he had already begun to pine and droop, could scarcely eat
and seldom opened his eyes. He missed his friend the sailor,
and his care and kindness; though whenever Mr. Moss
himself, or the sharpnosed, sallow-faced young man that
helped in the shop, looked in at his cage, and spoke to
him, he looked solemnly back, without showing either his
teeth or his temper. He never clutched at his food when it
was pushed in through the wire door, nor did he even attempt to make any sound in response to what they said to
him. He sat there, his hands folded under his gown, like
some small hairy king deprived of his kingdom. Mr. Moss
and his young man had never seen his like before; and
even in this short time, they had both discovered that they
could not face out the little creature's dwelling eyes.

But though Jasper sat for the most part so quiet
and motionless in his cage that he might seem, at first
sight, to be fast asleep, or even stuffed, all day long his
ears and wits (and now and then his eyes) were busy. He
would watch the Belgian canary birds which Mr. Moss, during their moulting, had fed on special seed and cayenne
pepper to brighten their feathers, for hours at a time. There
was an enormous python, too, coiled up in straw not far
away, and for a long time he hardly dared to look at it.
But at last he made himself watch that too; and he never
ceased to listen to the talk between Mr. Moss and his pale,
soft-footed assistant, and the strange human beings that

came into the shop. Strange talk in the shop too he heard
between his fellow-captives.

Mr. Moss himself, though if Jasper had been like other
ordinary monkeys he would have soon forgotten it, never
felt *wholly* at ease at the thought that he had stolen this
one. Odd, unlucky things began to happen in the shop. He
himself upset a glass case full of Death's Head Moths. It
frightened him—their tiny feet on his skin and the fanning
of their sepulchral wings. The python one night, having
managed to glide out of her tank, devoured a mandarin
duck at one gulp, and escaped into London. And when his
assistant, first thing in the morning, tripped over a broom
that had been left on the floor of the shop and broke his
left leg, his master began to think that it would be as well
to get rid of Jasper as soon as he could.

So when that afternoon an acquaintance of his, who
had once been a showman and trainer of animals for a cir-
cus, stepped into his shop and enquired how much he
wanted for Jasper, the price he asked him was so very
moderate that his friend paid it down at once, and carried
the monkey off with him, there and then. At first sight of
Jasper he too had become homesick—for the ring-lights
and the tan and the tinsel and the ambling horses—and
had determined to begin again.

"And what do you call him?" he asked Mr. Moss.

"Call him? Why, what he calls hisself, day in, day out,
and even in his sleep!—Jasper."

"Ah, now, 'Jasper'?" repeated his friend.

He too was a dark man, but hollow-cheeked and lean;
and he wore his hair long over his ears. His name was Mr.
J. Smith, but he changed this on the programmes and play-
bills, when he was showing his animals, to Signor Dolcetto

Antonio. Unlike one or two black-hearted miscreants who followed his trade, he believed in kindness and common sense. "There are five things," he would say to his wife, "all things breathing—buffaloes to bullfinches—*need;* like you and me, Amy: food, shelter, sleep, company, and freedom." And he gave his animals nearly as much as they could wish of them all except the last.

Away from the cold and noise and stench and darkness of Mr. Moss's shop, Jasper soon began to be himself again. His appetite returned, his eye brightened, he looked sleek and nimble. He was soon as well as could be expected —his bosom friend Mr. Bumps gone, and himself so far from his own land.

In order to take all possible care of his charge, Signor Antonio brought him home to where he lived with his wife—the upper parts of a house in Jay Street, Soho. Part of this house was a shop that sold wine and oil and coffee and macaroni and olives and sausages and other kinds of foreign meats and drinks. In the rest, first floor to roof, lived Mr. and Mrs. Smith. Here, beside the fire in their small parlour, they made Jasper as cosy as they could—in a little chamber to himself.

For two hours every morning, Signor Antonio would talk to Jasper, and teach him tricks. When he was gone out to do his business, Mrs. Smith, busy herself over her cooking and housework, would talk to him too. She was a very stout woman, even stouter than the Chief of the Mlango-Nlangoes. And, like the Chief, she was full of good humour, and had a kind heart. She took particular pleasure in children and animals; and at the zoo would not only cheep to the birds and stroke the gazelles, but nod and smile at the orang-outangs and hippopotami. She treated Jasper as if he were a long-lost son.

Her husband had soon discovered that Jasper was a monkey that had no equal. He was as different from other monkeys as day is from dusk. He learnt everything he was taught with ease and alacrity and could soon chatter away to his friend, almost as if he had known English all his life. If he *looked* five, he could certainly *talk* like two-and-a-half. But, though he was so teachable and sweet-tempered and serious in his manners, there was something about him that never ceased to perplex Mr. Smith.

He felt this in particular when, his lessons done, Jasper would sit quietly in his chair, waiting for his mid-day meal. He had an air, at such times, as if he were brooding on something of which Mr. Smith had not the least notion. He seemed to be so far away that even Mr. Smith never ventured to ask him what he was thinking about, or to summon him back to dark Soho.

Merely to look at, Jasper was a comfort to the eye. Mr. Smith, though he was a good-natured man, was as awkward and clumsy as a saucepan with too long a handle to it. He was all angles. Mrs. Smith, too, who was even more good-natured than her husband, sat and talked with no more grace than a feather bed. But Jasper, even in the least motion of his small body, turn of the head, of the hand, of the foot, was quiet as flowing water and delicate as the flowers beside it. When he touched, it was as if thistledown had settled at his finger-tips. When he stretched out his fingers to take an apple, it was like the movement of a shadow through the air. He would sidle along Mrs. Smith's curtain-rod without stirring a single ring; and if she were near, would be allowed to follow her out onto the roof where she sometimes sat—in spite of smoke and smuts —sewing a hem and looking over London. Jasper would balance himself in his gown on the edge of the tallest of the red chimney-pots, glancing north, south, east, and west, and not a finger-tip to keep his balance!

If he was this to look at, what can he then have *been* in his secret mind—with its memories and dreams and sedate ponderings, river and forest, the terrors and dangers and delights of vast dark Africa, or rather of his own particular dark green corner of it?

"What I feel about our friend over there," Mr. Smith said to his wife one day, when Jasper sat asleep in his chair, "what I feel is, that he could learn me a sight more than I can learn *him*—of what, I mean, *matters*, my love. He's that privy yet polite you don't know where you are. And what I feel *too* is that there's something little short of shameful in letting a mere mob of humans come paying their half-crowns and shillings and sixpences just to stare at him. He talks to us; but, bless you, he only talks to us about what he knows we can understand. He don't tell us his secrets. Never. The truth is, he ought not to have been took away from where he came from, though where *that* was, nobody knows. No Moss ever got such a mystery by rights. Never. He's had a queer past, has that little monk; mark *me*."

And Mrs. Smith, though in her heart she agreed with her husband, thought it would be unwise to say so.

"Don't you fret, Jim," she replied. "He has plenty to eat and keep him busy. Worry! Not he! Look at him there, sleeping as peaceful as a babby, as if there wasn't a coconut or a black man in the world. He's as happy as the day is long."

"Coconuts!" said her husband, but he was not convinced.

At last, one early morning, a happy thought came into Mrs. Smith's mind.

"What by and by would be really fair and square, Jim," she said as she was combing her hair by the glass, "what by and by would be nice and proper, would be for you to take half of what you make out of Jasper, and him take the other half. Once he began to earn a bit of money, we could teach him what money *means*. After all, Jim, it's only a sort of short cut for bread and cheese and tables and chairs and clothes and houses—not to mention the time and trouble taken in making them; and he would soon pick it up. Then, mebbe, he might like to get a few little things for himself. He might like to set up, with *some* cash in the bank, as an independent gentleman. Judging from what I've seen of the world, he has twice as much sense as most such, and not a shadow of any vices; and I don't see *any-thing* against it."

Mr. Smith looked at his wife in astonishment. Nor was it merely because she had been speaking with her mouth full of hairpins. It was because she would seem for days together not to agree with a single word he said, and then, of a sudden, like a knife from its sheath, out would come a notion that made everything plain and easy. So it was with what she had said about Jasper.

About nine months after he had brought him home, Mr. Smith became perfectly certain that there was nothing else he could teach his charge. Jasper could make a speech; could sing; and draw pictures of forests and ships with a box of coloured chalks. He could scribble down simple sums up to fractions on a blackboard, and find an answer. He could manage everything to the last nicety with his clothes. During the week he was dressed in scarlet breeches and a green coat, with ivory buttons. On Sundays he wore a lightly-starched ruff round his neck, a velvet gown to his heels, made out of an old Sunday dolman of Mrs. Smith's, and fine shoes. For out-of-doors he had two or three different kinds of cloak. Not that Mr. Smith *kept* him to human clothes, or human ways either. Jasper agreed he must grow used to them. Whenever he so fancied he went bare; and, if he wished, he kept two Sunday-clothes days in one week. But this was very seldom.

He knew many simple rhymes, and Mr. Smith had made a little harp for him—rough, of course, but tunable. To this he would sing these rhymes, and other airs, and a curious music also, whose meaning he kept to himself. More than once, indeed, Mr. Smith had been awakened early in the morning to hear Jasper playing on his harp in the next room. And *then,* while both the words and tune seemed to be of Jasper's own making or remembering, there sounded a cadence in them that almost made him weep. By good fortune Mrs. Smith slept far heavier of nights than he did.

Anyhow, there was no doubt at all, that if Signor Antonio and Dr. Jasper—as they were going to call themselves in the play-bills—were ever to get rich, now was the time to begin. Mr. Smith had long ago been to see the Manager of the Bank in which he kept his savings, and had arranged with him to open an account in Dr. Jasper's name. Into this each week he afterwards paid Jasper's share of their takings which mounted up by leaps and bounds.

"You see," he had first explained to the Manager, "it may be some time before my young friend is able to come and pay his money in himself. But I want everything open and aboveboard. When he makes his debboo, which will be shortly, he will take half the fees and I shall take half. And when we have made what he thinks is enough, then he shall choose as he thinks best."

The Manager, Mr. Johnson, who until then had seen

only a few photographs of Dr. Jasper, not very good like-
nesses either, smiled at this arrangement. But there was no
doubt that it *was* all open and aboveboard, and he fell in
with Mr. Smith's wishes.

It was in the month of December that Dr. Jasper made
his first appearance on the stage. This was in London.
There was sleet that Christmas, and a cold wind was blowing in the lamplit London streets, when Signor Antonio and
Mrs. Smith set off together in a four-wheeled cab bound for
the *Fortune,* a famous theatre which had been named after
the old *Fortune* in the days of Queen Bess, and the Merry
Wives of Windsor. "And not much more than twenty years
after it was built," Mr. Smith told Jasper, "it was burned
down to the very ground—in two hours."

"In two hours!" said Jasper.

Still, Mrs. Smith, as she reclined quietly but firmly
against the purple velvet of the cab, her back to the horse
and her face to Jasper, and her husband beside her to keep
out the draught, might herself have been one of those
merry wives come to life again!

In the bleak cold north wind, the tiny snowflakes
vanishing as they fell through the dark air, and with its
multitudes of people going off about their pleasure in their
furs and wraps and winter clothes, London looked as bright
as a peep-show.

Jasper trembled a little, and not from cold, as he
gazed out of the glass cab-window at the passers-by, while
Mr. and Mrs. Smith talked cheerfully to keep his spirits up,
and sometimes made wonderfully good fun together about
some over-dressed lady or gentleman they could admire
from their little inside gloom in the cab without themselves
being seen. For *their* hearts too were beating high. But
Jasper himself, in his warm dark corner, said nothing. The

crowd of humans and the brightly-lit windows of the shops, reflected in his round dark eyes, the noise and cold, alarmed and frightened him. He longed to be home again; or far, far away from this strange land. The cab trundled along down the Charing Cross Road and into Trafalgar Square. Mr. Smith had told the cabman to take this way round to the theatre because he wanted Jasper to see the lions.

"And look, Jasper," said Mrs. Smith, when her husband had pointed them out, "*that* there up there is the great Lord Nelson; and mighty sharp-set he must be in his cocked hat—and only one eye and one arm, pore feller—with all that sleet falling up among them stars."

Jasper lifted his quiet face and could but faintly detect the great silent granite figure aloft against the sky.

"Sea," he muttered. "Seaman." But, strangely enough, Mrs. Smith, who was usually quickness itself at following what he said, supposed he meant to spell the word *see* and not *sea*, and was afraid he must be very nervous indeed of what lay in front of him if he had gone back to his old childish way of speaking—*See . . . Man . . .* when he had first learnt English. But Jasper had other thoughts.

The cab rolled on along the Strand, and there was still enough melting sleet in the street almost to silence its iron-tyred wheels. On and on it went, past the great railway-station in its cobbled yard, and on towards Waterloo Bridge; and in a little while drew up in a back street where an iron lamp jutting out over the pavement lit up the "Stage Door."

Mr. Smith then got out of the cab. He paid the fare, and (as much for his own good luck as for the cabman's) gave him a half-crown over. And he asked him to be waiting for them at eleven. "Eleven sharp," he said.

Then, having handed out Mrs. Smith, he mounted the

three steps, pushed open the door, which clapped to after them with a bang that shook poor Jasper to the heart, and they all three entered the theatre.

"Good evening, Sam," said Mr. Smith to the stout man sitting in a box behind a little open window by the door.

"Good evening," he replied; but his watery grey eyes were fixed not on Mr. Smith but on Jasper. With a turn of his small head and a touch of his fingers, he had shown his friend that he wished to be put down. So, one after the other—Mr. Smith, Jasper, Mrs. Smith—the three of them ascended the flight of stone steps into the dressing-room that had been set apart for them by the Manager of the theatre. And here Mr. Smith helped Jasper to spell out the description of himself that had been printed in large capital letters on the play-bill, a copy of which was pinned to the wall. THE FIRST APPEARANCE OF THE LEARNED AND FA- MOUS DR. JASPER, he read out slowly, Jasper sagely nod- ding his head at every word, THAT MINUTE MARVEL OF MONKEYLAND, AND MASTER MIMIC OF MAN!

"There," said Mrs. Smith, "that's *you,* Jasper! What do you think of that?" But Jasper made no answer. At this moment, trembling a little, he was gazing at the picture of himself underneath the print. It had taken him straight home again—since the artist, though no doubt he had done his best, had made him look very much like a small gorilla!

When with deft fat hands Mrs. Smith had put the fin- ishing touches to his toilet, and her husband was ready, they all three went down the stone steps again and made their way to the wings of the stage. There, in shadow and in silence, they waited. Soon it would be Jasper's turn. In this nook of the painted scenery—all flowers and trees and butterflies—the framework of which went up into the blaze of lights above, Jasper peered about him. It was the night after Christmas, and the theatre, from the floor up to its very roof, was packed with human beings of all ages, but particularly human children.

By standing on tiptoe and peering through a tiny hole in the canvas Jasper could see row above row of strange faces mounting higher and higher, their eyes fixed on the five *Exceptionally Elegant Ethiopian Elephants Engaged at Enormous Expense* which were now seated around their trainer on the stage. At sight of all these faces a sigh shook him from head to foot. And he turned away his head—and peered out to see the elephants themselves.

Four of these mighty animals, garlanded with mistletoe, were caparisoned in bright green and silver. The fifth, and the smallest, was dressed up as a clown, his face whitewashed, and one eye surrounded with a diamond in red. They sat on their tubs. They wreathed their proboscises. They greeted their trainer in a chorus that drowned even the blare of the band. They walked on their hind legs; they passed the bottle; they turned the handle of their hurdy-gurdies; and the two senior elephants danced a cumbrous polka, while the two junior sat fanning themselves, and the youngest with a painted poker beat time.

Then, one by one, these sage and monstrous beasts, their tiny eyes alight with excitement, stumpy tails a-swing, trailed off the stage to their own quarters. The curtain descended. It was Jasper's turn.

And soon all was made ready for him. A table, with books upon it, an empty inkstand, some foolscap and a dinner bell; two gilt chairs covered in bright blue satin beside it, and a sofa—this was the only furniture, apart from an umbrella stand, a palm in a pot, and a red and green Axminster rug.

The music stopped. The curtain slowly rose again. And there, in the middle of the stage, was Signor Antonio, dressed up like a lackey in a black tail-coat, and as if engaged in putting the room in order in preparation for the coming home of his master. And while he tidied the books and gave a last flick of his featherbrush over the fleckless satin chairs and the palm in the pot, he kept talking to himself, though loud enough for everybody to hear. He was explaining who he was—the faithful servant of the great Dr. Themistocles Marmoset Jasper, the kindest and wisest master manservant ever had, and the most famous medico in Europe. "In Europe, did I say?" he cried to himself, slapping his leg with his brush. "Nay, in the WORLD!"

"Now, Jasper," whispered Mrs. Smith, stooping over her small friend's head. *"World,* Jasper: that's your word, that's your cue! On you go, and bless you, Jasper! And if, poor mite," she breathed to herself, "you're half as nervous of the business as I am, in spite of my size, well. . . . *Now,* Jasper!"

Jasper looked up at her; he let go her hand. Out of the shadows he went, and into the light.

In his striped trousers, French-grey waistcoat, long black morning-coat, with his gold watch chain and starched collar, high hat in hand, he minced gently forward. His patent-leather shoes were a little too long for him, but he managed them with ease.

At sight of his master, Jennings at once stepped forward. Dr. Jasper gave him his hat, his cane, and his canary-coloured gloves. "Thank you, sir. Very good, sir," said Jennings. He hung the hat on a peg, and stood the cane in the stand.

The Doctor lifted his head a little as he came to the low table, and reaching up, laid his hand upon a book. "It's a fine ssunny morning, Jennings," he said. "Who iss my firsst pay-sshent today?"

So dead a silence hung in the theatre at first sound of these small treble words and their soft-hissed esses one could not only have heard a pin drop, but could have declared whether it had fallen on its head or its point! Then a little girl, in a seat high up in the dress circle, began to whimper a little. But she was soon hushed, and Jennings was explaining to his master that his first patient was the Right Honourable the Countess of Crumpet; "and a very nice lady too, sir, as I have been told; closely related to Lord Muffin, sir, of Teacake Castle."

Thereupon his master drew his watch from his pocket, and said: "It iss five minut'ss after ten, Jennings, I fear her lady-sshipp iss late."

"I will see, sir," said Jennings; "she may be in the ante-room." And he retired.

"It's all right, Ma; it's all right," he whispered to Mrs. Smith, as, swift and quiet as a shadow, he went whisking by. "Don't worry. He's *safe*."

Meanwhile, and while he was gone, Jasper, having taken a chair at the gilded table, drew the long goose-quill pen from out of the dry inkpot, and bending his small head till his flat nose almost touched the paper, pretended to write on it.

"That will be three guine'ss," he sighed to himself almost like a miser as he scrawled with the pen. "Three more guine'ss!" But though he said these words *as if* to himself, they were loud enough, like Mr. Smith's, for everybody in the theatre to hear; and yet they were said so solemnly that nobody laughed.

At this moment Signor Antonio came onto the stage again, from behind the wings. But while he had been gone he had dressed himself up in a bonnet, a flounced purple skirt and bustle, with a long train, and he carried a green striped parasol. He was now of course the Countess of Crumpet. Dr. Jasper bowed to the Countess, and they both sat down. And Dr. Jasper said to the Countess, "It iss a fine morning. Would your lady-sship, pleess, kindly put out the tongue?"

Then he stood up on his chair to look at her tongue, and said, "Ah! excussing me, your lady-sship, a ssorry tongue, a dreadful tongue." And still nobody laughed. But when the Countess, with a simper, thrust out a great man's hand in a white cotton glove from under her Paisley shawl for Dr. Jasper to feel her pulse—then *every*body laughed; and after that—except when Dr. Jasper was all alone on the stage—they hardly stopped to take breath.

And so the play went on, Jasper saying his part as if it were as simple and easy a thing to do as it is for other apes and monkeys to crack nuts and skin bananas. But though he seemed to all who watched from high and low in the theatre to be as the Manager had said he was—the Master Mimic of Man—this was not really true. This was only the human way of looking at him.

All the time he was really and truly himself, and only himself—thinking his own thoughts, gazing out of his bright, darting, round, dark-deepened, and now almost amber-coloured eyes over the glare of the footlights at the people beyond, and at Signor Antonio in his shawl and gloves and bonnet and bustle. And though he smiled as he chattered, and even grinned with laughter when owing to a mistake made on purpose the Countess sat down on the floor instead of on her chair, he looked gravity itself underneath, if one could have seen him close.

It was cold to him in London—this wintry weather; and though he liked Mr. and Mrs. Smith, who had been very kind to him, and though he knew quite well in his own way of thinking what *a pot of money* meant, he had *not* liked the large, fat, black-moustached face of the Manager of the theatre, and had consented to shake hands with him only out of politeness. He took everything in good part. And yet, he pined still for a long-lost friend, and to return again to his own people.

And when the curtain fell at the end of his performance his face shrunk up as if into a mask, and his eyes suddenly shut, at sound of the roar of voices that had broken out beyond it. Up went the curtain again—himself and Signor Antonio in the middle of the stage: and yet again and yet again—Dr. Jasper alone now; and again and again, now hand in hand with the Manager on one side of him and Mr. Smith on the other. It seemed as if the audience would shout themselves to a whisper and clap their hands off!

When at last the curtain came down and stayed down, he walked off a little dizzily and unsteadily, and clutched at Mrs. Smith's skirt. "Bless *me,* you poor poor mite!" was all she could say to him, for there were tears in her eyes, part of rejoicing and part for pity, and she fondled his cold fingers as if he had been a child. But small though he was, even as monkeys of his kind go, he had been a gigantic success, and the Manager's face was one wide, dark, greasy smile when once more he shook hands with him, bowed to the ground, though it was not much more than in mockery, and said good-night.

So the money—Jasper's share—poured into the bank until he was by far the richest monkey in the world, even though he was also the only monkey in the world that knew it. Mr. and Mrs. Smith in all their dealings with him were as honest as the day, and they of course were soon rich too.

Now one day John Bumps came home again from sailing round the world, as he had sailed many times before, though never without pleasure. And even though he lived so far away from London as Portsmouth is, he had not been two days with his family before in large print in his newspaper he saw the name of Dr. Jasper, and read of what he had done.

"Jasper," he repeated to himself, "why that's queer, now, *that* is! *Jasper!*" He read it again, and slapped his leg. "The same name, right enough," he said to himself. "And, Solomon Davy, surely there can't be two Jaspers, not like this! And if there are *not* two Jaspers, then this Jasper must be my Jasper!"

And there and then, he'd made up his mind, for he still had a good deal of money in his pocket after his voyage, that he would take Mrs. Bumps and Topsy and Emmanuel and Kate right up to London so that they could go to the *Fortune,* and see this Jasper with their own eyes. Even if he were not his old friend of the Mlango-Nlangoes and only a coincidence, it would be a Treat. And Mr. Bumps always gave his family a Treat when he came home from sea. He said nothing whatever to the children meanwhile about his friend Jasper in case it should prove a disappointment, though he told Mrs. Bumps. The following Saturday morning, having locked up the house, they all set out together in their best clothes, and caught an early train.

Emmanuel and Kate had never been to London before. They sat, each of them in a corner, staring out of the carriage window so intently at the fields and meadows and villages and churches and hills and farms gliding by that they both of them had only just finished the buns Mrs. Bumps had bought for them to eat on the journey when the train steamed into the great glass-roofed cavern of a station called Waterloo—after (as Mr. Bumps explained) the great Duke of Wellington, the Iron Duke, Old Nosey.

They had the whole day before them, and Mr. Bumps, when he gave them a Treat, never wasted a minute. He at once led them all off into an omnibus and they went, first to Westminster Abbey, then to see the soldiers on their horses in Whitehall, then to St. Paul's Cathedral. And there Mr. Bumps showed them through the brass grating where the body of Lord Nelson reposed in his tomb made of the cannon he had captured from the French. "He was a great sailor, was Lord Nelson," said Mr. Bumps.

"Do you mean a sailor just like you, Daddy?" piped out Topsy.

"Ssh! Topsy!" whispered Mrs. Bumps. "You mustn't call out like that. It's a church."

In St. Paul's churchyard, on a seat in the open—for the sun was shining, though it was rather cold—they ate the lunch which Mrs. Bumps had packed into her wicker basket. Then, after seeing where the two little Princes had slept for the last time in the Tower of London, they had tea in a tea-shop. The three children had a boiled egg each, but Mr. and Mrs. Bumps preferred theirs poached. After that they had some Bath buns and plenty of cake. Then they all went out again; and after letting them look for a little while into the shop windows in Cheapside, and especially a top-shop bowered in with a great plane tree

like an immense umbrella, Mr. Bumps—as if he had suddenly made up his mind—packed them all into a hackney
cab and off they went to the *Fortune*.

Though Mr. Bumps was now first-mate of *The Old
Lion,* he was not yet a rich man, so he could not afford to
take tickets for the seats downstairs, except in what is
called the Pit. And he did not take tickets for the Pit because Mrs. Bumps said she always liked to look down when
she went to a theatre. They were extremely early and by
good luck there were five seats available in the Upper
Circle, and these in the very middle of the front row. Very
pleased they were to be able to sit quietly in these stuffed
easy seats and to rest and watch the people, after walking
about such a long time in London. Indeed, they had hardly
settled themselves in when little Kate, who was only five
and tired out, fell fast asleep in her chair.

Topsy and Emmanuel however stayed wide awake,
sucking their peardrops (because Mrs. Bumps had thought
the seats too dear for bull's-eyes), and whispering and
chattering and watching everything that went on. They
had never in all their lives seen so many fine ladies with
bare shoulders, and diamonds in their hair, or so many
gentlemen in long black coats and tall collars.

One by one the members of the band, some carrying
their instruments, came edging their way to their seats in
front of the stage, and began to tune up or softly tootle on
their oboes and trombones. The drummer too thumped
softly on his drums, but not on his triangle or cymbals. And
last came the conductor with his ivory wand.

"What's that for?" chirped Emmanuel.

"That," said Mrs. Bumps, "is to do the music with."

The conductor sat down on his little velvet seat and
waited.

Mr. Bumps took out his silver watch. "Sharp on the hour," he whispered to Mrs. Bumps; "I wonder what they are waiting for."

He had no need to wonder long. For suddenly at a signal the conductor with white-gloved hand lifted his wand, and to a crash of music that nearly startled poor little Kate out of her wits, everybody in the theatre stood up and the band played the National Anthem. Sure enough, in a moment or two there came in to a great box beside the stage which had been trimmed up with holly and mistletoe, first the King of England himself, then the Queen, then their son, the Prince of Wales, and then a little foreign princess with black ringlets and a tiny fan. They were followed by a few nice-looking but splendid ladies and gentlemen; and the King stood in front of the box, in the middle of it, while the anthem went on.

"That's the King," whispered Mr. Bumps to Emmanuel.

"And that's the Queen," said Mrs. Bumps. "And there, see, Topsy, see, Manny, see, Kitty, that's the Prince of Wales!"

It was a long time before little Kate could see at all, she had been so dead asleep. When the last note had been played, they all five cheered as loud as they could, and so did the other people in the theatre. The King bowed. They cheered again. Then he sat down; and slowly, quietly, in heavy folds, the curtain ascended and the performance began.

First came acrobats, in tights and spangles. Next came a juggler and his small daughter. It looked as if the balls and hoops and dinner-plates they juggled with were things alive. After the juggling there came a man who sang "The Bay of Biscay," though Mr. Bumps knew a good deal more about the Bay than he did. And after him the five silent-footed Ethiopian Elephants debouched one after the other onto the stage.

At sight of them, though the three children opened their mouths like O's and clapped till it hurt, Mr. Bumps himself could scarcely breathe. But not, of course, because he had never seen elephants before. Far from that. He had seen quantities of elephants—either walking about, wild and tranquil, in the black man's swamps in Africa, or lying caked with mud in the heat of the tropic sun, or fountaining one another with cascades of silvery water at the close of day. And even though these five did clever tricks, he had watched others at far more useful ones in their own country. Not that he despised the elephants, he was only used to them.

No; Mr. Bumps was waiting for Dr. Jasper and could scarcely endure the delay. He was waiting for Dr. Jasper in his "Grand New Act"—as the play-bills said, an act "especially invented for the August Amusement of Royalty; and patronised by the Shah of Persia, the Emperor of Abyssinia, and other all-powerful Potentates." And he knew now that before he could count fifty it would begin.

The huge ponderous beasts, having bowed, kneeling in their green and silver, to express their thanks for the applause, were shuffling off towards the back of the stage. There, as the lights dimmed, they stood in a row, their trunks uplifted above their heads. There came a pause; and then a slender shaft of pearly light struck down from on high towards the wings. A sudden shawm-like trumpeting broke out from the elephants' throats, a trumpeting loud enough to drown the strains of twenty orchestras.

And into the beam of light—it moving with him as he went—there came tripping softly forward—a trailing cloak of crimson velvet edged with gold lace upon his shoulders, a tall cap of sable surmounted by a plume of *aracatan* feathers pinned with a diamond in front of it upon his head, a little silver-gilt sceptre in his right hand —Jasper. No longer now a medico of fashion, prescribing pills for the Countess of Crumpet, but himself *Almighty Emperor of All the Ethiopians,* the All-Excellent Ammanabi Nana Dah.

Following in his train came two small fuzz-wigged pygmy blackamoors in ostrich feathers and in robes of silk—of yellow and vermilion. One of these was carrying the Emperor's royal sunshade, and the other (for it was very light in weight) his gilded throne. And these were followed by Signor Antonio (Mr. Smith), no longer either a man-servant or a countess, but one of the Emperor's tallest and lankiest wives!

When the trumpeting of the elephants had died down and the cymbals and drums had ceased to sound, there went up such a roar of voices in the theatre from the people in it that it was heard outside for half a mile in all directions. Even the King of England, seated smiling in his Royal Box, could not remember to have been greeted with a louder *Huzza*. And then, almost as if this prodigious noise itself had caused it, an utter quiet fell. The Emperor, having gathered his crimson skirts around him, his scarlet sunshade like a huge mushroom over his head, had taken his seat upon his throne. The royal twelve-whiskered leopard-skins had been laid about his feet.

He sat there a moment—small, upright—perfectly still, and looked on them all. Not a tongue wagged, not a sigh or a cough sounded in all the theatre. The *only* stir, and no one noticed it, was that little Kate, who had never before seen such things or anything like them, ducked down her head out of sight of the stage and hid her face in her mother's lap.

The Emperor Jasper looked around him. He was accustomed now to the glare and the sea of faces, and the plaudits and the laughter. He knew where he was, and he knew too—though he himself alone could tell it—*who* and *what* he was. And perhaps for this reason, as he sat there peering out of his splendour, the host of those who were looking at him felt a peculiar coldness stealing into their blood.

It was not only as if they were uneasy in his presence —the tiny motionless head, the intent eyes—but also as if they were frightened. Even the Queen, in her disquiet, glanced sidelong at the King, but the King was looking at the Emperor. And the Emperor at this moment, having very gently lifted his minute left hand, had opened his lips to speak. . . .

Perhaps if Mr. Bumps had thought all this over for a moment or two he would have remained quietly seated with his family in the front row of the Upper Circle and would have said nothing. He would have waited till the end of the performance, and then found his way round to the Stage Door, and sent in to the Manager his cards—his visiting card—which he had had printed when he was made first-mate of *The Old Lion: Mr. John Bumps, First-Mate of* THE OLD LION, 7 *The Transoms, Portsmouth*. That would have been the right thing to do. But Mr. Bumps, being a seaman and not used to holding himself back when anything that needed doing was to be done, couldn't wait to think.

Out loud, the only sound in the theatre, except that the Emperor having opened his lips had said, "WE," he called "Jasper! . . ." And as if on one hinge every face in the theatre and every face even in the Royal Box had

turned round to look at him. Moreover the puny Emperor
on the stage in his gold and crimson finery had said not
a syllable after that first clear "We"—which he had pro-
nounced as if it were spelt Oo-*ee*—but had looked at him
too. All else then but rapture had vanished out of his mind.
And, in the twinkling of an eye, without the least haste, or
word, or sound, or nod, he had risen from his throne, and
was softly pattering towards the footlights, or rather to the
side of the footlights opposite the Royal Box.

Now the stage was framed in, top and sides, with a
shimmering arch of carved wood and painted plaster. All
kinds of knobbly fruits and flowers and little cupids and
ribbons and dolphins and birds adorned it, glistening bright
with gilt and colours. It was behind this arch that the curtain rolled down, and the *Fortune* was one of the handsom-
est theatres in London.

In all that quiet, then, slowly and without haste, Jasper began to climb this arch, his royal robes swinging free
behind him. They were heavy with their gold lace, and he
climbed slowly. But he climbed none the less surely, on and
on, and up and up, and watched by every eye, until he
had reached to where Mr. Bumps's gallery began. Here
there ran a low wooden wall to keep the people from falling out of the gallery. Those in the front row of this gallery
sat in their seats with their knees bent, looking over this
low wall at the stage, and—to make it comfortable for their
elbows as well as to look nice—the top of it had been padded
with horsehair and covered with a maroon-coloured stuff
called plush.

So it was with no sound at all from his small five-toed
feet that Jasper came—hastening, now—alone along this
wall in front of the people seated there, their faces in the
reflected glow of the footlights looking as white as china.

Straight along this dizzy path he silently tippeted until he reached the place where Mr. Bumps was sitting. There he stopped. He looked at Mr. Bumps and bowed his head. Then he said something that few heard and nobody understood. He put out his hands towards Mr. Bumps. And the two friends were restored to one another.

Now all this time the people had sat perfectly still, watching. But when they witnessed what had happened— and these two there, Jasper and Mr. Bumps—though they didn't really know what to say or think, they all began to talk, and some to shout, even to hoot. They were angry. They were being cheated. *This* was not what they had paid all that money to see! Poor Mrs. Bumps could even hear what those near by were saying. She was growing more and more hot and discomfited. "Oh, John! Oh, John!" she kept repeating.

And now the Manager, whom Jasper had come to like even less and less as his nights had gone by, appeared, marching on to the stage. He bowed to the King, he bowed to the Queen, he bowed to the Prince of Wales, and he called out in a loud voice that he was very sorry for what had happened. He said he was very sorry to them all. He said that he had paid pounds and pounds of money for Jasper to come and amuse them, and now here was this man up there enticing him away. He bawled out, "Emperor Jasper, Emperor Jasper, come down, sir!"

Then some voices in the back parts of the theatre shouted, "Turn him out!" and a great clamour began, some yelling this and some that, and the Manager standing alone, fat and black and helpless in the middle of the stage, cajoling in vain Jasper to come back. As for Mr. Smith— since he was dressed up as one of the Emperor's wives, and was a born actor, he felt that it was not his place to speak; especially before Royalty. His eyes rolled in his black-dyed face, but he said nothing.

Meanwhile, safe with his Mr. Bumps again, Jasper had made not the faintest sign that he had even heard the Manager's call. And now, louder and louder, many voices were shouting, "Send him back!" and some were bellowing, "Let him stay!" and the uproar grew worse and worse.

At last the King himself stood up in the Royal Box and raised his hand. There was at once a great hush in the theatre. Everybody fell silent. The King said, "Whose monkey is this marvel?"

With a frowning countenance he looked down upon the Manager. And the Manager answered not a word. Then the King turned his eyes towards Mr. Bumps. He said, "Let that man stand up."

And Mr. Bumps stood up.

"Who are you?" said the King.

"I am John Bumps, may it please your Majesty," said Mr. Bumps simply. "First-mate of *The Old Lion,* now lying at Portsmouth."

"What are you doing here?" said the King.

"I came, your Majesty—and this is Mrs. Bumps beside me with the children—I came in hopes of seeing an old friend again."

"Who?" said the King.

Mrs. Bumps was now clutching tight her husband's hand, since it was hidden by the plush-topped wooden wall. His voice faltered. He touched with his other hand Jasper's sable cap.

"This, sir," he said.

"You mean," said the King, smiling, "his Serene Mightiness, the All-Excellent Ammanabi Nana Dah? Beseech his Mightiness to stand forth."

This good-humour of the King greatly pleased all the people present, and every eye was now fixed on Mr. Bumps.

"*Now*, Jasper," whispered he, "the King of England is speaking to 'ee."

Jasper blinked but once at his old friend, pressed the finger clasped tight in his hand, and stood up on the plush parapet, before them all.

And the King, his eye twinkling, said, "Is it your wish, cousin, that you remain with our loyal subject, Mr. Bumps, or—" and he swept his hand towards the Manager and the footlights.

An instant's silence followed.

And then, "Thissee Misster Bumpss, ssir," piped Jasper, for he had never quite mastered his s's, "thissee Misster Bumpss, ssir, iss my *firsst* friend. Mr. Ssmith iss my o-ther friend. My *firsst* iss. . . ." But the next word which was *firsst* was almost drowned by the shout of delight from a thousand throats that went up to the roof of the theatre like the roar of an avalanche. It was fortunate for the Manager that he had already left the stage and gone into the back parts of the theatre.

And then and there Mr. Bumps and Mrs. Bumps and the three children and Jasper were conducted down to the Royal Box and were presented to His Majesty. And first the King and then the Queen and then the Prince of Wales and then the little foreign princess shook hands with Jasper, and he spoke to them. And the King slipped a ring off his own finger and hung it round the neck of the Ethiopian Emperor. They met, one might say, as equals.

But Mr. Bumps being a sailor and an honest man, when the theatre was empty and the lights were out and the

people gone away, sat down in a little back room behind
the stage with the Manager and Mr. and Mrs. Smith, while
Mrs. Bumps and the children waited for them in Jasper's
dressing-room. Here, the four of them, over a bottle of
port wine, made a bargain together, so that the Manager
should not lose too much money. The bargain was that for
the whole of the next three days, except when it was time
for Dinner or Tea, Jasper should sit on the stage of the
Fortune in his gold and crimson, the King's ring dangling
round his neck, his cap of sable on his head, while every
man, woman or child who wished and could pay to see
him, passed along—in at one door and out at another—
before his throne. And of the cash they might take at the
doors, it was agreed that the Manager should keep half,
Mr. Smith a quarter, and Jasper a quarter. Mr. Bumps
would take nothing. In those three days the Manager made
more profit than he had ever made before in a whole
month!

When the three days were over, Mr. Bumps's leave
from his ship was over too, and they all went down to
Portsmouth. By the kindness of the captain of *The Old Lion,*
it had been arranged that Jasper should come aboard—it
was his wish—and return to Africa. He might, if he had so
chosen, have stayed in England and lived in a palace for
the rest of his life. His fame had run like wildfire through
the Kingdom, and far beyond it. Telegrams had come from
Paris and Rome and Vienna and Budapest, and all parts
of America, entreating him to visit them.

Apart from telegrams, the postman brought Jasper a
small sack of letters every morning—from old ladies in
the country who wished to adopt him, from learned pro-
fessors of Oxford and Cambridge who wished to share his

wisdom, from cunning men who hoped to make money out of him, and from all kinds of people grown-up and otherwise who asked him to put his name in their birthday books. And the King did not forget him. But Jasper refused everything—except the birthday books; he pined only for home.

In the meantime he himself made many presents to all his friends, and especially to little Kate, according to what he thought they would like best. The rest of his money—after he had said goodbye to Mr. Johnson—had been packed in the cellar at the Bank into twenty-eight small chests or coffers. These were piled up in the cabin that had been prepared for him on *The Old Lion.* And a nice pile they made.

Besides this, with the captain's consent, Jasper and Mr. and Mrs. Bumps had bought a large quantity of all kinds of trinkets, toys, linen and silk, dainties and beverages that would not rust or tarnish or go bad upon the voyage, whatever weather they might encounter. Jasper had thought of everything that his own people round about Dondo might fancy and enjoy. And the King had commanded that on this voyage *The Old Lion* should fly not the red ensign but at the main truck the Royal Standard.

A crowd of people so vast thronged the quay and the windows and the roofs of the houses near by to see Jasper off that some of those in the front row were tumbled into the water. All except one had nothing worse than a sousing and were picked up by row-boats. But the Manager unfortunately, who had pushed past some small boys for a better view, was drowned.

The best brass band in Portsmouth played *Rule Britannia,* and to the strains of *Rio Grande* the men of *The Old Lion* weighed anchor.

Oh *say*, were you ever in Rio Grande?—
    Awa-ay, Rio!
It's there that the rivers run down golden sand—
    And we're bound for the Rio Grande.
And awa-ay, Rio!—away, Rio!
Sing, fare you well, my bonny young gal,
    We're bound for the Rio Grande!

She shook, she stirred. Softly a gentle breeze between
the blue sky and the sparkling water bellied out the sails of
the ship. She drew away upon the water, past Nomansland
Fort, where a gun puffed out to greet her, and smalled
more and more. By the time Mrs. Bumps and the three
children sat down to tea, she was out of sight of land.

Mr. Bumps had many a quiet and private talk with
Jasper in his cabin as the days went by. Never had the old
ship seen fairer weather. The two friends were sad at
heart, for Mr. Bumps knew that nothing he could say now
would dissuade Jasper from returning to his own people.
That, Jasper assured him, as well as what words he had
could do so, was his *one* wish; and Mr. Bumps could say
no more.

Now the head village where Mr. Bumps's friend the
Chief of the Mlango-Nlangoes lived was a mile or more
from the banks of the Quanza. It lay beyond a swamp where
there is a forest of mangroves, the abode of countless crocodiles, though the two-horned rhinoceroses keep to the
river. Between the river and the swamp (where, if there
were hundreds of crocodiles there must have been thou-
sands of monkeys!) was a stretch of sand and green.

In this spot, out of sight of the river, but well in reach
of the trees, the black men whom Mr. Bumps's friend, the
Chief of the Mlango-Nlango tribe, had very kindly lent

him for the purpose, brought up not only Jasper's crates and tubs and boxes and barrels of rare nuts and fruits, fruits in syrup, biscuits, beads and gewgaws, etc., but also his money chests crammed tight with sovereigns and silver. For nothing that Mr. Bumps or Mr. Johnson or Mr. and Mrs. Smith could say, could persuade Jasper that all this money of his was just that and nothing more, and would be of no more use to his friends in their treetops, except perhaps for the beauty of it, than nut-shells or pebble-stones. It had been given to him, he kept saying, for what he had done; and therefore he would like to take it all back to his people—except of course what he wished to spend on the presents he had given to Mr. Bumps and his other friends.

Since, then, Jasper, however much they argued, still wished to take back his money with him, Mr. Bumps had said of course, "Let it be so." Just as the King had said.

When all Jasper's possessions had been piled up in the open space between the hidden river and the forest which he had chosen for his camping-place, and when a small bell-tent had been pitched for him beside them, it was evening. Strange voices of all manner of animals and birds sounded in their ears when Mr. Bumps bade his friend good-night.

"I hope, Jasper," he said, "ay, and more than hope, that your kith and kin over there will be pleased to see you. I hope so. But they have been keeping mighty quiet."

He said it with a faint heart, smiling at his little friend dressed up, as he had himself decided, in his robes of gold and crimson, his sable cap on his head. Still, since Mr. Bumps had promised to come back in the morning, this was not good-bye. It was only good-night.

When Mr. Bumps did come back in the morning,

Jasper greeted him sadly enough. Though he had heard in the night faint chatterings and shufflings, not a single friend of all he had known in past times—not one—had come near him. So at Mr. Bumps's advice they unpacked some of the boxes and crates containing the dainties that smelt sweetest and strongest and strewed them about in enticing piles some little distance away from Jasper's tent and nearer the forest.

Next morning these had vanished; and yet Jasper had remained solitary and unvisited in his tent all the night long. He had not slept a wink. Never mind, he told Mr. Bumps; his friends were no doubt shy and timid. He was sure they would be pleased to see him and longed to speak to him and welcome him back.

But morning after morning the piles grew less and less; the food was all gone; the toys and trinkets were scattered out of the boxes; only the money, the sovereigns and the silver, were left. And these the monkeys, having smelt and fingered them, left disowned.

Jasper thought at last it must be his royal robes, his antelope slippers, his cap and his colours that kept his people from knowing who he was. He said this smiling, to his friend Mr. Bumps, but not as if he quite believed it.

That evening when they parted again, the air over Africa was heavy and stagnant and the sky lowering. Silent lightnings gleamed ever and again above the distant forests, and they could hear the tom-toms of the Mlango-Nlangoes sullenly drumming from their hidden dancing-places. Jasper had stripped himself of all his finery, and stood up beside his tent only in his own fur—a little monkey, as he was before. Mr. Bumps shook him by the hand.

"Good-night, old friend," he said, "and God-speed."

But when he came back the next morning after the

storm, the cap and the robes and the slippers and the gilded sceptre were gone. The tent had been blown away. And Jasper was gone too. Mr. Bumps called and called and called. He came back in the evening and called again. No voice answered him. The forest lay dark and silent. Three days, by the kindness of the captain, to whom he had sent a black man as messenger, he waited and waited. But he waited in vain. And on the fourth *The Old Lion* sailed away.

Miss Jemima

It was a hot, still evening; the trees stood motionless; and not a bird was singing under the sky when a little old lady and a child appeared together over the crest of the hill. They paused side by side on the long, green, mounded ridge, behind which the sun was now descending. And spread out flat beneath them were the fields and farms and the wandering stream of the wide countryside. It was quite flat, and a faint thin mist was over it all, stretching out as if to the rim of the world. The stooping old lady and the child presently ventured a few further paces down the hillside, then again came to a standstill, and gazed once more, from under the umbrella that shaded them against the hot sun, on the scene spread out beneath them.

"Is *that* the house, Grannie," said the child, "that one near the meadow with the horses in it, and the trees? And is that *queer* little grey building right in the middle of that green square field the church?"

The old lady pressed her lips together, and continued to gaze through her thick glasses at the great solitary country scene. Then she drew her umbrella down with a click, placed it on the turf beside her, and sat down on it.

"I don't suppose the grass *is* damp, my dear, after this long hot day; but you never know," she said.

"It's perfectly dry, Grannie dear, and *very* beautiful," said the child, as if she could hardly spare the breath for the words. Then she too sat down. She had rather long fair hair, and a straight small nose under her round hat with its wreath of buttercups. Her name was Susan.

"And *is* that the house, Grannie?" she whispered once more. "And *is* that the church where you did really and truly see it?"

The old lady never turned her eyes, but continued to overlook the scene as if she had not heard the small voice questioning; as if she were alone with her thoughts. And at that moment, one after another, a troop of gentle-stepping, half-wild horses appeared on a path round the bluff of the hill. Shyly eyeing these two strange human figures in their haunts, one and another of them lifted a narrow lovely head to snort; and a slim young bay, his mane like rough silk in the light, paused to whinny. Then one by one they trotted along the path, and presently were gone. Susan watched them out of sight, then sighed.

"This is a lovely place to be in, Grannie," she said, and sighed again. "I wish I had been here too when I was little. Please do tell me again about the—*you* know."

Her voice trailed off faintly in the still golden air up there on the hill, as if she were now a little timid of repeating the question. She drew in closer beside her grannie, and pushing her small fingers between those of the bent-up, black-gloved hand in the old lady's lap, she stooped forward after yet another pause, looked up into the still grey face with its spectacles, and said very softly, *"How* many years ago did you say?"

There was a mild far-away expression in the slate-grey eyes into which Susan was looking, as if memory were retracing one by one the years that had gone. Never had Susan sat like this upon a green hill above so immense a world, or in so hushed an evening quiet. Her busy eyes turned once more to look first in the direction in which the trotting comely horses had vanished, then down again to the farmhouse with its barns and byres and orchard. They then rested once more on the grey stone church—which from this height looked almost as small as an old cottage —in the midst of its green field.

"How many years ago, Grannie?" repeated Susan.

"More than I scarcely dare think of," said the old woman at last, gently pressing her fingers. "Seventy-five, my dear."

"Seventy-five!" breathed Susan. "But that's not so very many, Grannie dear," she added quickly, pushing her head against her grannie's black-caped shoulder. "And now, before it is too late, please will you tell me the story. You see, Grannie, soon we shall have to be going back to the cab, or the man will suppose we are not coming back at all. *Please."*

"But you know most of it already."

"Only in pieces, Grannie; and besides, to think that here we are—here, in the very place!"

"Well," began the old voice at last, "I will tell it you all again, if you persist, my dear; but it's a little *more* than seventy-five years ago, for—though you would not believe it of such an old person—I was born in May. My mother, your great-grandmother, was young then, and in very delicate health after my father's death. Her doctor had said she must go on a long sea voyage. And since she was not able to take me with her, I was sent to that little farm-house down there—Green's Farm, as it was called—to spend the months of her absence with my Uncle James and his house-keeper, who was called Miss Jemima."

"Miss Jemima!" cried the little girl, stooping over suddenly with a burst of laughter. "It *is* a queer name, you know, Grannie."

"It is," said the old lady. "And it belonged to one to whom it was my duty to show affection, but who never cared much for the little girl she had in her charge. And when people don't care for you, it is sometimes a little difficult, Susan, to care for them. At least *I* found it so. I don't mean that Miss Jemima was unkind to me, only that when she was kind, she seemed to be kind on purpose. And when I had a slice of plum cake, her face always seemed to tell me it was *plum* cake, and that I deserved only plain. My Uncle James knew that his housekeeper did not think me a pleasant little girl. I was a shrimp in size, with straight black hair which she made me tie tightly back with a piece of velvet ribbon. I had small dark eyes and very skimpy legs. And though he himself was kind, and fond of me, he showed his affection only when we were alone together, and not when she was present. He was ill, too, then, though I did not know *how* ill. And he lay all day in a long chair with a check rug over his legs, and Miss Jemima had charge not only of me, but of the farm.

"*All* the milking, and the ploughing, and the chickens, and the pigs, Grannie?" asked Susan.

The old lady shut her eyes an instant, pressed her lips together and said, "All."

"The consequence was," she went on, "I was rather

a solitary child. Whenever I could, I used to hide myself away in some corner of the house—and a beautiful house it is. It's a pity, my dear, I am so old and you so young and this hill so steep. Otherwise we could go down and—well, never mind. That row of small lattice windows which you can see belong to a narrow corridor; and the rooms out of it, rambling one into the other, were walled in just as the builders fancied, when they made the house three hundred years or more ago. And that was in the reign of Edward VI."

"Like the Bluecoat boys," said Susan, "though I can't say I like the yellow stockings, Grannie, not that *mustard* yellow, you know."

"Like the Bluecoat boys," repeated her grandmother. "Well, as I say, the house was a nest of hiding-places; and as a child I was small—smaller even than you, Susan. I would sit with my book; or kneel up on a chair and watch from a window, lean *out* too sometimes—as if by so doing I might be able to see my mother in India. And whenever the weather was fine, and sometimes when it was not, I would creep out of the house and run away down that shaggy lane to the little wood down there. There is a brook in it (though you can't see that) which brawls continuously all day long and all the night too. And sometimes I would climb up this very hill. And sometimes I would creep across the field to that little church.

"It was there I most easily forgot myself and even my little scrapes and troubles—with the leaves and the birds, and the blue sky and the clouds overhead; or watching a snail, or picking kingcups and cowslips, or staring into the stream at the fish. You see I was rather a doleful little creature: first because I was usually alone; next because my Uncle James was ill and so could not be happy; and last because I was made to feel more homesick than ever by the cold glances and cold tongue of Miss Jemima."

"Miss Jemima!" echoed Susan, burying her face in her amusement an instant in her hands.

"Miss Jemima," repeated the old voice solemnly. "But I was not only dismal and doleful. Far worse: I made little attempt to be anything else, and began to be fretful too. There was no company of my own age, for, as you see, the village is a mile or two off—over there where the sun is lighting the trees up. And I was not allowed to play with the village children. The only company I had was a fat little boy of two, belonging to one of the farm-hands. And he was so backward a baby that even at that age he could scarcely say as many words."

"I began to talk at one," said Susan.

"Yes, my dear," said her grannie, "and you are likely, it seems, to go on talking the clock round."

"Grannie, dear," said Susan, "I simply *love* this story —until—*you* know."

"Well, of all the places strictly forbidden me to play in," continued the old lady, "that peaceful little churchyard came first. My 'aunt,' as I say, thought me a fantastic silly-notioned little girl, and she didn't approve of my picking flowers that grow among tombstones. Indeed, I am not now quite sure myself if such flowers belong to the living at all. Still, once or twice in the summer the old sexton—Mr. Fletcher he was called, and a very grumpy old man he was—used to come with his scythe and mow the lush grasses down. And you could scarcely breathe for the sweet smell of them. It seemed a waste to see them lying in swathes, butterflies hovering above them, fading in the sun. There never were such buttercups and dandelion-clocks and meadow-sweet as grew beneath those old grey walls. I was happy there; and coming and going, I would say a prayer for my mother. But you will please understand, Susan, that I was being disobedient; that I had no business to be there at all at any time. And perhaps if I had never gone, I should never have known that there was somebody else in the churchyard."

"Ah! somebody else," sighed Susan, sitting straight up, her eyes far away.

"It was one evening, rather like this one, but with a mackerel sky. The day before I had been stood in the corner for wearing an orange ribbon in my hair; and then sent to bed for talking to the grandfather's clock. I did it on purpose. And now—*this* evening, I was being scolded because I would not eat blackberry jam with my bread for tea. I was told it was because I had been spoilt, and was a little town child who did not know that God had made the wild fruits for human use, and who thought that the only things fit to eat grew in gardens.

"Really and truly I disliked the blackberry jam because of the pips, and I had a hollow tooth. But I told my 'aunt' that my mother didn't like blackberry jam either, which made her still more angry.

" 'Do you really think, James,' she said to my uncle, 'we should allow the child to grow up a dainty little minx like that? Now, see here, Miss, you will just stay there until you have eaten up the whole of that slice on your plate.'

" 'Well, then, Miss Jemima,' I said pertly, 'I shall stay here till I am eighty.'

" 'Hold your tongue,' she cried out at me, her eyes blazing.

" 'I can't bear the horrid——' I began again, and at that she gave me such a slap on my cheek that I overbalanced, and fell out of my chair. She lifted me up from the floor with a shake, set me in my chair again, and pushed it against the table till the edge was cutting into my legs. 'And now,' she said, 'sit there till you are eighty!'

"A look I had never seen before came into my uncle's face; his hands were trembling. Without another word to me, Miss Jemima helped him rise from his chair, and I was left alone.

"Never before had I been beaten like that. And I was at least as much frightened as I was hurt. I listened to the tall clock ticking, 'Wick-ed child, stubborn child,' and my tears splashed slowly down on the odious slice of bread-and-jam on my plate. Then all of a sudden I clenched and shook my ridiculous little fist at the door by which she had gone out, wriggled back my chair, jumped out of it, rushed out of the house, and never stopped to breathe or to look back, until I found myself sitting huddled up under the biggest tomb in the churchyard; crying there, if not my heart out, at least a good deal of my sour little temper."

"Poor Grannie!" said Susan, squeezing her hand.

"There was not much 'poor' about that," was the reply. "A pretty sight I must have looked, with my smeared face, green-stained frock and hair dangling. At last my silly sobbing ceased. The sky was flaming with the sunset. It was in June, and the air was cool and mild and sweet. But instead of being penitent and realizing what a bad and foolish child I was, I began to be coldly rebellious. I stared at the rosy clouds and vowed to myself I'd give Miss Jemima a fright. I'd rather die than go back to the house that night. And when the thought of my mother came into my mind, I shut it out, saying to myself that she could not have cared how much I loved her, to leave me like this. And yet only a fortnight before a long letter had come to me from India!

"Well, there I sat. A snail came out of his day's hiding-place; little moths were flitting among the grasses; the afternoon's butterflies had all gone to rest. Far away I heard a hooting—and then a step. Cautiously peering up above my tombstone, I saw Maggie, one of the girls that helped on the farm. Her face was burning hot, and she was staring about her round the corner of the little church tower with her saucer-blue eyes. She called to me, but couldn't see me, and at that my mouth opened and I let out, as they say, a shrill yelping squeal. It alarmed even me a little to hear it. She screeched; her steel-tipped boot slipped on the flagstones; in an instant she was gone. And once more I was alone."

"Ah, but you weren't *really* alone, Granny," whispered Susan, "*were* you?"

"That is just what I was going to tell you, my dear. Immediately in front of my face stood a few late dandelion stalks, with their beautiful clocks, grey in the still evening light. And there were a few other gently nodding flowers. As I stared across them, on the other side of the flat gravestone a face appeared. I mean it didn't rise up. It simply came into the air. A very small face, more oval than round, its gold-coloured hair over its wild greenish eyes falling on either side its head in a curious zigzag way—like this, I mean." The old lady took the hem of her skirt, and three or four times folded it together, then loosened it out.

"You mean, Grannie, as if it had been pleated," said Susan.

"Yes," said her grannie. "And strange and lovely it looked in the reddish light. The face was not smiling, and she did not appear to see me. And yet I knew *she* knew that I was there. And though I did not think she minded my being there, I felt more frightened than I had ever been in my life. My mouth opened; I was clutching tight the grass on

either side. And I saw nothing else as I stared into that face."

"That was the Fairy, Grannie," said Susan, stooping forward again as if to make her words more impressive. The old lady glanced fixedly at the two blue eyes bent on her from under the brim of the round straw hat.

"At that moment, my dear, I did not know *what* it was. I was far too frightened to think. Time must have been passing, too, very quickly, for as I stared on, it was already beginning to be gloaming between us, and silent. Yes, much more silent even than this. Then, suddenly, behind me a low, sweet, yet sorrowful voice began to sing from out of the may-bushes, the notes falling like dewdrops in the air. I knew it was a nightingale. And at the very moment that the thought came to me—'That is a nightingale'—the face on the other side of the rough grey stone vanished.

"For a few minutes I sat without moving—not daring to move. And then I ran, straight out of the churchyard by the way I had come as fast as my legs could carry me. I hardly know what I thought, but as soon as I saw the lights in the upper windows of the farm, I ran even faster. Up under the ilexes and round through the farmyard to the back door. It was unlatched. I slipped through, quiet as a mouse, into the kitchen, climbed into the chair, and at once devoured every scrap of that horrid bread-and-jam!

"And still, my dear, I don't believe I was really thinking, only dreadfully afraid, and yet with a kind of triumph in my heart that Miss Jemima should never know anything at all about the face in the churchyard. It was all but dark in the kitchen now, but I still sat on in my chair, even at last lifted the plate, and insolently licked up with my tongue every jammy crumb that was left.

"And then the door opened, and Miss Jemima stood there in the entry with a lighted brass candlestick in her hand. She looked at me, and I at her. "Ah, I see you have thought better of it," she said. "And high time too. You are to go straight to bed."

"If you can imagine, Susan, a cake made almost entirely of plums, and every plum a black thought of hatred, I was like that. But I said never a word. I got down from my chair, marched past her down the flagstone passage, and she followed after. When I came to my uncle's door, I lifted my hand towards the handle. 'Straight on, Miss,' said the voice behind me. 'You have made him too ill and too unhappy to wish you good-night.' Straight on I went, got into bed with all my clothes on, even my dew-wet shoes, and stared at the ceiling till I fell asleep."

"You know, Grannie," said Susan, "it was very curious of you not even to undress at all. Why do you think you did that?"

"My dear," said her grannie, "at that moment I had such a hard, hot heart in me, that there was not any room for a why. But you see that little jutting attic window above the trees—it was in the room beyond that and on the other side of the house that I lay. And it's now seventy-five years ago. It may be there was even then a far-away notion in my mind of getting up in the middle of the night and running away. But whether or not, I was awakened by the sun streaming through my lattice window, for my bedroom lay full in the light of the morning.

"I could think of but one thing—my disgrace of the night before, and what I had seen in the churchyard. It was a dream, I thought to myself, shutting my eyes, yet knowing all the time that I did not believe what I was saying. Even when I was told at breakfast that my uncle was no better, I thought little of him, and gobbled down my porridge, with the one wish to be out of the house before I could be forbidden to go. But the only sign of Miss Jemima was my dirty jam-stained plate of the night before, upon which she had put my hunch of breakfast bread. Yet although I was so anxious to get out, for some reason I chose very carefully what I should wear, and changed the piece of ribbon in my hat from blue to green. A rare minx I was."

"You were, Grannie," said Susan, clasping her knees. "And then you went out to the churchyard again?"

"Yes. But all seemed as usual there; except only that a tiny bunch of coral-coloured berries lay on a flat leaf, on the very tombstone where I had hid. Now though I was a minx, my dear, I was also fairly sharp for my age, and after the first gulp of surprise, as I stood there among the nodding buttercups, the sun already having stolen over the grey roof and shining upon the hot tombstones, I noticed a beady dewdrop resting on the leaf, and the leaf of as fresh a green as lettuce in a salad. Looking at this dewdrop I realised at once that the leaf could not have been there very long. Indeed, in a few minutes the sun had drunk up that one round drop of water, for it was some little time before I ventured to touch the berries.

"Then I knew in my heart I was not alone there, and that the green dish had been put there on purpose, just before I had come. The berries were strange yet beautiful to look at, too; of a coral colour edging into rose: I could not guess from what tree they had come. And I don't think it was because I had long ago been warned not to taste any wild fruit—except blackberries!—but because I was uneasy in conscience already, that I did not nibble one then and there.

"It was very quiet in that green place, and on and on I watched, as still as a cat over a mouse's hole, though I myself really and truly was the mouse. And then, all of a sudden, flinging back my green dangling hat-ribbon, I remember, over my shoulder, I said half aloud, in an affected little voice, 'Well, it's very kind of you, I am sure,' stretched my hand across, plucked one of the berries, and put it into my mouth.

"Hardly had its juice tartened my tongue when a strange thing happened. It was as if a grasshopper was actually sitting in my hair, the noise of that laughter was so close. Besides this, a kind of heat began to creep into my cheek, and it seemed all the colours around me grew so bright that they dazzled my eyes. I closed them. I must have sat there for a while quite unconscious of time, for when I opened them again, the shadow had gone perceptibly back from the stone, and it was getting towards the middle of the morning.

"But there was still that dazzle in my eyes, and everything I looked at—the flowers and the birds, even the moss and lichen on the old stones—seemed as if they were showing me secrets about themselves that I had not known before. It seemed that I could share the very being of the butterfly that was hovering near; and could almost hear not only what the birds were singing but what they were saying."

"Just like the fairy-tales, Grannie."

"Yes," said the little old woman, "but the difference is that I was not happy about it. The flush was still in my cheek, and I could hear my heart beating under my frock, and I was all of an excitement. But I knew in my inmost self that I ought not to feel like that at all; that I had crept into danger through my wicked temper; that these little unknown coral fruits on the tombstone had been put there for a trap. It was a bait, Susan; and I was the silly fish."

"Oh, Grannie, a 'silly fish!' " said Susan. "I can see

you *might* feel wicked," she added, with a sage little nod, "but I don't *exactly* see why."

"That is just when it's most dangerous, my child," said her grandmother, sharply closing her mouth, very much indeed like a fish. "But I must get on with my story, or we shall never get home.

"I sat on, keeping my eyes as far as I could fixed on the invisible place in the air where I had seen the face appear, but nothing came, and gradually the scene lost its radiance, and the birds were chirping as usual again, and the buttercups were the same as ever. No, not the same as ever, because, although it was a burning, sunny day, it seemed now that everything was darker and gloomier than usual on so bright a morning, and I skulked away home, feeling not only a little cold, but dejected and ashamed.

"As I went in through the gate between those two stone pillars you can just see by the round green tree down there, I looked up at the windows. And a dreadful pang seized me to see that their curtains were all drawn over the glass. And though I didn't know then what that meant, I knew it meant something sorrowful and tragic. Besides, they seemed like shut eyes, refusing to look at me. And when I went in, Miss Jemima told me that my uncle was dead. She told me, too, that he had asked to see me an hour or two before he died. 'He said, "Where is my little Susan?" ' 'And where you have been,' added Miss Jemima, 'is known only to your wicked, wilful self.' I stared at her, and seemed to shrink until she appeared to be twice as large as usual. I could not speak, because my tongue would not move. And then I rushed past her and up the stairs into a corner between two cupboards, where I used sometimes to hide, and I don't know what I did or thought there; I simply sat on and on, with my hands clenched in my lap, everything I looked at all blurred, and my lips trying to say a prayer that would not come.

"From that day on I became a more and more wretched and miserable little girl, and, as I think now, a wickeder one. It all came of three things. First, because I hated Miss Jemima, and that is just like leaving a steel knife in vinegar, it so frets and wastes the heart. Next, because of the thought of my poor uncle speaking of me so gently and kindly when he was at death's door; and my remorse that I could never now ask him to forgive me. And last, because I longed to see again that magical face in the churchyard, and yet knew that it was forbidden."

"But, Grannie dear, you know," said Susan, "I never can see why you should have thought that then."

"No," replied the old lady. "But the point was, you see, that I *did* think it, and I knew in my heart that it would lead to no good. Miss Jemima made me go next day into the room where my uncle lay in his coffin. But try as she might to persuade and compel me, she could not make me open my eyes and look at him. For that disobedience she sent me to my bedroom for the rest of the day.

"When all was still, I crept out across the corridor into another room, and looked out over the trees towards the little church. And I said to myself, as if I were speaking to someone who would hear, 'I am coming to you soon, and nobody, *nobody* here shall ever see me again.'

"Think of it; a little girl not yet nine, angry with the whole world, and hardly giving a thought to the mother who was longing to see her, and—though I didn't know it then—was very soon to be in England again.

"Well, then came the funeral. I was dressed—I can see myself now, as I stood looking into the looking-glass—

in a black frock trimmed with crape, with a tucker of white frilling round the neck, and an edging of it at the sleeves; my peaked white face and coal-black eyes.

"It was, as you see, but a very little distance to my poor uncle's last resting-place, and in those days they used a long hand-cart on wheels, which the men pushed in front of us, with its flowers. And Miss Jemima and I followed after it across the field. I listened to the prayers as closely as I could. But at last my attention began to wander, and, kneeling there beside Miss Jemima in the church, my hands pressed close to my eyes, for an instant I glanced out and up between my fingers.

"The great eastern window, though you cannot see it from here, is of centuries-old stained glass, crimson, blue, green. But in one corner, just above the narrow ledge of masonry outside, it had been broken many, many years ago by the falling of a branch of a tree, and had been mended with clear *white* glass. And there, looking steadily in and straight across and down at me, was the face and form of the being I had seen beside the tombstone.

"I cannot tell you, Susan, how beautiful that face looked then. Those rich colours of the saints and martyrs surrounding that gold hair—living gold—and the face as pale and beautiful—far more beautiful than anything else I had ever seen in my life before. But even then I saw, too, that into the morning church a cold and shadowy darkness had come, and the stone faces on either side the window, with their set stare, looked actually to be alive. I peeped out between my fingers, hearing not a single word of what the old clergyman was saying, wondering when anyone else would see what I saw, and knowing that the coldly smiling lips were breathing across at me, 'Come away, come away!'

"My bones were all cramped, and at last I managed to twist my head a little and glance up at Miss Jemima. The broad face beneath her veil had its eyes shut, and the lips were muttering. She had noticed nothing amiss. And when I looked again, the face at the window had vanished.

"It was a burning hot day—so hot that the flowers beside the grave were already withering before Miss Jemima took me home. We reached the stone porch together, and in its cold shadow she paused, staring down on me through her veil. 'You will be staying on here for a while, because I don't know what else to do with you,' she said to me. 'But you will understand that this is my house now. I am telling your mother how bad a child you are making yourself, and perhaps she will ask me to send you away to a school where they will know how to deal with stubborn and ungrateful beings like yourself. But she will be sorry, I think, to hear that it was your wickedness that brought that poor kind body to its grave over there. And now, miss, as the best part of the day is over, you shall have your bread-and-butter and milk in your bedroom, and think over what I have said.' "

"I think, Grannie," cried Susan, suddenly bending herself over her knees, "that that Miss Jemima was the most dreadful person I have ever heard of."

"Well, my dear," said her grandmother, "I have lived a good many years, and believe it is wiser to try and explain to oneself people as well as things. Do you suppose she would have been as harsh to me if I hadn't hated her? And now she lies there too, and I never had her forgiveness either."

Susan turned her head away and looked out over the countryside to the north, to where the roving horses had vanished, and where evening was already beginning gradually to settle itself towards night.

"And *did* you think over what Miss Jemima had said, Grannie?" she asked in a low voice.

"The first thing I did was to throw the bread-and-butter out of the window, and while I watched the birds wrangling over it and gobbling it up, I thought of nothing at all. It was cooler in the shade on that side of the house. My head ached after the hot sorrowful walk to the church and back. I came away from the window, took off my black frock, and sat there on the edge of my bed, I remember, in my petticoat, not knowing what to do next. And then, Susan, I made up my mind that I could not bear to be in Miss Jemima's house for a day longer than I needed.

"I was just clever enough to realise that if I wanted to run away I must take care not to be brought back. I grew hot all over, remembering what she had said to me, never thinking how weak and silly I was not to be able to endure patiently what could only be a few more days or weeks before another letter came from my mother. Then I tore a leaf from a book that was in my room—a Prayer Book—and scrawled a few words to my mother, saying how miserable *and* wicked I had been and how I longed to see her again. It's a curious thing, Susan, but I was pitying myself while I wrote those words and thinking how grieved my mother would be when she read them and how well Miss Jemima would deserve whatever my mother said to her. But I didn't utter a word in the letter about where I was going."

"You didn't really *know* where you were going, Grannie," whispered Susan, edging a little nearer. "Did you? Not *then*, I mean?"

"No, but I had a faint notion whom I was going *to;* for somehow, from old fairy tales I had got to believe that human children could be taken away to quite a different world from this—a country of enchantment. And I remembered having read, too, about two children that had come back from there, and had forgotten their own English."

"I know two poems about it," said Susan. "One about 'True Thomas'—'Thomas the Rhymer,' you know, Grannie, who stayed with the Queen of Elfland for seven whole years, and another about . . . I do wonder—— But please, *please,* go on."

"Well, I hid my little letter in a cranny in the wainscot, after sewing a piece of cotton to it so that I might pull it out again when I wanted it. The next morning, I got up early, and slipping on my clothes, tiptoed out of the house before breakfast, and made my way to the church. I thought deceitfully that Miss Jemima would be sure to find out that I had gone, and that if for a morning or two she discovered me quietly sitting in the churchyard she would not suppose at another time, perhaps, that I was not safely there again. Plots, Susan, are tangled things, and are likely to entangle the maker of them too.

"The old man who took care of the church, Mr. Fletcher, to save himself the trouble of carrying the key of the door, used to hide it under a large stone beneath the belfry tower. I had watched him put it there. It was a fresh sparkling day, I remember, with one or two thin silver clouds high in the sky—angels, I used to call them—and I forgot for the moment in the brightness of it all my troubles, as I frisked along past the dewy hedges.

"My first thought was to make quite, quite sure about the strange being in the churchyard; my next, to plan a way of escape. I gathered a bunch of daisies, and having come to the belfry door, I somehow managed to open it with the key which I fetched out from beneath its stone, and crept into the still, empty coolness. I had come to the conclusion, too, Susan, young though I was, that if the elf or fairy or whatever she might be actually came into the church to me, it would be a proof there was no harm in her company, though I knew in my heart that I was in some mysterious danger.

"There are a few old oak pews in the little church, with heads carved upon them, and one or two have side seats that draw out from beneath into the aisle. On one of these I sat down, so that while I could be intent on my daisy-chain—just to show I had something to do there—I could see out of the corner of my eye the open door by which I had come in. And I hadn't very long to wait.

"In the midst of the faint singing of the wild birds, out of the light that lay beyond the stone church wall I spied her come stealing. My heart almost stopped beating, nor did I turn my head one inch, so that my eyes soon ached because they were almost asquint with watching. If you can imagine a figure—even now I cannot tell you how tall she was—that seems to be made of the light of rainbows, and yet with every feature in its flaxen-framed face as clearly marked as a cherub's cut in stone; and if you can imagine a voice coming to you, close into your ear, without your being able to say exactly where it is coming *from*— *that* was what I saw and heard beneath that grey roof down there on that distant morning, seventy-five years ago. The longer I watched her out of the corner of my eye, the more certain I became that she was using every device she knew to attract my attention, even that she was impatient at my stupidity, and yet that she could not or that she dared not cross the threshold. And so I sat and watched her, fumbling on the while with my limpening daisy-stalks. Many strange minutes must have passed like this.

"At last, however, having fancied I heard a footfall, I was surprised out of myself, and suddenly twisted my head. She too had heard, and was standing stiller than a shadow on snow, gazing in at me. I suppose thoughts reveal themselves in the face more swiftly than one imagines. I was partly afraid, partly longing to approach closer. I wished her to realise that I longed for her company, but that danger was near, for I was well aware whose step it was I had heard. And, as I looked at her, there came a sharpness into her face, a cold inhuman look—not of fear, but almost of hatred—and she was gone. More intent than ever, I stooped over my daisies. And in the hush there was a faint sound as of an intensely distant whistle.

"Then a shadow fell across the porch, and there was Miss Jemima. It's a strange thing, Susan, but Miss Jemima also did not enter the church. She called to me from where she stood, in almost a honeyed voice: 'Breakfast is ready, Susan.' "

"I can imagine *exactly* how she said that, Grannie," said the little girl, "because my name's Susan, too."

"Yes, my dear," said the old lady, squeezing her hand. "It was passed on to you from me by your dear mother just because it was mine. And I hope you will always be the Susan I have *now*." . . . From near at hand upon the hill a skylark suddenly took its flight into the evening blue. The old lady listened a moment before going on with her story.

"Well," she began again, "I gathered up my apron and walked towards Miss Jemima down the aisle. Suddenly there came a slight rumbling noise, which I could not understand. Then instantly there followed a crash. And at

Miss Jemima's very feet, in the sunlight, I saw lying a piece of stone about the size of a small plum pudding. Miss Jemima gave a faint scream. Her cheek, already pale, went white; and she stared from me to the stone and back again, as I approached her.

" 'You were talking in there to someone—in God's church,' she whispered harshly, stooping towards me. 'To whom?' "

"I shook my head, and stood trembling and gazing at the stone.

" 'Look into my face, you wicked child,' she whispered. 'Who were you talking to in there?'

"I looked up at last. 'It's empty,' I said.

" 'There's a lying look in your eyes!' cried Miss Jemima. 'And *you* are the child that goes into a sacred place to weave daisy-chains! Turn your face away from me. Do you hear me, miss? Miserable little *sorceress* that you are!'

"The word seemed to flame up in my mind as if it had been written in fire on smoke; and still I stared at the stone. I felt but did not see Miss Jemima steadily turn her head and look around her.

" 'A few inches,' she added in a low voice, 'and you would have killed me.'

" 'Me!' I cried angrily. 'What has it to do with *me,* Miss Jemima?'

" 'Ah!' said she. 'We shall know a little more about that when you have told me what company you find here where your poor uncle might hope to be at rest.'

"It's a dreadful thing to confess, Susan, but up to that moment, though I had again and again cried by myself at memory of him, though tears were always in my heart for him, I hadn't thought of my uncle that morning.

" 'And perhaps,' added Miss Jemima, 'bread and water

and solitude for a day or two will help to loosen your tongue.'

"I followed her without another word across the fields, and in a few minutes was alone once more in my bedroom with a stale crust and a glass of water to keep me company.

"I should think that if my angry tears had run into the water that morning they would have actually made it taste salt. But I cried so that not even a mouse could have heard me. Every other thought was now out of my mind—for I dared not even talk to myself about the stone—but that of getting away from the house for ever. One thing I could not forget, however. And that was the word 'sorceress.' It terrified me far more than I can tell you. I knew in my young mind that Miss Jemima was treating me wickedly, however wicked *I* had been, and I knew too, in fear and horror, that the stone might not have fallen by accident. I had seen the look on the Fairy's face and . . ." The old lady suddenly broke off her story at this point, and looked about her in alarm. "My dear, we must go at once; the dew is beginning to fall, and the air is already colder."

"Oh, Grannie," said the child, "how I wish we might stay—a little, *little* longer!"

"Well, my dear, so do I. For I am old, and I shall never see this place again. It brings many memories back. Who knows what might have happened if——"

"But, Grannie," interrupted the child hastily, picking up the umbrella from the grass. "Please tell me the rest of the story straight, straight, straight on as we go back." It seemed to Susan, so rapt was her grandmother's face at that moment, and so absent her eyes—that she could not have heard her. Those small aged eyes were once more looking carefully down on the scene below. For an instant they shut as if the old lady had thought so to remember it more completely. And then the two of them began slowly to climb the hill, and the story proceeded.

"No one disturbed me during that long morning," continued the quiet voice, "but in the afternoon the door was unlocked, and Miss Jemima opened it to show in a clergyman, Mr. Wilmot, who conducted the service in the church every other Sunday. I won't tell you all he said to me. He was a kind and gentle old man, but he didn't so much as think it possible there was any being or thing in the churchyard but its birds, its tombstones, and now and then a straying animal. He only smiled about all that, nor did he ask me Miss Jemima's question.

He took my hand in his great bony one and begged me to be a good little girl. And I see his smiling face as he asked it. 'Not only for your mother's sake,' he said, 'but *for "goodness sake."* '

" 'I am sure, my dear,' he went on, 'Miss Jemima *means* to be kind, and all that *we* have to do is to mean to be good.'

"I gulped down the lump in my throat and said, 'But don't you think *sorceress* is a very wicked word?'

"He stood up, holding both my hands in his. 'But my poor little lamb,' he cried. 'Miss Jemima is no more a sorceress than I am a Double Dutchman!' And with that he stooped, kissed the top of my head, and went out of the room.

In a minute or two his footsteps returned. He opened the door an inch and peeped in. 'Why, we are better already!' He smiled at me over his spectacles. Then he came in, carrying a plate with a slice of bread-and-jam upon it, and a mug of milk. 'There,' he said, 'there's no sorcery in that, is there? And now you will be an obedient and gentle child, and think how happy your mother will be to see you?' "

"I think," said Susan stoutly, "that that Mr. Wilmot is one of the kindest men I ever knew."

Her grandmother looked down on her with a peculiar smile on her face. "He was so kind, Susan, that I never mentioned to him that the blackberry-jam on the bread was not a great favourite of mine! A moment after the sound of his footsteps had died away I heard the key once more in the lock. And what did I say to myself when he was gone? I looked forlornly at the plate, then out of the window, and I believe, Susan, that I did what they sometimes describe in the story-books—I wrung my hands a little, repeating to myself, *'He doesn't understand. No! No! He doesn't understand.'*

In an hour or two, Miss Jemima herself opened the door and looked in. She surveyed me where I sat, and then her glance fell on the untouched slice of bread-and-jam.

" 'Ah,' said she, 'a good man like Mr. Wilmot cannot realise the hardness of a stubborn heart. I don't want to be unkind to you, Susan, but I have a duty to perform to your mother and to your poor dead uncle. You shall not leave this room until you apologise to me for your insolence of this morning, and until you tell me whom you were speaking to in the church.'

"The lie that came into my mind—'But I was not speaking to anyone, Miss Jemima'—faded away on my tongue. And I simply looked at her in silence.

" 'You have a brazen face, Susan,' said she, 'and if you grow up as you are now, you will be a very wicked woman.' "

"I think," said Susan, "that was a perfectly *dreadful* thing to say, Grannie."

"Times change, my dear," said the old lady. "And now—well, it is fortunate there is very little more to tell. For this hill has taken nearly all the breath out of my body!"

The two of them stood now on the crest of the hill. The light was beginning to die away in the sky, and the mists to grow milkier in the hollows of the flat country that lay around and beneath them. Far, far away, facing them across the world, a reddish-coloured moon was rising. From far beneath them a dog barked—it might be from dead Miss Jemima's farmyard. The little church surrounded by its low wall seemed to have gathered in closer to its scattered stones.

"Yes, Grannie, dear?" breathed Susan, slipping her hand into the cotton-gloved one that hung near. "What then?"

"Then," replied her grandmother, "the door was locked again. Anger and hatred filled that silly little body sitting in the bedroom, and towards evening I fell asleep. And I must have dreamed a terrifying dream, though when I awoke I could not remember my dream—only its horror. I was terrified at it in that solitude, and I knew by the darkening at the window that it must be at least nine or ten o'clock. Night was coming, then. I could scarcely breathe at the thought. Another mug of milk had been put beside the plate; but I could not even persuade myself to drink any of it.

"Then in a while I heard Miss Jemima's footsteps pass my room. She made no pause there, and presently after I knew that she had gone to bed, having not even troubled to look in on her wretched little prisoner. The hardness of that decided me.

"I waited until it seemed certain she was asleep. Then

I tiptoed over to the door, and with both hands softly twisted the handle. It was still locked. Then I went to the window and discovered, as if the fairy creature herself had magicked it there, that a large hay-wain half full of hay, its shafts high in the air, had been left drawn up within a few feet of my window. It looked dangerous, but it was not actually a very difficult jump even for a child of my age; and I believe I should have attempted it if there had been no cart at all. My one wild thought was to run away. *Any-where*—so long as there was no chance of Miss Jemima's ever finding me again. Could you ever have dreamed of such a little silly, Susan?

"But even in that excited foolish moment I had sense enough left—before I jumped out of the window—to take a warm woollen jacket out of my chest-of-drawers, and to wrap my money-box up in a scarf so that it should not jangle too much. I pulled my letter up from its cranny in the wainscot by its thread, and put it on the pink dressing-table. And at that moment, in the half dark I saw my face in the looking-glass. I should hardly have recognised it. It looked nearly as old, Susan, as I do now."

"Yes, dear Grannie," said Susan.

"Then I jumped—without the slightest harm to my-self. I scrambled down into the yard and, keeping close to the house, crept past the kennel, the old sheep-dog merely shaking his chain with his thumping tail a little as I passed. And then, as soon as I was beyond the tall stone gate-posts, I ran off through the farm-yard, past the barns, and along the cart-track as fast as I could."

"But *not*," cried Susan almost with a shout in the still air, "*not* to the churchyard, Grannie. I think that was the most wonderful thing of all."

"Not so very wonderful, my dear, if you remember

that I was now intensely afraid of the fairy, after seeing
that look of evil and hatred in her face when Miss Jemima
was approaching the church. Something in me, as you know,
had never ceased to counsel me, *Don't be deceived by her.*
She means you no good. I cannot explain that; but so it
was. Yet all the time I had been longing to follow wherever she might lead. Why she should wish to carry off a
human child I don't know, but that she really wanted me I
soon discovered for certain.

"If you follow the tip of my umbrella, you will now
just be able to see, Susan, that great meadow sloping upwards beyond the farm. But I don't think even your sharp
eyes will detect the circle of old grey stones there. They are
called the Dancers, and though I was dreadfully frightened
of passing them in the darkness, this was the only way to
take. Gradually I approached them, my heart beating beneath my ribs like a drum, until I had come near.

"And there, lovelier than ever, shining in that dark as
if with a light of her own, and sitting beneath the largest of
the Dancers directly in my path, was She. But this time I
knew she was not alone. I cannot describe what passed in
my heart. I longed to go on, and yet was in anguish at the
thought of it. I didn't dare to look at her, and all I could
think to do was to pretend not to have seen her at all. How I
found the courage I cannot think. Perhaps it was the courage that comes when fear and terror are almost beyond
bearing.

"I put my money-box on to the grass; the scarf was already wet with dew. Then, very slowly, I put my black
jacket on and buttoned it up. And then, with my eyes
turned away, I walked slowly on down the path, between
the Dancers, towards the one that is called the Fiddler, in
their midst. The night air here was cold and still. But as I

approached the stone, it seemed as if the air was full of voices and patterings and sounds of wings and instruments. It terrified and bewildered me; I could think of nothing.

"I just kept saying, 'Oh, please, God; oh, please, God!' and walked on. And when at last I came to the stone, the whole world suddenly seemed to turn dark and cold and dead. And then! Apart from the ancient stone, jutting up out of the green turf as it had done for centuries, there was not a sign, not a vestige, Susan, of anything or anybody there!"

"I think I can *just* see the stone, Grannie, but I don't think I could dare to be alone there in the dark, not for anything in the world. . . . I expect it was what you *said* made the Fairy go. And then, Grannie?"

"Then, Susan, my heart seemed to go out of me. I ran on, stumbling blindly for a little way, then lost my balance completely over a tussock of grass or a mole-heap and fell flat on my face. Nettles, too! Without any words that I can remember, I lay praying in the grass.

"But even that did not turn me back. I got up at last and ran on more slowly, and without looking behind me, across the field. Its gate leads into a by-road. It was padlocked, and as I mounted to the top my eyes could see just above a slight rise in the ground, for the lane lies beneath a little hill there.

"And coming along the road towards me there were shining the lamps of a carriage. I clambered down and crouched in the hedge-side, and in a few moments the lamps reappeared at the top of the incline, and the horse came plod-plodding along down the hill. It was a wonderful summer night, the sky all faint with stars. What would have happened if it had been cold or pouring with rain, I

cannot think. But because it was so warm, the air almost like milk, the hood of the carriage was down.

"And as it came wheeling round by the hedge-side, I saw in the filmy starlight who it was who was sitting there. Neither horse nor coachman had seen me. I jumped to my feet and ran after the carriage as fast as my legs could carry me, screaming at the top of my voice, 'Mother, Mother!'

"Perhaps the grinding of the wheels in the flinty dust and the thump of the hoofs drowned my calling. But I still held tight to my money-box, and though it was muffled by the scarf in which it was wrapped, at each step it made a dull noise like a birdscare, and this must at last have attracted my mother's attention. She turned her head, opened her mouth wide at sight of me—I see her now—then instantly jumped up and tugged at the coachman's buttoned coat tails. The carriage came to a standstill. . . .

"And that," said the old lady, turning away her head for one last glance of the countryside around her, "that is all, Susan."

Susan gave a last great sigh. "I can't think what you must have felt, Grannie," she said, "when you were safe in the carriage. And I can't——" But at this point she began to laugh very softly to herself, and suddenly stood still. "And I can't think either," she went on, "what Miss Jemima must have thought when you and *Great*-Grannie knocked at the door. You did tell me once that she opened her bedroom window at the sound of the knocking, and looked out in her nightdress. I expect she was almost as frightened as you had been, amongst those Dancers."

The two of them were now descending the hill on the side away from the farm and the church. And they could see not only their carriage standing beneath them, but the evening star had also come into view. There could not be a more peaceful scene—the silver birches around them standing motionless under the deep, pale sky, clothed with their little leaves, and the rabbits at play among the gorse and juniper.

"Bless me, Mum," said the old cabman as he opened the carriage door, "I was just beginning to think them *fairises* must have runned away with you and the young lady."

Susan burst completely out laughing. "Now don't you think, Grannie," she said, "that is a very, very, very curious quincidence?"

The Riddle

So these seven children, Ann and Matilda, James, William, and Henry, Harriet and Dorothea, came to live with their grandmother. The house in which their grandmother had lived since her childhood was built in the time of the Georges. It was not a pretty house, but roomy, substantial, and square; and a great cedar tree outstretched its branches almost to the windows.

When the children were come out of the cab (five sitting inside and two beside the driver), they were shown into their grandmother's presence. They stood in a little black group before the old lady, seated in her bow-window. And she asked them each their names, and repeated each name in her kind, quavering voice. Then to one she gave a work-box, to William a jackknife, to Dorothea a painted ball; to each a present according to age. And she kissed all her grandchildren to the youngest.

"My dears," she said, 'I wish to see all of you bright and gay in my house. I am an old woman, so that I cannot romp with you; but Ann must look to you, and Mrs. Fenn too. And every morning and every evening you must all come in to see your granny; and bring me smiling faces, that call back to my mind my own son Harry. But all the rest of the day, when school is done, you shall do just as you please, my dears. And there is only one thing, just one, I would have you remember. In the large spare bedroom that looks out on the slate roof there stands in the corner an old oak chest; aye, older than I, my dears, a great deal older; older than my grandmother. Play anywhere else in the house, but not there." She spoke kindly to them all, smiling at them; but she was very old, and her eyes seemed to see nothing of this world.

And the seven children, though at first they were gloomy and strange, soon began to be happy and at home in the great house. There was much to interest and to amuse them there; all was new to them. Twice every day, morning and evening, they came in to see their grandmother, who every day seemed more feeble; and she spoke pleasantly to them of her mother, and her childhood, but never forgetting to visit her store of sugar-plums. And so the weeks passed by. . . .

It was evening twilight when Henry went upstairs from the nursery by himself to look at the oak chest. He pressed his fingers into the carved fruit and flowers, and spoke to the dark-smiling heads at the corners; and then, with a glance over his shoulder, he opened the lid and looked in. But the chest concealed no treasure, neither gold nor baubles, nor was there anything to alarm the eye. The chest was empty, except that it was lined with silk of old-rose, seeming darker in the dusk, and smelling sweet of pot-pourri. And while Henry was looking in, he heard the softened laughter and the clinking of the cups downstairs in the nursery; and out at the window he saw the day darkening. These things brought strangely to his memory

his mother who in her glimmering white dress used to read
to him in the dusk; and he climbed into the chest; and the
lid closed gently down over him.

When the other six children were tired with their
playing, they filed into their grandmother's room for her
good-night and her sugar-plums. She looked out between
the candles at them as if she were uncertain of something
in her thoughts. The next day Ann told her grandmother
that Henry was not anywhere to be found.

"Dearie me, child. Then he must be gone away for a
time," said the old lady. She paused. "But remember, all of
you, do not meddle with the oak chest."

But Matilda could not forget her brother Henry,
finding no pleasure in playing without him. So she would
loiter in the house thinking where he might be. And she carried her wooden doll in her bare arms, singing under her
breath all she could make up about it. And when one
bright morning she peeped in on the chest, so sweet-scented
and secret it seemed that she took her doll with her into it
—just as Henry himself had done.

So Ann, and James, and William, Harriet and Dorothea were left at home to play together. "Some day maybe
they will come back to you, my dears," said their grandmother, "or maybe you will go to them. Heed my warning
as best you may."

Now Harriet and William were friends together, pretending to be sweethearts; while James and Dorothea liked
wild games of hunting, and fishing, and battles.

On a silent afternoon in October, Harriet and William
were talking softly together, looking out over the slate roof
at the green fields, and they heard the squeak and frisking
of a mouse behind them in the room. They went together
and searched for the small, dark hole from whence it had

come out. But finding no hole, they began to finger the carving of the chest, and to give names to the dark-smiling heads, just as Henry had done. "*I* know! let's pretend you are Sleeping Beauty, Harriet," said William, "and I'll be the Prince that squeezes through the thorns and comes in." Harriet looked gently and strangely at her brother but she got into the box and lay down, pretending to be fast asleep, and on tiptoe William leaned over, and seeing how big was the chest, he stepped in to kiss the Sleeping Beauty and to wake her from her quiet sleep. Slowly the carved lid turned on its noiseless hinges. And only the clatter of James and Dorothea came in sometimes to recall Ann from her book.

But their old grandmother was very feeble, and her sight dim, and her hearing extremely difficult.

Snow was falling through the still air upon the roof; and Dorothea was a fish in the oak chest, and James stood over the hole in the ice, brandishing a walking-stick for a harpoon, pretending to be an Esquimau. Dorothea's face was red, and her wild eyes sparkled through her tousled hair. And James had a crooked scratch upon his cheek. "You must struggle, Dorothea, and then I shall swim back and drag you out. Be quick now!" He shouted with laughter as he was drawn into the open chest. And the lid closed softly and gently down as before.

Ann, left to herself, was too old to care overmuch for sugar-plums, but she would go solitary to bid her grandmother good-night; and the old lady looked wistfully at her over her spectacles. "Well, my dear," she said with trembling head; and she squeezed Ann's fingers between her own knuckled finger and thumb. "What lonely old people, we two are, to be sure!" Ann kissed her grandmother's soft, loose cheek. She left the old lady sitting in her easy chair,

her hands upon her knees, and her head turned sidelong towards her.

When Ann was gone to bed she used to sit reading her book by candlelight. She drew up her knees under the sheets, resting her book upon them. Her story was about fairies and gnomes, and the gently-flowing moonlight of the narrative seemed to illumine the white pages, and she could hear in fancy fairy voices, so silent was the great many-roomed house, and so mellifluent were the words of the story. Presently she put out her candle, and, with a confused Babel of voices close to her ear, and faint swift pictures before her eyes, she fell asleep.

And in the dead of night she rose out of her bed in dream, and with eyes wide open yet seeing nothing of reality, moved silently through the vacant house. Past the room where her grandmother was snoring in brief, heavy slumber, she stepped lightly and surely, and down the wide staircase. And Vega the far-shining stood over against the window above the slate roof. Ann walked into the strange room beneath as if she were being guided by the hand towards the oak chest. There, just as if she were dreaming it was her bed, she laid herself down in the old rose silk, in the fragrant place. But it was so dark in the room that the movement of the lid was indistinguishable.

Through the long day, the grandmother sat in her bow-window. Her lips were pursed, and she looked with dim, inquisitive scrutiny upon the street where people passed to and fro, and vehicles rolled by. At evening she climbed the stair and stood in the doorway of the large spare bedroom. The ascent had shortened her breath. Her magnifying spectacles rested upon her nose. Leaning her hand on the doorpost she peered in towards the glimmering square of window in the quiet gloom. But she could not see far, because her sight was dim and the light of day feeble. Nor could she detect the faint fragrance as of autumnal leaves. But in her mind was a tangled skein of memories— laughter and tears, and children long ago become old-fashioned, and the advent of friends, and last farewells. And gossiping fitfully, inarticulately, with herself, the old lady went down again to her window-seat.

Lucy

Once upon a time there were three sisters, the Misses
MacKnackery—or, better still, the Miss MacKnackeries.
They lived in a large, white square house called Stoneyhouse; and their names were Euphemia, Tabitha, and Jean
Elspeth. They were known over Scotland for miles and
miles, from the Tay to the Grampians—from the Tay to
the Grumpy Ones, as a cousin who did not like Euphemia
and Tabitha used to say.

Stoneyhouse had been built by the Miss MacKnackeries's grandfather, Mr. Angus MacKnackery, who, from
being a poor boy with scarcely a bawbee in his breeches
pocket, had risen up to be a wealthy manufacturer of the
best Scotch burlap, which is a kind of sacking. He made
twine, too, for tying up parcels. He would have made almost anything to make money. But at last, when he was
sixty-six, he felt he would like to be a gentleman living in
the country with a large garden to walk about in, flowers
in beds, cucumbers in frames, pigs in sties, and one or two
cows for milk, cream, and butter.

So he sold his huge, smoky works and warehouse, and

all the twine and burlap, hemp, jute, and whalebone still in it, for £80,000. With this £80,000 he built Stoneyhouse, purchased some fine furniture and some carriages and horses, and invested what was over.

Jean Elspeth, when she was learning sums, and when she had come to Interest—having sometimes heard her father and mother speak of her grandfather and of his fortune, and how he had *invested* it—just to please her governess, Miss Gimp, thought she would make a sum of it. So she wrote down in her rather straggly figures in an exercise book:

$$£80,000 @ 4 \text{ per centum per annum}$$
$$= £80,000 \times 4 \div 100 = £3,200.$$

It was the first really enjoyable sum she had ever done. And yet Miss Gimp was a little put about when Jean Elspeth showed it to her father. Still, Mr. MacKnackery, senior, had been a really rich man, and regretted that the gentleman who bought his factory could never afterwards make such fine burlap as himself, nor even such durable twine.

He lived to be eighty, and then he died, leaving his money to his son, Robert Duncan Donald David, Jean Elspeth's father. And when *he* died, his dear wife Euphemia Tabitha being dead too, he left all that was over of the £80,000 (for, alas and alas! he had lost a good part of it) to his three daughters: Euphemia, Tabitha, and Jean Elspeth.

When Jean Elspeth was old enough to breakfast with the family in the big dining-room with the four immense windows, she used to sit opposite the portraits of her grandfather, her father, and her mother. They hung in heavy handsome gilt frames on the wall opposite the windows. And while in her high chair she gobbled up her porridge— and gobbled it up quickly, not so much because she liked it as because she hated being put in the corner for not eating it—she would sit and look at them.

Her grandfather's was by far the largest of the three portraits, and it hung in the very middle of the lofty wall, under the moulded ceiling. He was a stout and imposing man, with bushy whiskers and cold bright blue eyes. The thumb and first finger of his right hand held a fine thick Albert watch-chain, which the painter had painted so skilfully that you could see it was eighteen-carat gold at a single glance. So he hung: for ever boldly staring down on his own great dining-room and all that was in it—yet not appearing to enjoy it very much.

What was more, her grandfather always looked exactly as if he were on the point of taking out his watch to see the time; and Jean Elspeth had the odd notion that, if he ever did succeed in so doing, its hands would undoubtedly point to a quarter to twelve. But she could no more have told you why than she could tell you why she used to count each spoonful of her porridge or why she felt happier when the last spoonful was an odd number.

The portrait of her father was that of a man much less stout and imposing than her grandfather. He was dark, and smiling, and he had no whiskers. And Jean Elspeth had loved him dearly. Every morning when she had finished her breakfast (and if nobody was looking) she would give a tiny little secret wave of the spoon towards him, as if he might be pleased at seeing her empty plate.

On the other side of her grandfather's portrait hung a picture of her mother. And the odd thing about this picture was that, if you looked long enough, you could not help

seeing—as if it were almost the ghost of Jean Elspeth—
her very own small face, peeping out of the paint at you, just
like a tiny little green marmoset out of a cage all to itself
in the zoo. Jean Elspeth had discovered this when she was
only seven; but Euphemia and Tabitha had never noticed it
at all.

They knew they were far less like their mother (who
had been a Miss Reeks MacGillicuddy of Kelso) than their
grandfather. Still they were exceedingly proud of *that*. As
for Jean Elspeth, they didn't think she was like any of the
family at all. Indeed, Euphemia had more than once remarked that Jean Elspeth had "nae deegnity," and Tabitha
that "she micht jist as weel ha' been a changeling." Even
now, when they were elderly ladies, they always treated her
as if she were still not very far from being a child, though,
after all, Jean Elspeth was only five years younger than
Tabitha.

But then, how different she was in looks! For while
Tabitha had a long pale face a little like a unicorn's, with
mouse-coloured hair and green-grey eyes, Jean Elspeth
was dark and small, with red in her cheek and a tip to her
nose. And while Tabitha's face changed very little, Jean
Elspeth's was like a dark little glancing pool on an April
morning. Sometimes it looked almost centuries older than
either of her sisters', and then, again, sometimes it looked
simply no age at all.

It depended on what she was doing—whether she
was sitting at seven o'clock dinner on Great Occasions,
when the Bults, and the McGaskins, and Dr. Menzies
were guests, or merely basking idly in the sunshine at her
bedroom window. Jean Elspeth would sometimes, too, go
wandering off by herself over the hills a mile or two away
from the house. And *then* she looked not a minute older

than looks a harebell, or a whinchat, perched with his white eyebrow on a fuzz-bush near a lichenous half-hidden rock among the heather.

However sad, too, she looked, she never looked grim. And even though (at dinner parties) she parted her hair straight down the middle, and smoothed the sides over as sleek as satin, she simply could not look what is called "superior." Besides, she had lips that were the colour of cherries, and curious quick hands that she was sometimes compelled to clasp together lest they should talk even more rapidly than her tongue.

Now in Stoneyhouse nobody—except perhaps the tweeny-maid and the scullery-maid, Sally and Nancy Mc-Gullie, who were cousins—ever talked *much*. It was difficult even to tell exactly how wise and sagacious and full of useful knowledge Euphemia and Tabitha were, simply because except at meals they so seldom opened their mouths. And never to sing.

This, perhaps, was because it is impossible to keep order if everybody's tongue keeps wagging. It wastes time, too; for only very few people can work hard and talk hard both at the same moment. And in Stoneyhouse everything was in apple pie order (except the beds), and nobody ever wasted *any* time (except kissing-time).

And yet, although time was never wasted, nobody seemed to be very much the better off for any that was actually "saved." Nobody had ever managed to pack some of it up in neat brown-paper parcels, or to put it in a bank as Mr. MacKnackery, senior, had put his money, or to pour it into jars like home-made jam. It just went. And in Stoney-house (until, at least, Euphemia one morning received a certain letter) it went very very slowly. The big hands of its clocks seemed to be envious of the little ones. They crept like shadows. And between their "tick" and their "tock" at times yawned a huge hole, as dark as a cellar. So, at least, Jean Elspeth fancied.

One glance at Stoneyhouse, even from the outside, would tell you how orderly it was. The four high white walls, with their large square slate roof fixed firmly on top of them, stood stiff as bombardiers on extremely solid foundations, and they on even solider rock. No tree dared cast a shadow upon them, no creeper crept. The glossy windows, with their straight lines of curtains behind them, just stared down on you as if they said, "Find the faintest speck or smear or flaw in us if you can!" And you hadn't the courage even to try.

It was just so inside. Everything was frozen in its place. Not only the great solid pieces of furniture which Mr. Mac-Knackery had purchased with his burlap money—wardrobes, coffers, presses, four-posters, highboys, sideboards, tables, sofas, and oak chairs—but even all the little things, bead-mats, footstools, candle-snuffers, boot-trees, ornaments, knick-knacks, Euphemia's silks and Tabitha's watercolours. There was a place for everything, and everything was in its place. Yes, and it was kept there.

Except in Jean Elspeth's room. She had never never learned to be tidy, not even in her sums. She was constantly taking things out, and either forgetting to put them away again or putting them away again in their wrong places. And do you suppose she blamed herself for this? Not at all. When she lost anything and had been looking for it for hours and hours—a book, or a brooch, or a ribbon, or a shoe—she would say to herself, laughing all over, "Well now, there! That *Lucy* must have hidden it!" And presently *there* it would be, right in the middle of her dressing-table or under a chair, as if a moment before it had been put back there; just for fun.

And who was this *"Lucy"*? There couldn't be a more difficult question; and Jean Elspeth had never attempted to answer it. It was one of those questions she never even asked herself. At least, not out loud. This, perhaps, was because she hated the thought of hurting anybody's feelings. As if Lucy . . . but never mind!

It was Lucy, at any rate, who so unfortunately came into that dreadful talk over the porridge on the morning when the fatal letter came to Euphemia. It arrived just like any other letter. The butler, with his mouth as closely shut as usual, had laid it beside Euphemia's plate. Judging from its large white envelope, nobody could possibly have thought it was as deadly as a poison and sharper than a serpent's tooth. Euphemia opened it, too, just as usual—with her long, lean forefinger, and her eyebrows lifted a little under her grey front of hair. Then she read it—and turned to ice.

It was from her lawyer, or rather from her Four Lawyers, for they all shared the same office, and at the foot of the letter one of them had signed all their four names. It was a pitch-black letter—a thunderbolt. It said at the beginning that the Miss MacKnackeries must expect in future to be a little less well off than they had been in the past, and it said at the end that they were ruined.

You see, Euphemia's grandfather had lent what remained of his £80,000 (after building his great mansion) to the British Government, for the use of the British nation. The British Government of that day put the money into what were called the Consolidated Funds. And to show how much obliged they were to Mr. MacKnackery for the

loan of it, they used every year to pay him interest on it—
so many shillings for every hundred pounds. Not so much as
4 per centum, as Jean Elspeth had put down in her sum,
but as much as they could afford—and that was at least
1,000,000 bawbees. There couldn't have been a safer
money-box; nor could Mr. MacKnackery's income have
"come in" more regularly if it had come in by clockwork.
So far the British Government resembled Stoneyhouse itself.

But the Miss MacKnackeries's father was not only a
less imposing man than their grandfather, he had been
much less careful of his money. He enjoyed *helping* the
nation to use the Funds. He delighted in *buying* things
and giving presents, and the more he bought the more he
wanted to buy. So he had gradually asked for his money
back from the British Government, spending most of it
and lending the rest to persons making railways and gasworks in foreign parts, and digging up gold and diamonds,
and making scent out of tar, and paint which they said
would never wear off or change colour, and everything like
that.

These persons paid him for helping them like this a
good deal more than the Consolidated Funds could pay
him. But then gasworks are not always so *safe* as the British
nation. It is what is called a speculation to lend gentlemen
money to help them to dig up diamonds or to make waterworks in Armenia, which means that you cannot be perfectly sure of getting it back again. Often and often, indeed,
the Miss MacKnackeries's father had not got *his* money
back again.

And now—these long years after his death—the
worst had befallen. The Four Lawyers had been suddenly
compelled to tell the Miss MacKnackeries that nearly every

bit left of their grandfather's savings was gone; that their solid gold had vanished like the glinting mists of a June morning. They had for some time been accustomed to growing less and less rich; but that's a very different thing from becoming alarmingly poor. It is the difference between a mouse with a fat nugget of cheese and a mouse with a bread-crumb.

Euphemia, before opening the letter, had put on her pince-nez. As she read, the very life seemed to ebb out of her poor old face, leaving it cold and grey. She finished it to the last word, then with a trembling hand took the glasses off her nose and passed the letter to Tabitha. Tabitha could still read without spectacles. Her light eyes angled rapidly to and fro across the letter; then she, too, put it down, her face not pale, but red and a little swollen. "It is the end, Euphemia," she said.

Jean Elspeth was sitting that morning with her back to the portraits, and at the moment was gently munching a slice of dry toast and Scotch marmalade (made by the Miss MacKnackeries's cook, Mrs. O'Phrump). She had been watching a pied wagtail flitting after flies across the smooth shorn lawn on the white stone terrace. Then her gaze had wandered off to the blue outline of the lovely distant hills, the Grumpy Ones, and her mind had slid into a kind of day-dream.

Into the very middle of this day-dream had broken the sound of Tabitha's words, "It is the end, Euphemia"; and it was as if a trumpet had sounded.

She looked round in dismay, and saw her sisters, Euphemia and Tabitha, sitting there in their chairs at the table, as stiff and cold as statues of stone. Not only this, which was not so very unusual, but they both of them looked extremely unwell. *Then* she noticed the letter. And she knew at once that this must be the serpent that had suddenly bitten her sisters' minds. The blood rushed up into her cheeks, and she said—feeling more intensely sorry for them both than she could possibly express—"Is there anything wrong, Euphemia?"

And Euphemia, in a voice Jean Elspeth would certainly not have recognized if she had heard it from outside the door, replied, "You may well ask it." And then in a rush Jean Elspeth remembered her strange dream of the night before and at once went blundering on: "Well, you know, Euphemia, I had a dream last night, all dark and awful, and, in it, *there* was *Lucy* looking out of a crooked stone window over some water. And she said to me——"

But Tabitha interrupted her: "I think, Elspeth, neither myself nor Euphemia at this moment wishes to hear what Lucy, as you call her, said in your dream. We have received exceedingly bad news this morning, that very closely concerns not only Tabitha and me, but even yourself also. And this is *no* time for frivolity." And it sounded even more tragic in her Scots tongue.

Jean Elspeth had not meant to be frivolous. She had hoped merely, and if but for a moment, to turn her sisters' minds away from this dreadful news that had come with the postman, and to explain what her dream had seemed to promise. But no. It was just her way. Whenever she said anything to anyone—anything that came from the very bottom of her heart—she always made a muddle of it. It sounded as small and meaningless as the echo of a sparrow's cheeping against a bare stone wall. They would look at her out of their green-grey eyes, down their long pale noses, with an expression either grim or superior, or both. Of course, too, at such a moment, any mention of Lucy was a dreadfully silly mistake. Even at the best of times they despised Jean Elspeth for her "childishness." What must they think of her now!

For there never was and there never could be any *real* Lucy. It was only a name. And yet Jean Elspeth still longed to find *some* word of hope or comfort that would bring back a little colour into poor Euphemia's cheeks, and make her look a little less like an image in marble. But no word came. She had even failed to hear what her sisters were saying. At last she could bear herself no longer.

"I am sure, Euphemia, that you would like to talk the letter over with Tabitha in quiet, and that you will tell me if I can be of any help. I think I will go out into the garden."

Euphemia bowed her head. And though, by trying to move with as little noise as possible, Jean Elspeth made her heavy chair give a loud screech on the polished floor, she managed to escape at last.

It was a cold, clear, spring morning, and the trees in the distance were now tipped with their first green buds. The gardeners were already mapping out their rows of plants in the "arbaceous borders," in preparation for the summer. There never was a garden "kept" so well. The angles of the flower-beds on the lawn—diamonds and lozenges, octagons, squares, and oblongs—were as sharp as if they had been cut out of cardboard with a pair of scissors. Not a blade of grass was out of place.

If even one little round pebble pushed up a shoulder in the gravel path, up came a vast cast-iron roller and ground him back into his place. As for a weed, let but one poke its little green bonnet above the black mould, it would soon see what happened.

The wide light from the sky streamed down upon the

house, and every single window in the high white wall of it seemed to be scornfully watching Jean Elspeth as she made her way down to a little straight green seat under the terrace. Here, at least, she would be out of their sight.

She sat down, folded her hands in her lap, and looked straight in front of her. She always so sat when she was in trouble. In vain she tried to compose and fix her mind and to *think*. It was impossible. For she had not been there more than a moment or two before her heart knew that Lucy was haunting somewhere close beside her. So close and so much on purpose, it seemed, that it was almost as if she wanted to whisper something in her ear. . . .

Now it has been said that Lucy was only a name. Yet, after all, she was a little more than that. Years and years ago, when Jean Elspeth was only seven, she had "sort of" made Lucy up. It was simply because there was no one else to play with, for Tabitha was five years older, and at least fifty-five times more sensible and intelligent and grown-up. So Jean Elspeth had pretended.

In those days she would sometimes sit on one flowerpot on the long hot or windy terrace, and she would put another flowerpot for Lucy. And they would talk, or rather she would talk, and Lucy would look. Or sometimes they sat together in a corner of the great bare nursery. And sometimes Jean Elspeth would pretend she was holding Lucy's hand when she fell asleep.

And the really odd thing was that the less in those days she tried to "pretend," the more often Lucy came. And though Jean Elspeth had never seen her with what is called her naked eye, she must have seen her with some other kind of eye, for she knew that her hair and skin were fairer than the fairest of flax, and that she was dressed in very light and queer-fashioned clothes, though she could not say *how* queer.

Another odd thing was that Lucy always seemed to appear without warning entirely out of nothing, and entirely of herself, when anything mysterious or unexpected or sad or very beautiful happened, and sometimes just before it happened. That had been why she told Euphemia of her dream of the night before. For though everything else in the dream had been dark and dismal, and the water had roared furiously over its rocks, breaking into foam like snow, and Jean Elspeth had been shaken with terror, Lucy herself appearing at the window had been more beautiful than moonlight and as consoling as a star.

It was a pity, of course, that Jean Elspeth had ever even so much as mentioned Lucy at all. But that had been years and years ago, and then she could not really help doing so. For Tabitha had crept up behind her one morning—it was on her eighth birthday—while she herself was sitting in a corner by the large cupboard, with her back to the nursery door, and had overheard her talking to someone.

"Aha! little Miss Toad-in-the-hole! So here you are! And who are *you* talking to?" Tabitha had asked.

Jean Elspeth had turned cold all over. "Nobody," she said.

"Oh, Nobody, is it? Then you just tell me, Madame Skulker, Nobody's name!"

And Jean Elspeth had refused. Unfortunately, she had been wearing that morning a high-waisted frock, with sleeves that came down only to the elbow, and though Tabitha, with nips and pinches of her bare skinny arm, could not make Jean Elspeth cry, she had at least made her tell.

"Oh, so its name's Lucy, is it?" said Tabitha. "You horrid little frump. Then you tell her from me that if *I* catch her anywhere about, I'll scratch her eyes out."

After another pinch or two, and a good "ring-of-the-bells" at Jean Elspeth's plait, Tabitha had gone downstairs to her father.

"Papa," she said, "I am sorry to interrupt you, but I think poor Elspeth must be ill or in a fever. She is 'rambling.' Had we better give her some Gregory's powder, or some castor-oil, do you think?"

Mr. MacKnackery had been worried that morning by a letter about a Gold Mine, something like that which poor Euphemia so many years afterwards was to receive from the Four Lawyers. But when *he* was worried he at once tried to forget his worry. Indeed, even at sight of what looked like an ugly letter, he would begin softly whistling and smiling. So it was almost with a sigh of relief that he pushed the uncomfortable letter into a drawer and climbed the stairs to the nursery.

And when Jean Elspeth, after crying a little as she sat on his knee, had told him about Lucy, he merely smiled out of his dark eyes, and, poking his finger and thumb into a waistcoat pocket, had pulled out, just as if it had been waiting there especially for this occasion, a tiny little gold locket with a picture of a moss-red inside, which he asked Jean Elspeth to give to Lucy the very next time she came again. "My dear," he had said, "I have my Lucy, too, though I never, never talk about her. I keep her 'for best.' "

As for Tabitha, he thanked her most gratefully that

morning at luncheon for having been so thoughtful about her sister. "But I fear, my child," he said, "you must be fretting yourself without need. And for fretting there is nothing so good as Gregory's powder. So I have asked Alison to mix a good dose for you at bedtime, and if you are very generous, perhaps Jenny would like to lick the spoon."

The very moment he turned his face away, with as dreadful a grimace as she could manage, Tabitha had put out her long pale tongue at Jean Elspeth—which was about as much use as it would have been to put out her tongue for their old doctor, Dr. Menzies—*after* he had gone out of the room. . . .

Even now, years and years after she had become completely grown up, whenever Jean Elspeth thought of those far-away times she always began wool-gathering. And whenever she began wool-gathering Lucy was sure to seem more real to her than at any other time. The gravel path, the green lawn, the distant hills vanished away before her eyes. She was lost as if in a region of light and happiness. There she was happy to be lost. But spattering raindrops on her cheeks soon called her back to herself. A dark cloud had come over the world, and for the first time a foreboding came into her mind of what Euphemia's letter might really mean.

She turned sharply on the little green seat almost as if she had been caught trespassing. And at that instant she could have vowed that she actually saw—this time with her real naked eye—a child standing and looking at her a few paces beyond. It could not have been so, of course; but what most surprised Jean Elspeth was that there should be such a peculiar smile on the child's face—as if she were saying: "Never mind, my dear. Whatever happens, what-

ever they say, I promise to be with you more than *ever* before. You just see!"

And then, for the very first time in her life, Jean Elspeth felt ashamed of Lucy; and then, still more ashamed of being ashamed. When they were all in such trouble, was it quite fair to Euphemia and Tabitha? She actually went so far as to turn away in the opposite direction and would have hastened straight back to the house if, at that moment, she had not heard a small, curious fluttering behind her. She glanced swiftly over her shoulder, but it was to find only that a robin had stolen in on her to share her company, and was now eyeing her with his bead-black eye from his perch on the green seat which she had just vacated.

And now, of course, there was no Lucy. Not a trace. She had been "dismissed"—would never come back.

For lunch that day the butler carried in a small souptureen of porridge. When he had attended to each of the ladies, and had withdrawn, Euphemia explained to Jean Elspeth precisely what the lawyers' letter meant. It was a long letter, not only about the gentlemen who had failed to find water enough for their waterworks in Armenia, but also about some other gentlemen in Madagascar whose crops of manioc and caoutchouc had been seized with chorblight. Jean Elspeth did not quite grasp the details; she did not quite understand why the lawyers had ever taken such a fancy to caoutchouc; but she did perfectly understand Euphemia's last sentence: "So you see, Elspeth, we —that is Us—are ruined!"

And would you believe it? Once more Jean Elspeth said the wrong thing. Or rather it was her voice that was wrong. For far away in it was the sound as of a bugle rejoicing at break of day. "And does that mean, Euphemia, that we shall have to *leave* Stoneyhouse?"

"It means," said Tabitha tartly, "that Stoneyhouse may have to leave *us*."

"In either case we are powerless," added Euphemia. And the tone in which Euphemia uttered these words—sitting there straight and erect, with her long white face, in her sleek grey silk morning-gown with its pattern of tiny mauve flowers—brought tears, not to Jean Elspeth's eyes, but to somewhere deep down inside her. It was as if somebody was drawing water out of the very well of her heart.

"It is the *disgrace*," said Tabitha. "To have to turn our backs, to run away. We shall be the talk, the laughing-stock of the county."

"What! Laugh at us because we are ruined!" cried Jean Elspeth.

But this time Tabitha ignored her. "This is the house," she said, "our noble grandfather built for us. And here I will die, unless I am positively driven out of it by these systematic blood-suckers."

"Tabitha!" pleaded Euphemia. "Surely we should not demean ourselves so far as even to call them by their right name."

"Systematic blood-suckers," cried Tabitha fiercely. "I will sell the very rings off my fingers rather than be an exile from the house where I was born. And *he*—*he* at least shall never witness the ruin into which our father's folly has betrayed us."

She rose from the table, and mounting one of the expensive damask chairs that, unless guests were present, were accustomed to stand in a stately row along the wall, she succeeded, after one or two vain attempts, in turning the immense gilt-framed portrait of her grandfather with its face to the wall.

Then tears really came into Jean Elspeth's eyes. But

they were tears of anger rather than of pity. "I think," she said, "that is being dreadfully unkind to Father."

"By this time," said Tabitha sternly, "I should have supposed that you would have given up the notion that you are capable of 'thinking.' What right have you to defend your father, pray, simply because you take after him?"

Jean Elspeth made no answer. Her father at any rate continued to smile at her from *his* nail—though it was not a very good portrait, because the painter had been unable to get the hair and the waistcoat quite right. And if— even at this unhappy moment—Jean Elspeth had had her porridge spoon in her hand, she would certainly have given it a little secret wave in his direction.

But he was not to smile down for very long. The Miss MacKnackeries's grandfather continued to hang with his face to the wall. But the two other portraits, together with the wardrobes, coffers, presses, sideboards, bead-mats, samplers, and even the Indian workboxes, were all taken off in a few weeks, to be sold for what they would fetch. And Euphemia now, instead of five, wore but one ring, and that of turquoises.

In a month all the servants, from the butler to Sally McGullie, and all the gardeners were gone. Mrs. O'Phrump alone remained—first because she was too stout to be likely to be comfortable in any new place, and next, because she wasn't greedy about wages. That was all. Just Mrs. O'Phrump and the gardener's boy, Tom Piper, whose mother lived in the village, and who slept at home. But he was a lazy boy, was Tom Piper, and when he was not fast asleep in the tool-shed, he was loafing in the deserted orchard.

Nevertheless, it was from this moment that Jean Elspeth seemed to have become completely alive.

It was extraordinary to find herself so much herself in so empty a house. The echoes! Why, if you but walked alone along a corridor, you heard your own footsteps pit-a-pattering after you all the way down. If by yourself, in "your ain, ain companie," you but laughed out in a room, it was like being the muffled clapper of a huge hollow bell. All Stoneyhouse seemed endlessly empty now; and perhaps the emptiest place of all was the coachhouse.

And then the stables. It was simply astonishing how quickly stray oats, that had fallen by chance into the crannies, sprang up green among the cobble-stones in front of their walls. And if for a little while you actually stood in the stables beside one of the empty mangers, the call of a bird was as shrill as early cock-crow. And you could almost see ghostly horses with their dark eyes looking round at you out of their long narrow heads, as if to say: "So this is what you have done for us!"

Not that Jean Elspeth had very much time to linger over such little experiences. No; and she seemed to have grown even smaller in the empty house. But she was ten times more active. And, though she tried not to be selfish by showing it, she was more than ten times happier. Between Jean Elspeth herself and the eagle-surmounted gate-posts, indeed, she now secretly confessed that she had always hated Stoneyhouse. How very odd, then, that the moment it ceased to be a place in which *any* fine personage would be proud to be offered a pillow, she began to be friends with it. She began to pity it.

No doubt Tabitha was right. Their grandfather would assuredly have "turned in his grave," poor creature, at the sound of those enormous vans, those hideous pantechni-cons, as their wheels ground down the gravel in the lingering twilight evenings. And yet, after all, that grandfather had been born—a fact that very much shocked Tabitha, whenever her father had smilingly related it—their grandfather had been born in a two-roomed cottage so cramped that, if only you could have got it through the window, it would have fitted quite comfortably even into the breakfast-room of the great house he had lived to build.

Then there had been not two bawbees in his breeches pocket, and—having been such a good man, as both Euphemia and Tabitha agreed—he did not need a bawbee now. *"Would* he then—once the pantechnicons were out of the way—would he," thought Jean Elspeth, "have been so very miserable to see all this light and sunshine in the house and to listen to these entrancing echoes?"

There were other advantages, too. It was easy to sweep the dining-room; and much easier to dust it. And one day, more out of kindness than curiosity, after busily whisking over its gilt frame with her feather cornice-broom, Jean Elspeth climbed on to a chair, and, tilting it, looked in at the portrait. A spider had spun its web in one corner, but otherwise (it was almost disappointing) the picture was unchanged. Nor had Mr. MacKnackery yet taken his watch out of his pocket, even though (for his three granddaughters at any rate) the time was now—well, a good way past a quarter to twelve.

Jean Elspeth had had ridiculous thoughts like these as long as she could remember. But now they came swarming into her head like midsummer bees into a hive. Try as she might, she could not keep them all to herself, and though on this account alone Tabitha seemed to dislike her more than ever, Euphemia seemed sometimes to wish for her company. But then Euphemia was by no means well. She had begun to stoop a little, and sometimes did not hear what was said to her. To watch her visibly grow older like this gave Jean Elspeth dreadful anxiety. Still, in most things—and she all but said it out loud every morning at her first early look out of her window—she was far happier than when Stoneyhouse stood in all its glory. It seemed rather peculiar, but it was true.

Also, there was no time to be anything else; and even if there had been a complete cupboard *full* of neat packages of time *saved*, she would have used them all up in a week. Euphemia, being so poorly, did very little. She helped to make the beds and with the mending. Only the mending, for, fortunately, the making of any new clothes would be unnecessary for years and years to come; they had so many old ones. Tabitha did what she could manage of the lighter work, but although she had a quick tongue, she had slow, clumsy hands. And it is quite certain, though nobody, naturally, would have been so unkind as to say so, that she would never have got even as low wages as Sally McGullie, if she had been in need of a place.

Mrs. O'Phrump did the cooking; but sat on a chair in the kitchen for so many hours together that she became almost like a piece of furniture herself—the heaviest piece in the house. For the cooking of water-porridge and potatoes does not require very much time, and these were now pretty much all that the Miss MacKnackeries had to eat, except for the eggs from Jean Elspeth's three Cochin-Chinas. And Mrs. O'Phrump needed most of these, as there was so much of her to sustain. As for the apples and pears in the orchard, since Mrs. O'Phrump was too stout to stoop to make dumplings, Jean Elspeth, having two wonderful rows of small sharp teeth, shared these raw with Tom Piper—though *he* had all the stomach-aches.

All the rest of the work fell to Jean Elspeth. She slaved from morning till night. And to slave the more merrily, she had taught herself to whistle. She never asked herself why she was so happy. And no doubt it was chiefly by contrast with having been so cramped in, and kept under, and passed over in days gone by.

Still, certain things did now happen in Stoneyhouse that had not happened before, and some of these may have helped. For one thing, Jean Elspeth had always dreaded "company." Dressing up made her feel awkward. The simplest stranger made her shy. She much preferred the company even of her two sisters. None came now, except Dr. Menzies, who of his kindness sometimes called to feel Euphemia's pulse and mutter, "H'm h'm—" though he did not charge for it.

Jean Elspeth, too, had never liked servants, not because they were servants, but because Euphemia and Tabitha seemed to think they oughtn't to be talked to much. Just given their orders. Now Jean Elspeth could easily have given everything else in the world: but not orders. And if there ever *had* been an interesting creature in Stoneyhouse, even though she was so stupid in some things, it was Sally McGullie.

Then, again, Jean Elspeth, being by nature desperately untidy, never showed it now. For it's all but impossible to be untidy in a room that contains only a table and three chairs!

Then, yet again, Jean Elspeth, before the gentlemen in Armenia and Madagascar had been disappointed in their waterworks and caoutchouc, had had very little to do. She was scarcely even allowed to read. For Tabitha was convinced that most reading was a waste of time, and trash at that; while improving books had never the least bit improved Jean Elspeth. But now she had so many things to do that it was a perfect joy to fit them all in (like the pieces of a puzzle). And the perfectest joy of all was to scramble into her truckle bed, which had formerly been Sally Mc-Gullie's bed, and, with a tallow candle stuck by its own grease to the lefthand knob, to read and read and read.

The hours she spent like this, with no living company but roving mice and flitting moths and, in autumn, perhaps a queen wasp. When her upper parts grew cold in winter weather, she spread her skirt over the quilt. One thin blanket, indeed, is not much comfort on cold nights when one is lying up North there, almost in positive view of the Grumpy Ones. As for her feet, she used to boil some water in the great solitary kitchen in a kettle and fill a wine-bottle.

This, of course, broke a good many bottles; and it was an odd thing that until there was only one left, Tabitha (whose feet were like slabs of ice) refused to hear of anything so vulgar. And *then* she changed her mind. And medicine-bottles are too small.

Apart from all this, queer things now happened in Stoneyhouse. Little things, but entrancing. The pantechnicon men, for example, had broken a window on a lower staircase as they were heaving down old Mr. MacKnackery's best wardrobe. A sweetheart pair of robins in the springtime noticed this hole, and decided to build their nest in a nook of the cornice. Jean Elspeth (with her tiny whistling) was accepted as the bosom friend of the whole family.

There was, too, a boot cupboard, one too far from the kitchen for Mrs. O'Phrump to range. Its window had been left open. And when, by chance, Jean Elspeth looked in one sunny afternoon, there hung within it a marvellous bush of Traveller's Joy, rather pale in leaf, but actually flowering there; and even a butterfly sipping of its nectar.

After that, not a day passed now but she would peep in at this delicate green visitor, and kiss her hand. It was, too, an immense relief to Jean Elspeth to have said good-bye for ever to lots of things in the house that seemed to her to have been her enemies ever since she was five years old.

She wandered up into rooms she had never seen before, and looked out of windows whose views had never before lain under her eyes. Nor did she cease to day-dream, but indulged in only tiny ones that may come and go, like swifts, between two ticks of a clock. And although, of course, Tabitha strongly disapproved of much that delighted Jean Elspeth now, there was not nearly so much time in which to tell her so.

Besides, Jean Elspeth was more useful in that great barracks of a place than ten superior parlour-maids would have been. She was much more like a steam-engine than a maiden lady. And, like a steam-engine, she refused to be angry; she refused to sulk; and she usually refused to answer back. When nowadays, however, she *did* answer back, her tongue had a sting to it at least as sharp (though never so venomous) as that of the busy bee.

And last, but no less, there was the *outside* of the house. As soon as ever Mr. McPhizz and his under-gardeners had departed with their shears and knives and edging-irons and mowing machines, wildness had begun to creep into the garden. Wind and bird carried in seeds from the wilderness, and after but two summers, the trim barbered lawns sprang up into a marvellous meadow of daisies and buttercups, plantains, dandelions, and fools' parsley, and then dock, thistle, groundsel and feathery grasses. Ivy, hop, briony, convolvulus roved across the terrace; Hosts of the Tiny blossomed between the stones.

Moss, too, in mats and cushions of a green livelier than the emerald, or even than a one-night-old beech-leaf. Rain-stains now softly coloured the white walls, as if a stranger had come in the night and begun to paint pictures there. And the roses, in their now hidden beds, rushed back as fast as ever they could to bloom like their wild-briar sisters again.

And not only green things growing. Jean Elspeth would tiptoe out to see complete little immense families of rabbits nibbling their breakfast or supper of dandelion leaves on the very flagstones under the windows. Squirrels nutted; moles burrowed; hedgehogs came beetle-hunting; mice of every tiny size scampered and twinkled and danced and made merry.

As for the birds—birds numberless! And of so many kinds and colours and notes that she had to sit up half the night looking out their names in the huge birdbook her father had given her on her eleventh Christmas. This was the one treasure she had saved from the pantechnicon men. She had wrapped it up in two copies of the *Scotsman,* and hidden it in the chimney. She felt a little guilty over it at times, but none the less determined that the Four Law-yers should never hear of *that*.

It was strange, exceedingly strange, to be so happy; and Jean Elspeth sometimes could hardly contain herself, she was so much ashamed of it in the presence of her sisters. Still, she now drew the line, as they say, at Lucy.

And that was the strangest and oddest thing of all. After the dreadful shock of the Four Lawyers' letter, after the torment and anxiety and horror, the pantechnicons and the tradespeople, poor Tabitha and Euphemia—however brave their faces and stiff their backs—had drooped within like flowers in autumn nipped by frost. In their pride, too, they had renounced even the friends who would have been faithful to them in their trouble.

They shut themselves more than ever, like birds in cages. They scarcely ever even looked from the windows. It was only on Sundays they went out of doors. Euphemia, too, had sometimes to keep her bed. And Jean Elspeth would cry to herself, "Oh, my dear! oh, my dear!" at the sight of Tabitha trailing about the house with a large duster and so little to dust. To see her sipping at her water-porridge as if she were not in the least hungry, as if it was the daintiest dish in Christendom, was like having a knife stuck in one's very breast.

Yet, such was Tabitha's "strength of mind" and hardihood, Jean Elspeth never dared to comfort her, to cheer her up, to wave her spoon by so much as a quarter of an inch in *her* direction.

In these circumstances it had seemed to Jean Elspeth it would be utterly unfair to share Lucy's company, even in her hidden mind. It would be like stealing a march, as they say. It would be cheating. At any rate, it might hurt their feelings. They would see, more stark than ever before, how desolate they were. They would look up and realize by the very light in her eyes that her old playmate had not deserted her. No. She would wait. There was plenty of time. She would keep her wishes down. And the little secret door of her mind should be left, not, as it once was, wide open, but just ajar.

How, she could not exactly say. And yet, in spite of all this, Lucy herself, just as if she were a real live ghost, seemed to be everywhere. If in her scrubbing Jean Elspeth happened to glance up suddenly out of the window— whether mere fancy or not—that fair gentle face might be stealthily smiling in. If some moonlight night she leaned for a few precious sweet cold moments over her bedroom sill, as likely as not her phantom would be seen wandering, shadowless, among the tall whispering weeds and grasses of the lawn.

Phantoms and ghosts are usually very far from welcome company. Lucy was nothing but gentleness and grace. The least little glimpse of her was like hearing a wild bird singing—blackbird or black-cap, not in the least like the solitary hoot-owl whose long, bubbling, grievous notes seem to darken the darkness. Having this ghost, then, for company, however much she tried not to heed it, all that Jean Elspeth had to do in order just to play fair—and she did it with all her might—was not to *look* for Lucy, and not to *show* that she saw her, when there she was, plain to be seen, before her very eyes. And when at last she realized her plan was succeeding, that Lucy was gone from her, her very heart seemed to come into her mouth.

And so the years went by. And the sisters became older and older, and Stoneyhouse older and older too. Walls, fences, stables, coach-house, hen-house, and the square lodge crept on steadily to rack and ruin. Tabitha kept more and more to herself, and the sisters scarcely spoke at meal-times.

Then at last Euphemia fell really ill; and everything else for a while went completely out of Jean Elspeth's life and remembrance. She hadn't a moment even to lean from her window or to read in her bed. It was unfortunate, of course, that Euphemia's bedroom was three stair-flights up. Jean Elspeth's legs grew very tired of climbing those long ladders, and Tabitha could do little else but sit at the window and knit—knit the wool of worn-out shawls and stockings into new ones. So she would stay for hours together, never raising her eyes to glance over the pair of horn-rimmed spectacles that had belonged to her grandfather, and now straddled her own lean nose. Dr. Menzies, too, was an old man now, and could visit them very seldom.

Jean Elspeth herself seldom even went to bed. She sat on a chair in Euphemia's room and snatched morsels of sleep, as a hungry dog snatches at bits of meat on a butcher's tray. It was on such a night as this, nodding there in her chair, that, after having seemed to fall into a long narrow nightmare hole of utter cold and darkness, and to have stayed there for centuries without light or sound, she was suddenly roused by Euphemia's voice.

It was not Euphemia's usual voice, and the words were following one another much more rapidly than usual, like sheep and lambs running through a gate. Daybreak was at the window. And in this first chill eastern light Euphemia was sitting up in bed—a thing she had been unable to do for weeks. And she was asking Jean Elspeth to tell her who the child was that was now standing at the end of her bed.

Euphemia described her, too—"A fair child with straight hair. And she is carrying a bundle of gorse, with its prickles, and flowers wide open. I can smell the almond smell. And she keeps on looking and smiling first at me, and then at you. Don't you *see*, Elspeth? Tell her, please, to go away. Tell her I don't want to be happy like that. She is making me afraid. Tell her to go away at once, please."

Jean Elspeth sat shivering, colder than a snail in its winter shell. The awful thing was to know that this visitor must be Lucy, and yet not to be able to see her—not a vestige, nothing but the iron bed and the bedpost, and Euphemia sitting there, just gazing. How, then, could she tell Lucy to go away?

She scurried across the room, and took Euphemia's cold hands in hers. "You are dreaming, Euphemia. *I* see nothing. And if it is a pleasant dream, why drive it away?"

"No," said Euphemia, in the same strange, low, clear voice. "It is not a dream. You are deceiving me, Elspeth. She has come only to mock at me. Send her away!"

And Jean Elspeth, gazing into her sister's wide light eyes, that now seemed deeper than the deepest well that ever was on earth, was compelled to answer her.

"Please, please, Euphemia, do not think of it any more. There is nothing to fear—nothing at all. Why, it sounds like Lucy—that old silly story; do you remember? But I have not seen her myself for ever so long. I *couldn't* while you are ill."

The lids closed gently down over the wide eyes, but Euphemia still held tight to Jean Elspeth's work-roughened hand. "Never mind, then," she whispered, "If that is all. I had no wish to take her away from you, Elspeth. Keep close to me. One thing, we are happier now, you and I."

"Oh, Euphemia, do you mean that?" said Jean Elspeth, peering closer.

"Well," Euphemia replied; and it was as if there were now two voices speaking: the old Euphemia's and this low, even, dreamlike voice. "I mean it. There is plenty of air now—a different place. And I hope your friend will come as often as she pleases. There's room for us all."

And with that word "room," and the grim smile that accompanied it, all the old Euphemia seemed to have come back again, though a moment after she dropped back upon her pillow and appeared to be asleep.

Seeing her thus quiet once more, Jean Elspeth very, very cautiously turned her head. The first rays of the sun were on the window. Not the faintest scent of almond was borne to her nostrils on the air. There was no sign at all of any company. A crooked frown had settled on her forehead. She was cold through and through, and her body ached; but she tried to smile, and almost imperceptibly lifted a finger just as if it held a teaspoon and she was waving it in her own old secret childish way to her father's portrait on the wall.

Now and again after that Jean Elspeth watched the same absent far-away look steal over Euphemia's face, and the same fixed smile, dour and grim, and yet happy—like still deep water under waves. It was almost as if Euphemia were amused at having stolen Lucy away.

"You see, my dear," she said suddenly one morning, as if after a long talk, "it only proves that we all go the same way home."

"Euphemia, please don't say that," whispered Jean Elspeth.

"But why not?" said Euphemia. "So it is. And *she* almost laughing out loud at me. The hussy! . . ."

None of their old friends knew when Euphemia died, so it was only Dr. Menzies and his sister who came to Stoneyhouse for the funeral. And though Jean Elspeth would now have been contented to do *all* the work in the house and to take care of Tabitha and her knitting into the bargain, they persuaded her at last that this would be impossible. And so, one blazing hot morning, having given a little parting gift to Tom Piper and wept a moment or two on Mrs. O'Phrump's ample shoulder, Jean Elspeth climbed with Tabitha into a cab, and that evening found herself hundreds of miles away from Stoneyhouse, in the two upper rooms set apart for the two ladies by Sally McGullie, who had married a fisherman and was now Mrs. John Jones.

Jean Elspeth could not have imagined a life so different. It was as if she had simply been pulled up by the roots. Whenever Tabitha could spare her—and that was seldom now—she would sit at her window looking on the square stone harbour and the sea, or in a glass shelter on its narrow front. But now that time stretched vacantly before her, and she was at liberty if she pleased to "pretend" whenever she wished, and to fall into day-dreams one after another just as they might happen to come, it was life's queer way that she could scarcely picture Lucy now, even with her inward eye, and never with her naked one.

It was, too, just the way of this odd world that she should pine and long for Stoneyhouse beyond words to tell. She felt sometimes she must die—suffocate—of homesickness, and would frown at the grey moving sea, as if that alone were the enemy who was keeping her away from it. Not only this, but she saved up in a tin money-box every bawbee which she could spare of the little money the Four Lawyers had managed to save from the caoutchouc. And all for one distant purpose.

And at length, years and years afterwards, she told Mrs. Jones that she could bear herself no longer, that—like the cat in the fairy-tale—she must pay a visit, and must go alone. . . .

It was on an autumn afternoon, about five o'clock, and long shadows were creeping across the grasses of the forsaken garden when Jean Elspeth came into sight of Stoneyhouse again, and found herself standing some little distance from the gaunt walls beside a shallow pool of water that now lay in a hollow of the garden. Her father had delighted in water; and, putting to use a tiny steam that coursed near by, had made a jetting fountain and a fish-pond. The fountain having long ceased to flow and the pond having become choked with water-weeds, the stream had pushed its way out across the hollows, and had made itself this last dark resting-place. You might almost have thought it was trying to copy Jean Elspeth's life in Sallie Jones's seaside cottage. On the other hand, the windows of the great house did not stare so fiercely now; they were blurred and empty like the eyes of a man walking in his sleep. One of the chimney-stacks had toppled down, and creepers had rambled all over the wide expanse of the walls.

Jean Elspeth, bent-up old woman that she now was, in her dingy black bonnet and a beaded mantle that had belonged to Euphemia, stood there drinking the great still scene in, as a dry sponge drinks in salt water.

And after hesitating for some little time, she decided to venture nearer. She pushed her way through the matted wilderness of the garden, crossed the terrace, and presently peered in through one of the dingy dining-room windows. Half a shutter had by chance been left unhasped. When her eyes were grown accustomed to the gloom within, she discovered that the opposite wall was now quite empty. The portrait of her grandfather must have slowly ravelled through its cord. It had fallen face upwards on to the boards beneath.

It saddened her to see this. She had left the picture hanging there simply because she felt sure that Euphemia would so have wished it to hang. But though she wearied herself out seeking to find entry into the house, in order, at least, to lean her grandfather up again against the wall, it was in vain. The doors were rustily bolted; the lower windows tight-shut. And it was beginning to be twilight when she found herself once more beside the cold, stagnant pool.

All this while she had been utterly alone. It had been a dreadful and sorrowful sight to see the great house thus decaying, and all this neglect. Yet she was not unhappy, for it seemed with its trees and greenery in this solitude to be uncomplaining and at rest. And so, too, was she. It was as if her whole life had just vanished and flitted away like a dream, leaving merely her body standing there in the evening light under the boughs of the great green chestnut-tree overhead.

And then by chance, in that deep hush, her eyes wandered to the surface of the water at her feet, and there fixed themselves, her whole mind in a sudden confusion. For by some curious freak of the cheating dusk, she saw gazing back at her from under a squat old crape bonnet, with Euphemia's cast-off beaded mantle on the shoulders beneath it, a face not in the least like that of the little old woman inside them, but a face, fair and smiling, as of one eternally young and happy and blessed—Lucy's. She gazed and gazed, in the darkening evening. A peace beyond understanding comforted her spirit. It was by far the oddest thing that had ever happened to Jean Elspeth in all the eighty years of her odd long life on earth.

Visitors

One of the very last things that Tom Nevis was to think about in this world was a sight he had seen when he was a child of about ten. Years and years were to pass by after that March morning; and at the last Tom was far away from home and England in the heat and glare of the tropics. Yet this one far-away memory floated up into his imagination to rest there in its peace and strangeness as serenely as a planet shining in its silver above the snows of remote hills. It had just stayed on in the quiet depths of his mind—like the small insects that may be seen imprisoned in lumps of amber, their wings still glistening ages after they were used in flitting hither-thither in their world as it was then.

Most human beings have little experiences similar to Tom's. But they come more frequently to rather solitary people—people who enjoy being alone, and who have daydreams. If they occur at other times, they may leave little impression, because perhaps one is talking or laughing or busy, working away at what has to be done, or perhaps reading or thinking. And then they may pass unnoticed.

But Tom had always been a funny solitary creature.

Even as a child he enjoyed being alone. He would sit on a gate or a stile for an hour at a time just staring idly into a field, following with his eyes the shadows of the clouds as they swept silently over its greenness, or the wandering wind, now here, now there, stooping upon the taller weeds and grasses. It was a pleasure to him merely even to watch a cow browsing her way among the buttercups, swinging the tuft of her tail and occasionally rubbing her cinnamon-coloured shoulder with her soft nose. It seemed to Tom at such times—though he never actually put the feeling into words—almost as if the world were only in his mind; almost as if it were the panorama of a dream.

So too Tom particularly enjoyed looking out of his window when the moon was shining. Not only in winter when there is snow on the ground, and clotting hoar-frost, but in May and summer too, the light the moon sheds in her quiet rests on the trees and the grass and the fields like a silver tissue. And she is for ever changing: now a crescent slenderly shining—a loop of silver or copper wire in the western after-glow of sunset; and now a mere ghost of herself, lingering in the blue of morning like a lantern burning long after the party is over which it was meant to make gay.

Tom was more likely to be left alone than most boys, owing to a fall he had had when he was three. He had a nurse then, named Alice Jenkins. One morning she sat him up as usual close to the nursery table and his bowl of bread and milk; and had then turned round an instant at the sound of something heard at the window. And he, in that instant, to see perhaps what she was looking at, had jumped up in his chair, the bar had slipped out, and he had fallen sprawling on to the floor.

The fall had injured his left arm. And try as the doctors might, they had never been able to make it grow like his right arm. It was lean and shrunken and almost useless, and the fingers of the hand were drawn up a little so that it could be used only for simple easy things. He was very little good at games in consequence, and didn't see much of other boys of his own age. Alice had cried half the night after that miserable hour; but the two of them loved each other the more dearly for it ever afterwards. Even now that she was married and kept a small greengrocer's shop in a neighbouring town, Tom went to see her whenever he could, and munched her apples and pears and talked about everything under the sun.

This accident had happened so long ago that he had almost forgotten he had ever at all had the full use of his arm. He grew as much accustomed to its hanging limply from his shoulder as one may become accustomed to having a crooked nose, prominent ears, or a squint. And though he realized that it kept him out of things like climbing trees or playing such games as other boys could do with ease, though it had made a kind of scarecrow of him, it was simply because of this that he was left more to himself and his own devices than most boys. And though he never confessed it to himself, and certainly not to anybody else, he immensely enjoyed being in his own company. It was not a bit—as it well might be—like being in an empty house, but rather in an enchanted one; wherein you never knew what might not happen next, even though everything was still and quiet—the sun at the windows, the faint shadows in the corridors, the water in the green fishpond and the tangled branches in the orchard.

Tom, too, beside being for this reason rather odd in his body—small for his age, with narrow shoulders, a bony face, light grey-blue eyes and a stiff shock of yellow hair

standing up on his high head—was also a little odd in
mind. He was continually making up stories, even when
there was no one to listen to them. For his black-eyebrowed
elder sister very seldom had time to do so; and the nurse
he had after Alice was married had not much patience with
such things. But he almost as much enjoyed telling them
to himself. And when his sister Emily died he seemed to get
into the habit of mooning and daydreaming more than ever.

He had other queer little habits too. Whenever he went
downstairs from his bedroom—unless he was in a violent
hurry or his father had called him—he always sat down for
a few moments on a narrow stair from which he looked out
from a tall landing window over the garden. It seemed to
him you could never tell what you might *not* see at such
a moment; though as a matter of fact he never saw anything very unusual: just the grass and the lawn and the
currant-bushes and the monkey-puzzle; perhaps a cat walking gingerly on its errand, and the usual thrushes and blackbirds, tits and robins, and the light of the sun on the red-
brick wall. And what you don't actually see you cannot put
a name to.

Another fancy of his was, whenever he passed it, to
stoop down and peer through the keyhole of a cellar that
spread out underneath the old Parsonage. He might just as
well have looked up a chimney for there was even less
light to be seen through the keyhole. And nothing was
stowed away in the cellar except a few old discarded pieces
of furniture, some bottles of wine, empty hampers, an old
broken rocking-horse, and such things as that. None the
less, whenever he passed that door, Tom almost invariably
stooped on his knees, puckered up one eye and peered
through its keyhole with the other, and smelt the fusty
smell.

There was no end to his cranky comicalities. Long ago, for example, he had made a rule of always doing certain things on certain days. He cared no more for washing in those early days than most boys: but he always had a "thorough good wash" on Fridays; even though it was "bath night" on Saturdays. He went certain walks on certain evenings, that is, evenings after it had been raining, or maybe when some flower or tree was just out. And he always went to see his sister Emily's grave once a month.

She had died on the twelfth of April; and apart from her birthday, he always kept her month day—all the twelfths throughout the year. If he could, and if he had time, he would take a bunch of flowers along with him, choosing those which Emily had liked the best or those he liked the best, or both together. The churchyard was not far away, as the crow flies, but it was yet another of his odd habits not to go there direct—as if that might be too easy— but to go round by a meadow path that was at least three-quarters of a mile further than the way by the village lane.

Except when he happened to be by himself at evenings just after the sun was set, Tom always felt more alone on these monthly journeys than at any other time. And for as long a time as he could spare he would sit on an old bench under the churchyard yew. At first he had been exceedingly wretched and miserable on these visits. The whole Parsonage, his father and his sister and the maids—it was just as if a kind of thick cold mist had come over them all when Emily died. Everything that was familiar in the house had suddenly stood up strange and exclamatory, as if to remind them something was gone that would never come back again. And though none of the others, of course, really forgot what had happened, though he often actually noticed his father desisting from what he was just about to say simply because he could not bear the grief of mentioning Emily's name, as time went on, things began to be much as ever again.

In the early days Tom's black-haired elder sister, Esther, used to come with him to the churchyard now and then; but she soon had so many things to think about and to amuse herself with that there was very little time to spend with him. Besides, they agreed about nothing and spent most of the time arguing and wrangling. So for a good many months Tom had gone alone. He knew his own particular monthly walk to the churchyard as well as he knew his own clothes or anything else in the world. He never set out on it without wishing he could see his sister Emily again, and he never came home again to the Parsonage without thinking to himself that it was better perhaps he could *not* bring her back. For he was somehow sure, wherever her body might be, that she herself was perfectly happy, and, as it were, always to be young. Now and then, indeed, it seemed as if some wraith of herself had actually whispered this into his ear as he sat on his bench looking out across the tombstones and sometimes wondering how long it would be before he was dead too. But then Tom's little moperies came very near at times to being a little mad.

That was another odd thing about Tom. He enjoyed thinking and puzzling over everything that came into his head, whereas most people will not allow hard or disagreeable thoughts to stay in their minds. They drive them out like strange dogs out of a garden, or wasps out of a sunny room. Tom thought of them, however, in the most practical way possible. He knew, for example, as much about grave-digging when he was ten as the old sexton could tell him at sixty. The thought of the bones beneath the turf did not frighten him a bit. Surely, he thought to himself, nothing could be as ugly as all that if it were just the truth. And if it was, why, then it *was*.

Not that he did not enjoy being alive in this world. He fairly ached sometimes with delight in it. He had talked to Alice about it, and to Emily too, sitting on a green bank in the sunshine or in the hayfields, or by the banks of their secret pond in the woods. He loved also to brood on what might happen to him in the future; though he never had the faintest notion in those days that he was going to travel, that he was going to leave England when he was still a young man, for good and all, and never come back. He had no notion of that at all until there came a talk one afternoon in her husband's shop with his nurse Alice. After that he knew he had been born to be a traveller in spite of his arm and his cranky meagre body. And what led up to the talk was what happened to him that March morning as he came back from his customary visit to the churchyard.

A faint but bleak east wind was blowing. Except for a light silvery ridge of cloud in the south the sky was blue all over, and the sunlight was as bright as if a huge crystal reflector behind it were casting back its beams from the heavens upon the earth. A few daffodils were out in the fields, and the celandine with its shovel-shaped glossy leaves too; and the hedges were beginning to quicken, looking from a distance as if a faint green mist hung over them. The grass was already growing after its winter's rest, and the birds of the countryside were busy flying hither and thither as if time were something that melted in the sun. Instead of returning from the churchyard to the house by the way he had come, Tom had turned in through a wicket gate into a straggling wood of birch and hazel, and so came out at the corner of a large meadow which lay over against the Old Farm.

There had been heavy rains during the previous week, and as Tom—absent-minded as ever—came edging along the path of the meadow, he lifted his eyes and was astonished to see a pool of water in the green hollow of the meadow beneath him, where none had lain before. Its waters were evidently of the rains that had fallen in the past few days. They stretched there grey and sparkling, glassing the sky, and the budding trees which grew not far from their margin. And floating upon this new wild water he saw two strange birds. Never had he seen their like before, though he guessed they might be straying sea-birds. They were white as snow, and were disporting themselves gently in this chance pool as if it were a haven or refuge or meeting-place which they had been seeking from the first moment they had come out of their shells.

Tom watched them, fixed motionless where he stood, afraid almost to blink lest he should disturb their happy play. But at last he took courage, and gradually, inch by inch, he approached stealthily nearer until at last he could see their very eyes shining in their heads, and the marvellous snow of their wings and their coral beaks reflected in the shallow wind-rippled pool. They appeared to be companions of all time. They preened their feathers, uttering faint cries as if of delight, as if they were telling secrets one to the other. And now and again they would desist from their preening and float there quietly together on the surface of the water, in the silvery sunshine. And still Tom continued to gaze at them with such greedy eagerness it was a marvel this alone did not scare the wild creatures away. It seemed to Tom as if he had been looking at them for ages and ages under the huge shallow bowl of the March sky. He dreaded every instant they would lift their wings and fly away. That would be as if something had gone out of his own inmost self.

He was whispering too under his breath, as if to persuade them to remain there always, and let there be no change. Indeed they might be human creatures, they floated there on the water so naturally and happily in their devotion to one another's company. And it seemed once more to Tom as if the whole world and his own small life had floated off into a dream, and that he had stood watching their movements and their beauty for as many centuries as the huge oak that towered above the farm had stood with outflung boughs, bearing its flowers and its acorns from spring on to spring, and from autumn to autumn, until this very morning.

What was curious too, the two strange birds seemed at last to have no fear of his being there, even though the bright shallow basin of rain on which they rested in the meadow was not more than eleven paces wide. They eyed him indeed with a curious sharp brightness, almost as if they wished to be sharing their secret with him, one brought from the remote haunts from which they had set out overnight; as if this was the end of their journey. The drops they flung with their bills over their snowy plumage gleamed like little balls of changing silver or crystal, though not brighter than their eyes. The red of their webbed feet showed vividly beneath the grey clear water. And the faint soft cries uttered in their throats rather than with open bills were not sweet or shrill as a peewit or a linnet singing, but were yet wonderfully gentle and tender to listen to.

And Tom's odd mind slipped once more into a deep daydream as he stood there—in his buttoned-up jacket,

with his cap over his short springy hair—in the light but bleak east wind that swept out of the clouds across the meadow and the roof and chimneys of the old red-brick farm. . . . In the middle of that night he woke up: as suddenly almost as if a voice had called him. And the scene was still as sharp and fresh in his imagination as if he were looking at it again spread out in actuality in the morning light before his very eyes.

It was just like ridiculous Tom not to visit the meadow again for many days afterwards. Once or twice he actually set out in that direction, but turned off before the farmyard came into view. And when at last he did go back again, towards evening, the whole scene had changed. No longer was the wind from the east, but from the south. Lofty clouds towered up into the intense blue of the sky, like snow-topped mountains. The air was sweet with spring. The tight dark buds had burst in the hedges into their first pale-green leaf; thrushes were singing among the higher branches of the elms. But the pool of rainwater had sunk out of sight in its hollow, had been carried up by the wind and sun into the heavens, leaving only the greener and fresher grass behind it. The birds were flown. . . .

One day in the following July, Tom went off to see his old nurse, Alice Hubbard. She had grown a good deal stouter after her marriage, and Tom sat with her in the cramped parlour behind the shop, looking out into the street across the bins of green peas and potatoes, carrots and turnips, lettuces and cabbages and mint, the baskets of gooseberries and currants and strawberries and the last cherries. And while Alice was picking out for him a saucerful of strawberries, he told her all about himself: what he had been doing and thinking, and about the new maid, and about the Parsonage. And she would say as she paused with

finger and thumb over her basket, "Lor, Master Tom!"
"Did you ever, now, Master Tom!" or "There now, Master
Tom!" And all of a sudden the memory of the pool of water and the two strange birds flitted back into his mind, and
he fell silent. Alice put down before him the saucer of
strawberries, with a little blue-and-white jug of cream,
and she glanced a little curiously into his narrow, ugly
face.

"And what might you be thinking of now, I wonder?"
she said.

An old woman in a black bonnet and shawl who had
been peering about at the fruit from the pavement close to
the window outside, at this moment came into the shop, and
Alice went out to serve her with what she wanted. Tom
watched the two of them; watched the potatoes weighed
and the sprig of mint thrown into the scale; watched a huge
dapple-grey cart-horse go by, dragging its cartload of
bricks, with its snuff-coloured driver sitting on a sack on
top. And then Alice had come back into the little parlour
again, and he was telling her all about the birds and the
pool.

"Lor now, that *was* queer, Master Tom," said Alice.
"And where might you have been that morning?"

And Tom told her he had been to the churchyard.

"Now you know, my dear soul," she said in a hushed
voice as if somebody might be listening; "you know you
didn't ought to go there too often. It isn't good for you. You
think too much already. And Joe says—and you wouldn't
believe how happy I am, Master Tom, living here in this
little shop, though I never, never forget the old Parsonage
and the kindness of your dear mother—but Joe, he says
that one didn't ought to keep on thinking about such
things. Not keep on, he means. How would the world go

round, he says, if we was all of us up in the clouds all day. It looks to me as if you were more a bag of bones than ever, though p'raps you have been growing—sprouting up a good deal."

"But wasn't it funny about the birds?" said Tom.

"Why," said Alice, "what was funny?"

"Why," said Tom, "they weren't just ordinary birds. I am not sure now they were even quite live birds—real birds, I mean, though they might have come from the sea. And why didn't they fly away when I got near? They saw me right enough. And why, do you think, do I keep on thinking about them?"

"Lor bless me!" said Alice. "The questions he asks! And all them why's! You ain't much changed at that, Master Tom."

"Yes, but why?" Tom persisted, spoon in hand, looking up at her over his saucer of strawberries and cream.

Alice stood on the other side of the table, resting the knuckles of one hand upon it, and as she looked out across the shop a vacancy came into her blue eyes, just as if, like Tom himself, she too at times fell into daydreams. "Well, I suppose—I suppose," she said at last in a low far-away voice, "you keep on thinking about them because you can't get them out of your head."

"Oh, that's all right," said Tom a little impatiently; "but what I want to know is why they stay there?"

"Well," said Alice, "some things do. I can see those birds meself. And of course they were real, Master Tom. Of course they were real. Or else"—she gave a little gentle laugh—"or else, why you and me would be just talking about ghost birds. What I mean is that it doesn't follow even if they *was* real that they didn't mean something else

too. I don't mean exactly that such things do mean anything
else, but only, so to speak, it *seems* that they do. All depends, I suppose, in a manner of speaking, on what they
are to us, Master Tom. Bless me, when I stand here in
this shop sometimes, looking out at the people in the
street and seeing customers come in—even serving them,
too—I sometimes wonder if the whole *thing* mayn't mean
something else. How was I to know that I was ever going to get married to my Joe and keep a greengrocer's
shop too? And yet, believe *me,* Master Tom, it seems just
as ordinary and natural now as if I had been meant to do it
from my very cradle."

Tom looked at her curiously. "Then what do you
think the birds *mean?*" he repeated.

The soft lids with their light lashes closed down a little further over her blue eyes as Alice stood pondering over
the same old question. "Why," she whispered almost as if
she were talking in her sleep, "if you ask me, it means that
you are going to travel. That's what *I* think the birds mean.
But then I couldn't say where."

And suddenly she came back again, as it were—came
out of her momentary reverie or daydream, and looked
sharply round at him as if he might be in danger of something. She was frowning, as though she were frightened.
"You know, Master Tom," she went on in a solemn voice,
"I can never never forgive myself for that poor arm of
yours. Why you might by now. . . . But there! life *is* a
mystery, isn't it? I suppose in a sort of a way—though Joe
would say we oughtn't to brood on it—life itself is a kind of
a journey. That goes on too."

"Goes on where?" said Tom.

"Ah, that we can't rightly say," said Alice, smiling at

him. "But I expect if them birds of yours could find their way from over the sea, there is no particular reason why human beings should not find theirs."

"You mean Emily found hers?" said Tom.

Alice nodded two or three times. "That I do," she said.

"Well, all I can say is," said Tom, "I wish they'd come back, and the water too. They were more—more—well, I don't know *what,* than anything I have ever seen in the whole of my life."

"And that's a tidy-sized one too!" said Alice, smiling at him again. And they exchanged a long, still look.

And what she had said about his travelling came perfectly true. Quite early in his twenties Tom had pushed on up the gangway and into the bowels of the ship that was to take him across the sea to that far-away country from which he was never to come back. And though green peas and mint and the last of the cherries may not be quite such magical things in the memory as the sight of two strange sea-birds disporting themselves in a pool of rain-water on a bleak silvery March morning far from their natural haunts, these too when they came round each year always reminded Alice of that talk with Tom. Indeed she loved him very dearly, for Tom was of course—and especially after his accident —a kind of foster son. And when she heard of his going abroad she remembered the birds as well.

Broomsticks

Miss Chauncey's cat, Sam, had been with her many years
before she noticed anything unusual, anything *disturbing,*
in his conduct. Like most cats who live under the same roof
with but one or two humans, he had always been more
sagacious than cats of a common household. He had
learned Miss Chauncey's ways. He acted, that is, as nearly
like a small mortal dressed up in a hairy coat as one could
expect a cat to act. He was what is called an "intelligent"
cat.

But though Sam had learned much from Miss Chauncey, I am bound to say that Miss Chauncey had learned
very little from Sam. She was a kind, indulgent mistress;
she could sew, and cook, and crochet, and make a bed,
and read and write and cipher a little. And when she was a
girl she used to sing "Kathleen Mavourneen" to the piano.
Sam, of course, could do nothing of this kind.

But then, Miss Chauncey could no more have caught
and killed a mouse or a blackbird with her five naked fingers than she could have been Pope of Rome. Nor could
she run up a six-foot brick wall, or leap clean from the

hearthmat in her parlour on to the shelf of her chimney-piece without disturbing a single ornament, or even tinkling one crystal lustre against another. Unlike Sam, too, she could not find her way in the dark, or by her sense of smell; or keep in good health by merely nibbling grass in the garden. If, moreover, she had been carefully held up by her feet and hands two or three feet above the ground and then dropped, she would have at once fallen plump on her back; whereas when Sam was only three months old he could have managed to twist clean about in the air in twelve inches and come down on his four feet, as firm as a table.

While, then, Sam had learned a good deal from Miss Chauncey, she had learned nothing from him. And even if she had been willing to be taught, and he to teach her, it is doubtful if she would have proved a promising pupil. What is more, she knew much less about Sam than he knew about his mistress—until, at least, that afternoon when she was doing her hair in the glass. And then she could hardly believe her own eyes. It was a moment that completely changed her views about Sam—and nothing after that experience was ever quite the same again. . . .

Sam had always been a fine upstanding creature, his fur jet-black and silky, his eyes a lambent gold, even in sunshine, and at night aglow like green topazes. He was now full five years of age, and had an unusually powerful miaou. Living as he did quite alone with Miss Chauncey at Post Houses, it was natural that he should become her constant companion. For Post Houses was a singularly solitary house, standing almost in the middle of Haggurdsdon Moor, just where two wandering byways cross each other like the half-closed blades of a pair of shears or scissors.

She was well over a mile from her nearest neighbour, Mr. Cullings, the carrier; and yet another mile from the straggling old village of Haggurdsdon itself. Its roads were extremely ancient. They had been sheep-tracks long before the Romans came to England and had cut *their* roads from shore to shore. But for many years few travellers on horse or foot, or even sheep with their shepherd had come Miss Chauncey's way. You could have gazed from her windows for days together without seeing so much as a tinker's barrow or a gipsy's van.

Post Houses too was perhaps the ugliest house there ever was. Its four corners stood straight up on the moor like a pile of nursery bricks. From its flat roof on a clear day the eye could see for miles and miles across the moor, Mr. Cullings's cottage being out of sight in a shallow hollow. It had belonged to Miss Chauncey's respectable ancestors for generations. Many people in Haggurdsdon indeed called it Chauncey's. And though in a blustering wind it was as full of noises as an organ, though it was cold as a barn in winter, and though another branch of the family had as far back as the 'seventies gone to live in the Isle of Wight, Miss Chauncey still remained faithful to the old walls. In fact she loved the ugly old place. Had she not lived in it ever since she was a little girl, with knickerbockers showing under her skirts, and pale-blue ribbon rosettes at her shoulders?

This fact alone made Sam's conduct the more reprehensible, for never cat had kinder mistress. Miss Chauncey herself was now about sixty years of age—fifty-five years older than Sam. She was tall and gaunt, and straight as a ramrod. On weekdays she wore black alpaca, and on Sundays a watered silk. Her large round steel spectacles straddling across her high nose gave her a look of being keen as well as cold. But truly she was neither. For even so stupid a man as Mr. Cullings could take her in over the cartage charge for a parcel—just by looking tired, or sighing as he glanced at his rough-haired, knock-kneed mare. And there was the warmest of hearts under her stiff bodice.

Post Houses being so far from the village, milk and cream were a little difficult. But Miss Chauncey could deny Sam nothing—in reason. She paid a whole sixpence a week to a little girl called Susan Ard, who brought these dainties from the nearest farm. They were dainties indeed, for though the grasses on Haggurdsdon Moor were of a dark sour green, the cows that grazed on it gave an uncommonly rich milk, and Sam flourished on it. Mr. Cullings called once a week on his round, and had a standing order to bring with him a few sprats or fresh herrings, or any toothsome fish that was in season; Miss Chauncey would not even withhold her purse from whitebait, if no other cheaper wholesome fish were procurable. And Mr. Cullings would eye Sam fawning about his cartwheel, or gloating up at his dish, and say, " 'Ee be a queer animal, Mum, shure enough; 'ee be a wunnerful queer animal, 'ee be."

As for Miss Chauncey herself, she was a niggardly eater, though much attached to her tea. She made her own bread and cookies. On Saturday a butcher-boy drove up in a striped apron with her Sunday joint; but she was no meat-lover. Her cupboards were full of home-made jams and bottled fruits and dried herbs—everything of that kind, for Post Houses had a nice long strip of garden behind it, surrounded by a high old yellow brick wall.

Quite early in life Sam, of course, had learned to know his meal-times—though how he "told" them was known only to himself, for he never appeared even to glance at the face of the grandfather's clock on the staircase. He was punctual, a dandy in his toilet, and a prodigious sleeper.

He had learned to pull down the latch of the back door, if, in the months when an open window was not to be found, he wished to go out. Indeed, he often seemed to prefer the latch. He never slept on Miss Chauncey's patchwork quilt unless his own had been placed over it. He was fastidious almost to a foppish degree in his habits, and he was no thief. He had a mew on one note to show when he wanted something to eat; a mew a semitone or two higher if he wanted drink (that is, cold water, for which he had a natural taste); and yet another mew—gentle and sustained— when he wished, so to speak, to converse with his mistress.

Not, of course, that the creature talked *English*. He liked to sit up on one chair by the fireside, especially in the kitchen—for he was no born parlour cat—and to look up at the glinting glasses of Miss Chauncey's spectacles, and then down a while at the fire flames (drawing his claws in and out as he did so, and purring the while), almost as if he might be preaching a sermon, or reciting a poem.

But this was in the happy days when all seemed well. This was in the days when Miss Chauncey's mind was innocent of doubts and suspicions.

Like others of his kind, too, Sam had delighted in his youth to lie in the window and idly watch the birds in the apple-trees—tits, thrushes, blackbirds, bullfinches—or to crouch over a mousehole, for hours together. Such were his house amusements (he never ate his mice), while Miss Chauncey with cap and broom, duster and dish-clout, went about her work. But he also had a way of examining things in which cats are not generally interested. He as good as told Miss Chauncey one afternoon that moths were at work in her parlour carpet. For he walked to and fro and back and forth with his tail up, until she attended to him. And he certainly warned her, with a yelp like an Amazonian monkey, when a red-hot coal had set her kitchen mat on fire.

He would lie or sit with his whiskers to the north before noonday, and due south afterwards. In general his manners were perfection. But occasionally, when she called him, his face would appear to knot itself into a frown—at any rate to assume a low sullen look, as if he expostulated: "Why must you be interrupting me, Madam, when I was attending to something else?" And now and then, Miss Chauncey fancied, he would deliberately secrete himself or steal out of (and into) Post Houses unbeknown.

Miss Chauncey too would sometimes find him trotting from room to room as if on a visit of inspection. On his second birthday he had carried in an immense mouse and laid it beside the shiny toecap of her boot as she sat knitting by the fire. She smiled and nodded merrily at him, as usual, but on this occasion he looked at her intently, and then deliberately shook his head. After that he never paid the smallest attention to mouse or mousehole or mousery, and Miss Chauncey was obliged to purchase a cheese-bait trap, else she would have been overrun.

Almost any domestic cat may do things of this nature, and all this of course was solely on Sam's domestic side. For he shared house with Miss Chauncey and, like any two beings that live together, he was bound to keep up certain appearances. He met her half-way, as the saying goes. When, however, he was 'on his own,' he was no longer Miss Chauncey's Sam, he was no longer merely the cat at Post Houses, but just *himself*. He went back, that is, to his own free independent life; to his own private habits.

Then the moor on which he roved was his own country, and the "humans" and their houses on it were no more

to him in his wild privy existence than mole-hills or badg-
ers' earths or rabbit warrens are to ourselves. Of this side
of his life his mistress knew practically nothing. She did not
consider it. She supposed that Sam behaved like other cats,
though it was evident that at times he went far afield, for
he now and again brought home a young Cochin China
pullet, and the nearest Cochin China fowls were at the
vicarage, a good four miles off. Sometimes of an evening,
too, when Miss Chauncey was taking a little walk herself,
she would see him—a swiftly moving black speck—far
along the road, hastening home. And there was more purpose expressed in his gait and appearance than ever Mr.
Cullings or even the vicar showed!

It was pleasant to observe, too, when he came within
miauoing distance, how his manner changed. He turned at
once from being a Cat into being a Domestic Cat. He was
instantaneously no longer the Feline Adventurer, the Noc-
turnal Marauder and Haunter of Haggurdsdon Moor
(though Miss Chauncey would not have so expressed it),
but simply his mistress's spoiled pet, Sam. She loved him
dearly. But, as again with human beings who are accustomed to live together, she did not *think* very much about
him. It could not but be a shock then that late evening,
when without the slightest warning Miss Chauncey discovered that Sam was deliberately deceiving her.

She was brushing her thin brown front hair before her
looking-glass. At this moment it hung down over her face
like a fine loose veil. And as she always mused of other
things when she was brushing her hair, she was somewhat
absent-minded the while. On raising her eyes from her
reverie behind this screen of hair, she perceived not only
that Sam's reflection was in sight in the looking-glass, but
also that something a little mysterious was happening.

Sam was sitting up as if to beg. There was nothing in that. It had been a customary feat of his since he was a few months old. Still, for what might he be begging, no one by?

Now the window to the right of the chintz-valanced dressing-table was open at the top. Outside, it was beginning to grow dark. All Haggurdsdon Moor lay hushed and still in the evening's thickening gloom. And apart from begging when there was nothing to beg for, Sam seemed, so to speak, to be gesticulating with his paws. He appeared, that is, to be making signs, just as if there were someone or something looking in at the window at him from out of the air—which was quite impossible. And there was a look upon his face that certainly Miss Chauncey had never seen before.

She stayed a moment with hair-brush uplifted, her long lean arm at an angle with her head. On seeing this, Sam had instantly desisted from these motions. He had dropped to his fours again, and was now apparently composing himself for another nap. No; this too was a pretence; for presently as she watched, he turned restlessly about so that his whiskers were once again due south. His backward parts towards the window, he was now gazing fixedly in front of him out of a far from friendly face. Far indeed from friendly for a creature that had lived with her ever since he opened the eyes of his blind kittenhood.

As if he had read her thoughts, Sam at that moment lifted his head to look at his mistress; she withdrew her eyes to the glass only in the nick of time, and when she turned from her toilet there sat he—so serene in appearance, so puss-like, so ordinary once more that Miss Chauncey could scarcely believe anything whatever had been amiss. Had her eyes deluded her—her glass? Was that peculiar motion of Sam's fore-paws (almost as if he were knitting), was that wide excited stare due only to the fact that he was catching what was, to her, an invisible fly?

Miss Chauncey having now neatly arranged her "window-curtains"—the sleek loops of hair she wore on either side her high forehead—glanced yet again out of the window. Nothing there but the silence of the Moor; nothing there but the faint pricking of a star as the evening darkened.

Sam's supper cream was waiting on the hearthrug in the parlour as usual that evening. The lamp was lit. The red blinds were drawn. The fire crackled in the grate. There they sat, these two; the walls of the four-cornered house beside the crossroads rising up above them like a huge oblong box under the immense starry sky that saucered in the wide darkness of the Moor.

And while she sat so—with Sam there, seemingly fast asleep—Miss Chauncey was thinking. What had occurred in the bedroom that early evening had reminded her of other odd little bygone happenings. Trifles she had scarcely noticed, but which now returned clearly to memory. How often in the past, for example, Sam at this hour would be sitting as if fast asleep (as now), his paws tucked neatly in, looking very much like a stout alderman after his dinner. And then suddenly, without warning, as if a distant voice had called him, he would leap to his feet and run straight out of the room. And somewhere in the house—door ajar or window agape, he would find his egress and be up and away into the night. This had been a common thing to happen.

Once, too, Miss Chauncey had found him squatting on his hindquarters on the window-ledge of a little room that had been entirely disused since, years ago, Cousin Milly had stayed at Post Houses when Miss Chauncey was a child of eight. She had cried out at sight of him, "You foolish Sam, you; come in, sir! You will be tumbling out of the window next!" And she remembered as though it were yesterday that though at this he had stepped gingerly in at once from his dizzy perch, he had not looked at her. He had passed her without a sign.

On moonlight evenings, too—why, you could never be sure *where* he was! You could never be sure from what errand he had *returned*. Was she sure indeed where he was on *any* night? The longer she reflected, the gloomier grew her doubts and misgivings. This night, at any rate, Miss Chauncey determined to keep watch. But she was not happy in doing so. She hated all manner of spying. They were old companions, Sam and she; and she, without him in bleak Post Houses, would be sadly desolate. She loved Sam dearly. None the less, what she had witnessed that evening had stayed in her mind, and it would be wiser to know all that there was to be known, even if for Sam's sake only.

Now Miss Chauncey always slept with her bedroom door ajar. She had slept so ever since her nursery days. Being a rather timid little girl, she liked in those far-away times to hear the grown-up voices downstairs and the spoons and forks clinking. As for Sam, he always slept in his basket beside her fireplace. Every morning there he would be, though on some mornings Miss Chauncey's eyes would open gently to find herself gazing steadily into his pale green ones as he stood on his hind paws, resting his front ones on her bedside, and looking into her face. "Time for breakfast, Sam?" his mistress would murmur. And Sam would mew, as distantly almost as a seagull in the heights of the sky.

To-night, however, Miss Chauncey only pretended to

be asleep. It was difficult, however, to keep wholly awake, and she was all but drowsing off when there came a faint squeak from the hinge of her door, and she realised that Sam was gone out. After waiting a moment or two, she struck a match. Yes, there was his empty basket in the dark silent room, and presently from far away—from the steeple at Haggurdsdon Village—came the knolling of the hour.

Miss Chauncey placed the dead end of the match in the saucer of her candlestick, and at that moment fancied she heard a faint *whssh* at her window, as of a sudden gust or scurry of wind, or the wings of a fast-flying bird—of a wild goose. It even reminded Miss Chauncey of half-forgotten Guy Fawkes days and of the sound the stick of a rocket makes as it slips down through the air—while its green and ruby lights die out in the immense vacancy above. Miss Chauncey gathered up her long legs in the bed, got up, drew on the blue flannel dressing-gown that always hung on her bedrail, and lifting back the blind an inch or two, looked out of the window.

It was a high starry night; and a brightening in the sky above the roof seemed to betoken there must be a moon over the backward parts of the house. Even as she watched, a streak of pale silver descended swiftly out of the far spaces of the heavens, and fading into the darkness dwindled and vanished away. It was a meteorite; and at that very instant Miss Chauncey fancied she heard again a faint remote dwindling *whssh* in the air. Was *that* the meteorite too? Could she have been deceived? Was she being deceived in everything? She drew back.

And then, as if in deliberate and defiant answer, out of the distance and from what appeared to be the extreme end of her long garden where grew a tangle of sloe bushes, there followed a prolonged and as if half-secret caterwaul: very low—contralto, one might say—*Meearou-rou-rou-rou-rou!*

Heaven forbid! Was *that* Sam's tongue? The cater-wauling ceased. Yet still Miss Chauncey could not suppress a shudder. She knew Sam's voice of old. But surely not that! Surely not that!

Strange and immodest though it was to hear herself, too, in that solitary place calling out in the dead of night, she nevertheless at once opened the window and summoned Sam by name. There was no response. The trees and bushes of the garden stood motionless; their faint shadows on the ground revealing how small a moon was actually in the sky, and how low it hung towards its setting. The vague un-dulations of the Moor stretched into the distance. Not a light to be seen except those of the firmament. Again, and yet again, Miss Chauncey cried, "Sam, Sam! Come away in! Come away in, sir, you bad creature!" Not a sound. Not the least stir of leaf or blade of grass.

When, after so broken a night, Miss Chauncey awoke a little late the next morning, the first thing her eyes beheld when she sat up in bed was Sam—couched as usual in his basket. It was a mystery, and an uneasy one. After supping up his morning bowl, he slept steadily on until noonday. This happened to be the day of the week when Miss Chaun-cey made bread. On and on she steadily kneaded the dough with her knuckled hands, glancing ever and again towards the motionless creature. With fingers clotted from the great earthenware bowl, she stood over him at last for a few mo-ments, and eyed him closely.

He was lying curled round with his whiskered face to one side towards the fire. And it seemed to Miss Chauncey that she had never noticed before that faint peculiar grin on his face. "Sam!" she cried sharply. An eye instantly opened, wide and ferocious, as if a mouse had squeaked. He stared at her for an instant; then the lid narrowed. The gaze slunk away a little, but Sam began to purr.

The truth of it is, all this was making Miss Chauncey exceedingly unhappy. Mr. Cullings called that afternoon, with a basket of some fresh comely young sprats. "Them'll wake his Royal Highness up," he said. "They'm fresh as daisies. Lor, m'm, what a Nero that beast be!"

"Cats *are* strange creatures, Mr. Cullings," replied Miss Chauncey reflectively; complacently supposing that Mr. Cullings had misplaced an *h* and had meant to say, *an hero*. And Sam himself, with uplifted tail, and as if of the same opinion, was rubbing his head gently against her boot.

Mr. Cullings eyed her closely. "Why, yes, they be," he said. "What I says is that as soon as they're out of your sight, you are out of their mind. There's no more gratitood nor affection in a cat than in a pump. Though so far as the pump is concerned, the gratitood should be on our side. I knew a family of cats once what fairly druv their mistress out of house and home."

"But you wouldn't have a cat *only* a pet?" said Miss Chauncey faintly, afraid to ask for further particulars of this peculiar occurrence.

"Why, no, m'm," said the carrier. "As the Lord made 'em, so they be. But I'll be bound they could tell some knotty stories if they had a human tongue to their heads!"

Sam had ceased caressing his mistress's foot, and was looking steadily at Mr. Cullings, his hair roughed a little about the neck and shoulders. And the carrier looked back.

"No, m'm. We wouldn't keep 'em," he said at last, "if they was *four* times that size. Or, not for long!"

Having watched Mr. Cullings's little cart bowl away

into the distance, Miss Chauncey returned into the house, more disturbed than ever. Nor did her uneasiness abate when Sam refused even to sniff at his sprats. Instead, he crawled in under a low table in the kitchen, behind the old seaman's chest in which Miss Chauncey kept her kindling wood. She fancied she heard his claws working in the wood now and again, and once he seemed to be expressing his natural feelings in what vulgar people with little sympathy for animals describe as "swearing."

Her caressing "Sams," at any rate, were all in vain. His only reply was a kind of sneeze which uncomfortably resembled "spitting." Miss Chauncey's feelings had already been hurt. It was now her mind that suffered. Something the carrier had said, or the way he had said it, or the peculiar look she had noticed on his face when he was returning Sam's stare in the porch, haunted her thoughts. She was no longer young, was she becoming fanciful? Or must she indeed conclude that for weeks past Sam had been steadily circumventing her, or at any rate concealing his wanderings and his interests? What nonsense. Worse still: was she now so credulous as to believe that Sam had in actual fact been making signals—and secretly, behind her back—to some confederate that must either have been up in the sky, or in the moon!

Whether or not, Miss Chauncey determined to keep a sharper eye on him. Their future was at stake. She would at least make sure that he did not leave the house that night. But then: "Why not?" she asked herself. "Why shouldn't the creature choose his own hour and season? Cats, like owls, *see* best in the dark. They go best a-mousing in the dark, and may prefer the dark for their private, social, and even public affairs." Post Houses, after all, was only rather more than two miles from Haggurdsdon Village, and there were cats there in plenty. Poor fellow, her own dumb human company must sometimes be dull enough!

Such were Miss Chauncey's reflections; and as if to reassure her, Sam himself at that moment serenely entered the room and leapt up on to the empty chair beside her tea-table. As if, too, to prove that he had thought better of his evil temper, or to insinuate that there had been nothing amiss between himself and Mr. Cullings, he was licking his chops, and there was no mistaking the odour of fish which he brought in with him from his saucer.

"So you have thought better of it, my boy?" thought Miss Chauncey, though she did not utter the words aloud. And yet as she returned his steady feline gaze, she realized how difficult it was to read the intelligence behind those eyes. You might say that, Sam being only a cat, there was no meaning in them at all. But Miss Chauncey knew better. There could be meaning enough if such eyes had looked out of a *human* shape at her.

Unfortunately, and almost as if Sam had overheard his mistress's speculations regarding possible cat friends in the village, there came at that moment a faint wambling mew beneath the open window. In a flash Sam was out of his chair and over the window-ledge, and Miss Chauncey rose only just in time to see him in infuriated pursuit of a slim sleek tortoiseshell creature that had evidently come to Post Houses in hope of a friendlier reception, and was now fleeing in positive fear of its life.

Sam returned from his chase as fresh as paint, and Miss Chauncey was horrified to detect—caught up between the claws of his right forefoot—a tuft or two of tortoiseshell fur, which, having composed himself by the fire, he promptly removed by licking.

Still pondering on these disquieting events, Miss

Chauncey took her usual evening walk in the garden. Candytuft and virginia stock were seeding along the shell-lined path, and late roses were already beginning to blow on the high brick wall which shut off her narrow strip of land from the vast lap of the moor. Having come to the end of the path, Miss Chauncey pushed on a little further than usual, to where the grasses grew more rampant, and where wild headlong weeds raised their heads beneath her few lichenous apple-trees. Still further down, for hers was a long, though narrow, garden—there grew straggling bushes of sloe and spiny whitethorn. These had blossomed indeed in the moor's bleak springs long before Post Houses had raised its chimney pots into the sky. Here, too, flourished a frowning drift of nettles—their sour odour haunting the air.

It was in this forlorn spot that—just like Robinson Crusoe, before her—Miss Chauncey was suddenly brought to a standstill by the appearance of what might be nothing other than a footprint in the mould. But not only this. A few inches away there showed what might be the mark of a walking-cane or even of something stouter and heavier—a crutch. Could she be deceived? The footprint, it was true, was of a peculiar kind. "A queer shoe that!" thought Miss Chauncey. Could the resemblance be accidental? *Was* it a footprint?

Miss Chauncey glanced furtively across the bushes towards the house. It loomed gaunt and forbidding in the moorland dusk. And she fancied she could see, though the evening light might be deluding her, the cowering shape of Sam looking out at her from the kitchen window. To be watched! To be herself spied upon—and watched!

But then, of course, Sam was always watching her. What oddity was there in that? Where else would his sprats come from, his cream, his saucer of milk, his bowl of fresh well-water? Nevertheless, Miss Chauncey returned to her parlour gravely discomposed.

It was an uncommonly calm evening, and as she went from room to room locking the windows, she noticed there was already a moon in the sky. She eyed it with misgiving. And at last bedtime came; and when Sam, as usual, after a lick or two, had composed himself in his basket, Miss Chauncey, holding the key almost challengingly within view, deliberately locked her own bedroom door.

When she awoke next morning Sam was asleep in his basket as usual, and during the day-time he kept pretty closely to the house. So, too, on the Wednesday and the Thursday. It was not until the following Friday that having occasion to go into an upper bedroom that had no fireplace, and being followed as usual by Sam, Miss Chauncey detected the faint rank smell of soot in the room. No chimney, and a smell of soot! She turned rapidly on her companion: he had already left the room.

And when that afternoon she discovered a black sooty smear upon her own patchwork quilt, she realized not only that her suspicions had been justified, but that for the first time in his life Sam had deliberately laid himself down there in her absence. At this act of sheer defiance she was no longer so much hurt as exceedingly angry. There could be no doubt. Sam was now openly defying her. No two companions could share a house on such terms as these. He must be taught a lesson.

That evening, in full sight of the creature, having locked her bedroom door, she stuffed a large piece of mattress ticking into the mouth of her chimney and pulled down the register. Having watched these proceedings, Sam rose from his basket, and with an easy spring, leapt up on to

the dressing-table. Beyond the window, the moor lay almost as bright as day. Ignoring Miss Chauncey, the creature crouched there, steadily and sullenly staring into the
empty skies, for a vast gulf of them was visible from where
he sat.

Miss Chauncey proceeded to make her toilet for the
night, trying in vain to pretend that she was entirely unin-
terested in what the animal was at. A faint sound—not exactly mewings or growlings—but a kind of low inward
caterwauling, hardly audible, was proceeding from his
throat. But whatever these sounds might imply, Sam himself
can have been the only listener. There was not a sign of
movement at the window or in the world without. And
then Miss Chauncey promptly drew down the blind. At this
Sam at once raised his paw for all the world as if he were
about to protest, and then, apparently thinking better of it,
he pretended instead that the action had been only for the
purpose of beginning his nightly wash.

Long after her candle had been extinguished, Miss
Chauncey lay listening. Every stir and movement in the
quiet darkness could be easily understood. First there came
a furtive footing and tapping at the register of the fireplace,
so clearly showing what was happening that Miss Chauncey
could positively see in her imagination Sam on the hearth-
stone, erecting himself there upon his hind legs, vainly at-
tempting to push the obstacle back.

This being in vain, he appeared to have dropped back
on to his fours. There came a pause. Had he given up his
intention? No: now he was at the door, pawing, gently
scratching. Then a leap, even, towards the latch: but only
one—the door was locked. Retiring from the door, he now
sprang lightly again on to the dressing-table. What now
was he at? By covertly raising her head a little from her pil-

low, Miss Chauncey could see him with paw thrust out, gently drawing back the blind from the moon-flooded window-pane. And even while she listened and watched, she heard yet again—and yet again—the faint *whssh* as of a wild swan cleaving the air; and then what might have been the night-cry of a bird, but which to Miss Chauncey's ears resembled a thin shrill pealing cackle of laughter. At this Sam hastily turned from the window, and without the least attempt at concealment pounced clean from the dressing-table on to the lower rail of her bed.

This unmannerly conduct could be ignored no longer. Poor Miss Chauncey raised herself in her sheets, pulled her nightcap a little closer down over her ears, and thrusting out her hand towards the chair beside the bed, struck a match and relit her candle. It was with a real effort that she then slowly turned her head and faced her night-companion. His hair was bristling about his body as if he had had an electric shock. His whiskers stood out at stiff angles with his jaws. He looked at least twice his usual size, and his eyes blazed in his head, as averting his face from her regard he gave vent to a low sustained *Miariou-rou-rou-rou!*

"I say you shall *not*," cried Miss Chauncey at the creature. At the sound of her words, he turned slowly and confronted her. And it seemed that until that moment Miss Chauncey had never actually seen Sam's countenance as in actual fact it really was. It was not so much the grinning tigerish look it wore, but the morose assurance in it not only of what he wanted but that he meant to get it.

All thought of sleep was now out of the question. Miss Chauncey could be obstinate too. The creature seemed to shed an influence on the very air which she could hardly resist. She rose from her bed and thrusting on her slippers

made her way to the window. Once more a peculiar inward
cry broke out from the bedrail. She raised the blind and the
light of the moon from over the moor swept in upon her
little apartment. And when she turned to remonstrate with
her pet at his ingratitude, and at all this unseemliness and
the deceit of his ways, there was something so menacing
and stubborn and ferocious in his aspect that Miss Chauncey hesitated no more.

"Well, mark me!" she cried in a trembling voice, "go
out of the *door* you shan't. But if you enjoy soot, soot it
shall be."

With that she thrust back the register with the poker
and drew down the bundle of ticking with the tongs. Before the fit of coughing caused by the smotheration that followed had ceased, the lithe black shape had sprung from
the bedrail, and with a scramble was into the hearth, over
the firebars, up the chimney, and away.

Trembling from head to foot, Miss Chauncey sat
down on a cane rocking-chair that stood handy to reflect
what next she must be doing. *Wh-ssh! Wh-ssh!* Again at
the window came that mysterious rushing sound; but now,
the flurrying murmur as of a rocket shooting up with its
fiery train of sparks thinning into space, rather than the
sound of its descending stick. And then in the hush that
followed, there sounded yet again like a yell of triumph
from the foot of the garden, a caterwauling piercing and
sonorous enough to arouse every sleeping cock in the Haggurdsdon hen-roosts, and for miles around. Out of the
distance their chanticleering broke shrill on the night air; to
be followed a moment afterwards by the tardy clang of
midnight from the church steeple. Then once more, silence;
utter quiet. Miss Chauncey returned to her bed, but that
night slept no more.

Her mind overflowed with unhappy thoughts. Her faith in Sam was gone. Far worse, she had lost faith even in her affection for him. To have wasted that! All the sprats, all the whitebait in the wide, wide seas were as nothing by comparison. That Sam had wearied of her company was at last beyond question. It shamed her to think how much this meant to her—a mere animal! But she knew what was gone; knew how dull and spiritless the day's round would seem—the rising, the housework, the meals, her toilet in the afternoon, her evening slippers, book or knitting, a dish of tea, her candle, prayers, bed. On and on. In what wild company was her cat, Sam, now? At her own refusal to answer this horrid question, it was as if she had heard the hollow clanging slam of an immense iron door.

Next morning—still ruminating on these strange events, grieved to the heart at this dreadful rift between herself and one who had been her trusted companion for so many years; ashamed too that Sam should have had his way with her when she had determined not to allow him to go out during the night—next morning Miss Chauncey, as if merely to take a little exercise, once again ventured down to the foot of her garden. A faint, blurred mark (such as she had seen on the previous evening) in the black mould of what *might* be a footprint is nothing very much. But now—in the neglected patch beyond the bushes of white-thorn and bramble—there could be no doubt in the world —appeared many strange marks. And surely no cats' pawprints these! Of what use, indeed, to a cat could a crutch or a staff be? A staff or a crutch which—to judge from the impression it had left in the mould—must have been at least as thick as a broomstick.

More disquieted and alarmed than ever over this fresh mystery, Miss Chauncey glanced up and back towards the chimneypots of the house clearly and sharply fretted against the morning light of the eastern skies. And she realized what perils even so sure-footed a creature as Sam had faced when he skirred up out of the chimney in his wild effort to emerge into the night. Having thus astonishingly reached the rim of the chimney—the wild burning stars above and the wilderness of the moor spread out far beneath and around him—he must have leaped from the top of the low pot to a narrow brick ledge not three inches wide. Thence on to the peak of the roof and thence down a steep, slippery slope of slates to a leaden gutter.

And how then? The thick tod of ivy, matting the walls of the house, reached hardly more than half-way up. Could Sam actually have plunged from gutter to tod? The very thought of such a peril drew Miss Chauncey's steps towards the house again, in the sharpest anxiety to assure herself that he was still in the land of the living.

And lo and behold, when she was but half-way on her journey, she heard a succession of frenzied yelps and catcalls in the air from over the moor. Hastily placing a flower-pot by the wall, she stood on tiptoe and peered over. And even now, at this very moment, in full flight across the nearer slope of the moor, she descried her Sam, not now in chase of a foolishly trustful visitor, but hotly pursued by what appeared to be the complete rabblement of Haggurdsdon's cats. Sore spent though he showed himself to be, Sam was keeping his distance. Only a few lank tabby cats, and what appeared to be a grey-ginger Manx (unless he was an ordinary cat with his tail chopped off), were close behind.

"Sam! Sam!" Miss Chauncey cried, and yet again, "Sam!" but in her excitement and anxiety her foot slipped on the flower-pot and in an instant the feline chase had fallen out of sight. Gathering herself together again, she clutched a long besom or garden broom that was leaning against the wall, and rushed down to the point at which she judged Sam would make his entrance into the garden. She was not mistaken, nor an instant too soon. With a bound he was up and over, and in three seconds the rabble had followed, in vehement pursuit.

What came after Miss Chauncey could never very clearly recall. She could but remember plying her besom with might and main amid this rabble and mellay of animals, while Sam, no longer a fugitive, turned on his enemies and fought them man to man. None the less, it was by no means an easy victory. And had not the over-fatted cur from the butcher's in Haggurdsdon—which had long since started in pursuit of this congregation of his enemies—had he not at last managed to overtake them, the contest might very well have had a tragic ending. But at sound of his baying, and at sight of teeth fiercely snapping at them as he vainly attempted to surmount the wall, Sam's enemies turned and fled in all directions. And faint and panting, Miss Chauncey was able to fling down her besom and to lean for a brief respite against the trunk of a tree.

At last she opened her eyes again. "Well, Sam," she managed to mutter at last, "we got the best of them, then?"

But to her amazement she found herself uttering these friendly words into a complete vacancy. The creature was nowhere to be seen. His cream disappeared during the day, however, and by an occasional rasping sound Miss Chauncey knew that he once more lay hidden in his dingy resort behind the kindling-wood box. There she did not disturb him.

Not until tea-time of the following day did Sam reappear. And then—after attending to his hurts—it was merely to sit with face towards the fire, sluggish and sullen and dumb as a dog. It was not Miss Chauncey's "place" to make advances, she thought. She took no notice of the beast except to rub in a little hog's-fat on the raw places of his wounds. She was rejoiced to find, however, that he kept steadily to Post Houses for the next few days, though her dismay was reawakened at hearing on the third night a more dismal wailing and wauling than ever from the sloe-bushes, even though Sam himself sat motionless beside the fire. His ears twitched; his fur bristled; he sneezed or spat but otherwise remained motionless.

When Mr. Cullings called again, Sam at once hid himself in the coal cellar, but gradually his manners towards Miss Chauncey began to recover their usual suavity. And within a fortnight after the full moon, the two of them had almost returned to their old friendly companionship. He was healed, sleek, confident and punctual. No intruder of his species had appeared from Haggurdsdon. The night noises had ceased. Post Houses to all appearance—apart from its strange ugliness—was as peaceful and calm as any other solitary domicile in the United Kingdom.

But alas and alas. With the very first peeping of the crescent moon, Sam's mood and habits began to change again. He mouched about with a sly and furtive eye. And when he fawned on his mistress, purring and clawing, the whole look of him was a picture of deceit. If Miss Chauncey chanced to enter the room wherein he sat, he would at once leap down from the window at which he had been perched as if in the attempt to prove that he had *not* been looking out of it. And once, towards evening, though she was no spy, she could not but pause at the parlour door. She had peeped through its crack as it stood ajar. And there on the hard sharp back of an old prie-Dieu chair that had belonged to her pious great-aunt Miranda, sat Sam on his hind quarters. And without the least doubt in the world he was vigorously signalling to some observer outside with his forepaws. Miss Chauncey turned away sick at heart.

From that hour on Sam more and more steadily ignored and flouted his mistress, was openly insolent, shockingly audacious. Mr. Cullings gave her small help indeed. "If I had a cat, m'm, what had manners like that, after all your kindness, fresh fish and all every week, and cream, as I understand, not skim, I'd—I'd *give* him away."

"To whom?" said poor Miss Chauncey.

"Well," said the carrier, "I don't know as how I'd much mind to who. Beggars can't be choosers, m'm."

"He seems to have no friends in the village," said Miss Chauncey, in as light a tone as she could manage.

"When they're as black as that, with them saucer eyes, you can never tell," said Mr. Cullings. "There's that old trollimog what lives in Hogges Bottom. She've got a cat that might be your Sam's twin."

"Indeed no, he has the mange," said Miss Chauncey, loyal to the end. The carrier shrugged his shoulders, climbed into his cart, and bowled away off over the Moor. And Miss Chauncey, returning to the house, laid the platter of silvery sprats on the table, sat down, and burst into tears.

It was, then, in most ways a fortunate thing that the very next morning—five complete days, that is, before the next full-moon-tide—she received a letter from her sister-in-law in Shanklin, in the Isle of Wight, entreating her to pay them a long visit.

"My dear Emma. You must sometimes be feeling very lonely [it ran] shut up in that grate house so far from any neighbours. We often think of you, and particularly these last few days. It's very nice to have that Sam of yours for company, but after all, as George says, a pet's only a pet. And we do all think it's high time you took a little holiday with us. I am looking out of my window at this very moment. The sea is as calm as a mill-pond, a sollem beautiful blue. The fishing boats are coming in with their brown sails. This is the best time of the year with us, because the *tripper* season is drawing to a close and there are fewer of those horrid visitors to be seen, and no crowds. George says you *must* come. He joins with me in his love as would Maria if she weren't out shoping, and will meet you at the station in the trap. And we shall all be looking forward to seeing you in a few days. Emmie is now free of her cough —only hooping when the memory takes her, and never sick. Your affec., (Mrs.) Gertrude Chauncey."

At this kindness, and with all her anxieties, Miss Chauncey all but broke down. When the butcher drove up in his cart an hour or two afterwards, he took a telegram for her back to the village, and on the Monday her box was packed, and all that remained was to put Sam in his basket in preparation for the journey. But I am bound to say it took more than the persuasions of his old protectress to accomplish this. Indeed Mr. Cullings had actually to hold the creature down with gloved hands and none too gently, while Miss Chauncey pressed down the lid and pushed the skewer in to hold it close. "What's done's durned done," said the carrier, as he rubbed a pinch of earth into his scratches. "And what *I* says is, better done for ever. Mark my words, m'm!"

Miss Chauncey took a shilling out of her large leather purse; but made no reply.

Indeed, all this trouble proved at last in vain. Thirty miles distant from Haggurdsdon, at Blackmoor Junction, Miss Chauncey had to change trains. Her box and Sam's

basket were placed together on the station platform beside
half a dozen empty milk-cans and some fowls in a crate,
and Miss Chauncey went to make inquiries of the station-
master in order to make sure of her platform.

It was the furious panic-stricken cackling of these
fowls that brought her hastily back to her belongings, only
to find that by hook or by crook Sam had managed to push
the skewer of the basket out of its cane loops. The wicker
lid gaped open—the basket was empty. Indeed one poor
gasping hen, its life fluttering away from its helpless body,
was proof enough not only of Sam's prowess but of his
pitiless ferocity.

A few days afterwards, as Miss Chauncey sat in the
very room to which her sister-in-law had referred in her
invitation, looking over the placid surface of the English
Channel, the sun gently shining in the sky, there came a
letter from Mr. Cullings. It was in pencil and written upon
the back of a baker's bag.

"Dear madam i take the libberty of riteing you in
reference to the Animall as how i helped put in is bawskit
which has cum back returned empty agenn by rail me
having okashun to cart sum hop powles from Haggurdsden
late at nite ov Sunday. I seez him squattin at the parlour
windy grimasin out at me fit to curdle your blood in your
vanes and lights at the upper windies and a yowling and
screetching as i never hopes to hear agen in a Christian
lokalety. And that ole wumman from Hogges Botom sitting in the porch mi own vew being that there is no good
in the place and the Animall be bewhitched. Mister flint
the boutcher agrees with me as how now only last mesures
is of any use and as i have said afore i am willing to take
over the house the rent if so be being low and moddrit
considering of the bad name it as in these parts around

Haggurdsden. I remain dear madam waitin your orders and oblige yours truely William Cullings.'

To look at Miss Chauncey you might have supposed she was a strong-minded woman. You might have supposed that this uncivil reference to the bad name her family house had won for itself would have mortified her beyond words. Whether or not, she neither showed this letter to her sister-in-law nor for many days together did she attempt to answer it. Sitting on the esplanade, and looking out to sea, she brooded on and on in the warm, salt, yet balmy air. It was a distressing problem. But "No, he must go his own way," she sighed to herself at last; "I have done my best for him."

What is more, Miss Chauncey never returned to Post Houses. She sold it at last, house and garden, and for a pitiful sum, to the carrier, Mr. Cullings. By that time Sam had vanished, had never been seen again. He had gone his way.

Not that Miss Chauncey was faithless to his memory. Whenever the faint swish of a seagull's wing whispered through the air above her head; or the crackling of an ascending rocket for the amusement of visitors broke the silence of the nearer heavens over the sea; whenever even she became conscious of the rustling frou-frou of her Sunday watered-silk gown as she sallied out to church from the neat little villa she now rented on the Shanklin Esplanade —she never noticed such things without being instantly transported in imagination to her old bedroom at Post Houses, and seeing again that strange deluded animal, once her Sam, squatting there on her bed, and as it were knitting with his fore-paws the while he stood erect upon his hind.

ABOUT THE AUTHOR

WALTER DE LA MARE, poet, novelist, short-story writer, critic, dramatist, and anthologist, was born in Kent in 1873. For many years he earned his living as a statistician in the office of the Anglo-American Oil Company. In 1908 the British government awarded him a small pension, thus setting him free to devote all his energies to writing.

An artist of complete integrity, he never considered the demands of the market. Few writers of any period have equalled his record for writing inspired verse over a very long period. Mr. de la Mare died at his home in Twickenham, England, on June 22, 1956.

A NOTE ON THE TYPE

The text of this book was set on the Linotype in a face called TIMES ROMAN, designed by Stanley Morison for *The Times* (London), and first introduced by that newspaper in 1932.

Among typographers and designers of the twentieth century, Stanley Morison has been a strong forming influence, as typographical advisor to the English Monotype Corporation, as a director of two distinguished English publishing houses, and as a writer of sensibility, erudition, and keen practical sense.